Nicolaes Nimbus

High Tech Science vs. Ancient Magic

By Koos Verkaik

Outer Banks Publishing Group
Raleigh/Outer Banks

www.outerbankspublishing.com

Edited by Dennis De Rose, Moneysaver Editing

FIRST EDITION - May 2020

Library of Congress Control Number: 2020937522

ISBN: 978-1-7341687-5-4
eISBN:978-0-4634046-6-9

Table of Contents

Chapter 1: False Identity, True Identity, and First Listing
Chapter 2: The Reading Man
Chapter 3: Fort Web
Chapter 4: A Name in a Diary
Chapter 5: A Timeless Phenomenon
Chapter 6: Regina and Karina
Chapter 7: The Society of Tamfana and Victor the Visionary
Chapter 8: Art Shop Remco Castor
Chapter 9: Empty Picture Frame
Chapter 10: Wood on Bone
Chapter 11: Rein Vulpes visits Fort Web
Chapter 12: Broken Glass
Chapter 13: Painting under Hypnotic Influence
Chapter 14: De Cup
Chapter 15: The Swimming Fox
Chapter 16: Like a Bird of Prey
Chapter 17: Under a Coffee Cup

Chapter 1

FALSE IDENTITY, TRUE IDENTITY, AND FIRST
LISTING

*Free interpretation of an article from the archives of The
Society of Tamfana.*

*Place: Leiden, Republic of the Seven United
Netherlands. Time: Around 1750.*

Book printer Geerten Jacobsz listened to the rattling
of wooden wheels on the cobblestones of De
Breestraat on the other side of the stained glass
window. Outside it was dreary, cloudy and rainy,
inside dim. Geerten sat on a dark wooden chair with
red velvet upholstery in a lavishly furnished up room.
Seated in the darkest corner, a man was nervously
twirling a cane around his fingers, making the copper
knob fly around like a huge, exotic beetle.

Not a word was spoken between them. It was
obvious both visitors took into account the walls were
thin in a fortuneteller's waiting room. Any trained
eavesdropper could distill useful information from a
cavalier conversation.

The silence gave Geerten an uncomfortable feeling: he noticed the man was constantly observing him. He heaved a sigh of relief when a door swung open and a maid stepped inside.

"Mr. Raes... Mrs. Reede will receive you now. Will you please follow me?"

The man clenched the fingers of his left hand around his cane and made a protesting gesture with his right hand. "I have all the time in the world. Let this gentleman go first. It is raining outside. I prefer to stay dry..."

"As you wish," said the maid, while she looked inquiringly at Geerten.

Geerten rose to his feet and gave the man a friendly nod when he started walking to the door.

I have been here before. Ada Reede came from a family of textile traders; several legacies had made her a wealthy woman. She dealt in anything that might be profitable and she provided loans to entrepreneurs. All her business decisions were complicated rituals; she would go into a trance, roll the dice and consult the cards. It was generally known that she was blessed with the gift of prophecy and made a lot of money because of it.

Anyone who wanted to make use of her gift wrote her a letter. If she replied with a rejection, it was useless to beg her to reconsider; she never gave anyone a second chance. Geerten Jacobsz had received an invitation, the fortuneteller had already helped him several times, issuing sage advice.

He recalled one of his recent visits. He remembered her saying, "I've learned much about this myself," she had explained to him. "Often I enjoy delving deeply into the problems of another person."

The maid led Geerten up a broad staircase to the first story, opening the door to a big stateroom at the front of the house. Ada Reede gave him a warm welcome. She wore an eccentric, shining silk robe, it was probably imported from Japan. Geerten, dressed in the fashion of his time, wore pastel justeaucorps, silk stockings, and shoes with silver buckles. His horsehair wig was short and full of curls. He had removed his three-cornered hat when he entered the room and put it on his knee after he had taken a seat at a table sitting opposite Ada. He noticed her studying every line in his face when he explained why he needed to consult with her again.

Geerten Jacobsz was the owner of a printing house and a bindery, a publisher as well. The freedom of the printed word was considered paramount in the Republic of the Seven United Netherlands, more than elsewhere in Europe. French Huguenots, political refugees, philosophers, and freethinkers had settled in Leiden to print their books, books that were banned elsewhere. Not so long ago a book had been published wherein man was compared with a machine and God was put on the sidelines. The book was not banned, but the patience of indignant, influential theologians had almost come to an end.

Someone had offered Geerten the opportunity to publish similar manuscripts, he told Ada about the shocking contents.

"My question to you is if I publish these works, will I risk long imprisonment or even worse? Must I fear getting involved in a lawsuit, will this cost me more than it will ever bring in?"

Ada had closed her eyes and leaned so far forward that her forehead rested on the tabletop. He had already been silent for quite a while, staring at her in surprise, when she slowly sat up and opened her eyes.

"Experimentum crucis..." she whispered, "an ordeal. The deciding test is..."

She opened a little wooden box and took out six dice made of walrus teeth, rolled them across the table, pushed them together, and stared at the spots. "What did I say, anything?"

"Experimentum crucis..." he repeated.

"Ah, but the dice tell me the opposite. It is not God who decides but the theologians will be wagging their tongues. They will be mild, Geerten Jacobsz, you can print the books and publish them. Yes, there will be a lot of commotion and that will draw attention to them. You will make a profit. People show little of even big flaws wherein man was compared with a machine and

God was put on the sidelines. The book was not banned, but the patience of indignant, influential theologians had almost come to an end.

Someone had offered Geerten the opportunity to publish similar manuscripts, he told Ada about the shocking contents.

"My question to you is if I publish these works, will I risk long imprisonment or even worse? Must I fear getting involved in a lawsuit, will this cost me more than it will ever bring in?"

Ada had closed her eyes and leaned so far forward that her forehead rested on the tabletop. He had already been silent for quite a while, staring at her in surprise, when she slowly sat up and opened her eyes.

"Experimentum crucis..." she whispered, "an ordeal. The deciding test is..."

She opened a little wooden box and took out six dice made of walrus teeth, rolled them across the table, pushed them together, and stared at the spots. "What did I say, anything?"

"Experimentum crucis..." he repeated.

"Ah, but the dice tell me the opposite. It is not God who decides but the theologians will be wagging their tongues. They will be mild, Geerten Jacobsz, you can print the books and publish them. Yes, there will be a lot of commotion and that will draw attention to them. You will make a profit. People show little of even big flaws and that is what makes them different. No opinions should remain unmentioned, especially not when they germinate in philosophical ground. Do what you have to do, present new insights for everyone who wants to read about them!"

Geerten felt relieved and stood up immediately. "It is clear to me that you can look into the future. I am very happy with your advice."

"Please don't go away yet," she put her dice back into the little wooden box. "I need your help now. There are only women in the house and I don't trust the man in the waiting room downstairs. His name is Tijn Raes, he is a cabinetmaker who urgently needs my help finding someone who stole money and merchandise from him. The name he gave as a reference is sound but can sense his presence clearly; it doesn't give me a good feeling. I am beginning to suspect he has evil intentions." She pointed to a door. "I would very much appreciate it if you step inside and leave the door ajar... you can come to the rescue when he becomes violent. Are you willing to help me?"

"Of course," he said firmly, "we have become good friends over time, you have given me your good advice once again."

He walked up to the door, opening it he was awed by imposing pieces of furniture that filled the room. Small silver objects shone behind the glass of a high display case, on top of other closets stood expensive china vases, there were chairs the size of thrones and splendid painting hung on the walls– portraits, landscapes and still lifes. A cabinet of curiosities containing an enormous amount of special objects that were probably collected by different generations – rare manuscripts, skulls of exotic animals, frightening little creatures in bottles, coins and crystals, a globe and a planetarium, indefinable little appliances, the statue of an Egyptian god, weapons and more paintings... dominated the center atop a fine silk rug.

Ada pulled a cord that hung near the wall behind her chair, a light tinkle could be heard below. The maid appeared and looked around. "I have time now to receive Mr. Raes."

The maid nodded, went downstairs, and came back not much later to announce Tijn Raes and let him in.

Ada rose to her feet but remained standing cautiously behind the big table. "Mr. Raes..."

The man walked up to her with large strides. Just before he reached her he let the cane twirl around his fingers allowing it skim across the tabletop. The copper knob broke the little box; the six dice flew into the air.

"Tijn Raes..., that's not my name... My true name is Nicolaes Nimbus; I came here to confront you and your scams. You are not a fortuneteller at all, you are a swindler. I will make your evil practices public unless you pay me hush money. And by that, I mean a lot of cash."

He held the cane in both hands and seemed ready to lash out. In the meantime, Geerten left the room of curiosities, carefully walking toward the table. He tried to walk lightly over the soft, thick carpets that lay strewn about like safe islands in a sea of shining parquet. The man stood with his back towards him, still screaming to Ada, who sat frozen in her chair. Geerten hit him with a left and a right in the neck. Tijn Raes tried to turn round quickly, but stumbled and fell, letting go of the cane. Geerten leaned forward and dealt him another blow. Tijn managed to avoid it by rolling to one side – then he jumped to his feet and ran up to the door.

The maid, who had run upstairs to see what was going on, was trampled in his haste to escape.

Geerten went after the man, rushing down the stairs and through the hall. The front door was open. Geerten looked outside, he watched from a distance as the man slipped on the wet cobblestones of De Breestraat, grazing his hands and knees as he scrambled to his feet and staggered along as if he'd had too much wine.

When he went upstairs again, the door to the stateroom closed. Another maid, whom he had not seen earlier, told him Ada had passed out, that he should wait till she managed to recover from her fright. After waited patiently for minutes, he was ushered inside.

Ada was leaning back in a dramatic pose on a sofa holding a perfume-sprinkled handkerchief under her nose. She gestured to an armchair opposite the sofa.

"Sit down, my friend. You have rescued me. I was right, my intuition didn't deceive me, that was a very bad man..."

"So his name is not Tijn Raes, I heard him tell you his real name, Nicolaes Nimbus."

Ada sat up straight and moved her forefinger to-and-fro. "No, no, the man is a liar!"

"How can you be so sure?" Geerten wanted to know.

"I will recognize the real Nicolaes Nimbus the moment I see him," she answered and quickly added, "but I understand you have no idea what I am talking about." He saw her shivering. "You rescued me," she repeated, "and that is why you deserve an explanation. Fortunetellers, the real visionaries, take their profession very seriously. All you can think up is already there. The past races away behind us, the future flies in front of us, and somewhere in the far distance they come together full circle. You can dream up everything and you can know everything. For most people this sounds crazy, for a small group it is a possibility, for us, it is a fact, we deal with it on a daily basis. Do you follow me, Geerten?"

"More or less..."

"Real fortune-tellers needn't fear anything. The charlatans among, things are quite different for them. Nicolaes Nimbus is a man of all times and when he turns up somewhere, it will be to punish someone for his boiler-room operation."

"What or who is a man of all times?" Geerten interrupted her.

"...Someone who is always there, there yesterday, tomorrow or a hundred years ago, perhaps a hundred years later. Nicolaes Nimbus is the macabre joke, worse than a satyr; he is someone with devilish traits. Thijs Raes must have heard about him. He might be a fortune-teller himself who doesn't take his customers very seriously, telling them what they want to hear to diddle them out of their money. He wanted to scare me, which he did. He accused me of evil practices and demanded hush money. That was what he was after – money! Now you know what was going on. You'd best forget that name; it is of no use for you. I would appreciate it if you'd stay for a time, I will order some wine and see to it that we eat a good meal. Let this subject be, talk about other things..."

About two hours later Geerten took leave of the fortuneteller, picking the cane up and taking it as a keepsake.

Ada Reed had given him good advice. He printed the books and published them. Leiden wasn't shaken to its foundations. Anyone able to read, laying a hand on the books, either found the contents revolting or agreed with the authors. The whole affair was no more than a ripple in the pond, caused by a tiny stone. Life went on.

✾✾✾

Free interpretation of an article from the archives of The Society of Tamfana.

Place: North Holland, The Netherlands. Time: Around 1950.

Her stage name was Mea Culpa (Latin for my fault) and she had the gift of faultless intuition. Even before someone said a single word, she received a torrent of information by looking at the person concerned only: attitude, look, the shape of face and fingers, their way of moving, clothes, hair, even their way of breathing. Her first impression always turned out to be the right one and the thoughts of the visitor were heard by her as if she was able to hear what was never said. Mea could dig into someone's past and see what was bound to happen in their future. Thanks to these miraculous gifts she had become rich. She abused information she received through her paranormal ways, she manipulated, intrigued, and blackmailed.

Businessmen and high government officials who asked for advice when they had to make difficult decisions soon became dependent on her guidance. She discovered lots of facts about them that should have remained secret forever. Mea was a fortuneteller who used black magic, nothing was off-limits for her to enrich herself. Having power over people gave her energy. Once a year at least she left her big canal house in Amsterdam to set up a fairground attraction. For seven days she sat in a big booth predicting the future of customers, using her crystal ball. She honed her skills, finding useful information as quickly as possible, staying alert as long as possible, and sharpening her special gifts. She only asked but a single guilder for her services, forcing herself to advise every visitor in less than five minutes.

She scared the hell out of everyone by describing secrets in short sentences:

"You broke into your neighbor's house and stole money. Someone else got blamed for it."

"She has passed away, your wife... You loved another woman when she was still alive."

"Your husband doesn't know your daughter isn't his child."

"Again and again you take money from your employer. Watch out, he is keeping an eye on you."

"Did you push someone? Have you murdered someone?"

"There is that letter you'd better tear to pieces before someone finds it."

While she spoke her big, dark brown eyes stared into the crystal ball; with every move of her head her long, black curls swung back-and-forth. And over and over again she showed her beautiful white teeth when she looked up, smiling, knowing she was right, having uncovered another deep dark secret.

Then she held up her hand, saying, "Give me money. You don't even have to confess because I already know everything. When I forgive you, here and now, all your sins will be washed away."

Those with no money left in tears, full of fear and more than often so sick that they had to throw-up not much later behind a shooting gallery or a haunted house; those who paid a sufficient number of guilders left feeling relieved.

❁ ❁ ❁

Five years after the Second World War fair days were celebrated exuberantly. Mea Culpa put up her booth on the square of a town in North Holland – it might have been Hoorn, Naarden, Den Helder, Enkhuizen, or Beverwijk, or perhaps somewhere in her own Amsterdam. The fairground people arrived in big trucks, many of their attractions were brand new, there were no villages of dwarfs or four-breasted women, but there was a boxing booth still where everyone with enough guts got invited to step into the ring and try to take down a tough fairground fighter. People enjoyed riding bumper cars, the Ferris wheel, the merry-go-round, throwing 10-cent Euros (dubbeltjes) in gambling machines, eating and drinking, being enchanted by the amazing jumble of movement, surprise, colors, scents, and ear-splitting noise.

A man shuffled along without looking around. He had put up the collar of his coat, the brim of his hat cast a shadow over his eyes. With his hands in his pockets, he went past the try-your-luck he-man attraction and a pastry stall. When he walked by the house of mirrors, he looked to the left and stepped inside. He hadn't bought a ticket, but no one stopped him. He didn't laugh along with the children and the adults standing in front of the mirrors, looking at their transformed images. Slowly, he leaned forward to study a skinny version of himself, seemingly fascinated by the impalpable world behind the glass. He stood there for a long time, till an impatient visitor nudged him, saying, "It's my turn, don't you think so?"

He moved to the next mirror. He remained standing there looking at his pseudo-fat self until he got pushed away. Ten minutes later he left and found his way between the crowd heading to the next attraction, Mea Culpa, Fortune-teller.

The man did not wait his turn in line. The moment a sad-looking woman with tears in her eyes stepped outside, he slipped in.

Mea sat down at a round table, stroking the surface of a crystal ball with her fingertips. She didn't know her new visitor but she sat up with a start and her jaw dropped when he took off his hat and greeted her, "Mea Culpa," he said in a deep dark voice, "It's about time I came."

Now she knew who he was. "Please, have mercy..." she stammered.

"Mea Culpa, you have only used your unique talents to enrich yourself, you have ruined the life of countless people. My name is Nicolaes Nimbus, I have come here to teach you a lesson."

❊ ❊ ❊

The next visitor, a middle-aged nervous woman, found two empty chairs in the booth. She heard sounds she could not place coming from behind a curtain. Sitting down at the little round table, she noticed a black Bakelite phone in the middle, no cord, no plug, just the phone. The women looked around skittishly... A phone all by itself and I wonder who's behind that curtain? I don't see a crystal ball either? All of a sudden she took the receiver from the hook and started dialing numbers with the forefinger of her left hand.

Not much later a clear voice sounded in her ear, "Henriëtte, so glad that you are here. I have some important things to tell you."

Henriëtte listened, fascinated by the powerful voice on the other end of the line. Wherever that is? She tried to relax, soon she felt totally at ease. No longer wondering who was talking to her, she let the words sink in.

Her character was revealed in flowing sentences, her fears were mentioned, explained, and wiped out. After a couple of minutes, she placed the receiver back on the hook, rose to her feet, and left the booth with a smile on her face.

"I am a totally different person now!" she shouted to the people standing in line. "Life is beautiful and I will be able to enjoy it for many, many years to come!"

Not much later, a young man entered the booth. He listened patiently to the sounds coming from behind the curtain and tried to guess what it was, perhaps a strangled cry, shuffling feet, the creaking of moving hinges, tapping on wood, knuckles knocking on glass. I think my imagination is running away with me. On a whim, he picked up the receiver and dialed an arbitrary number.

"Hello, Maarten," he heard, "how nice of you to come ..."

Tens of people sat down at the little table that day, felt the urge to pick up the receiver and press it to their ear. Listening to the voice, they were overwhelmed by an intense feeling of happiness and when they left the booth, they understood themselves better, became reconciled with all the mistakes they made and faced the future with confidence.

✵ ✵ ✵

White Dirk, a man with hair as white as snow, walked to Mea Culpa's booth for reasons unknown even to himself. He was the owner of the Ferris wheel. After he'd had coffee he'd gone back to the fairground walking past the attractions watching the gondolas of his Ferris wheel, high above the roofs of the houses behind it, moving through the blue sky. No one was standing near Mea's booth, as if an invisible wall prevented people from coming closer. But White Dirk walked up to it. Before he entered he threw away the stub of his cigar and took off his hat. What he saw inside made him so sick he started to retch, covering his mouth and nose with his free hand, looking with half-closed eyes passed his forefinger. There was no round table, no chairs. An oriental carpet decorated the floor, an apparatus Dirk immediately recognized as a fortunetelling machine stood in the middle of the room. The underside consisted of a dark wooded square box, the upper was made of glass and metal. Behind the glass, a puppet was supposed to be sitting there – a fortuneteller with a beard, a garment and a turban – that started to gesture the moment a coin was put the mechanism, movement ceased after a little card had come out of a slot with a prediction written on it in bold print.

The puppet was missing. Bilious green light shone around a damaged head. There were bruises on both cheeks, the chin was grazed, sticky hair and sweaty skin were there for all to see. Never in his life had White Dirk seen such frightened eyes – they bulged out of their sockets, staring at him. Her lips moved. He heard a voice, without understanding a word, and saw condensation appear on the inside of the glass. Mea Culpa's body had been crammed in the box; how her head could be sticking through a hole in wood that was just wide enough for her long, slender neck was a mystery. Her red-glassed earrings were like grotesque drops of blood that seemed to spatter about when she started to shake her head vigorously. White Dirk leaned forward and pressed his ear to the glass trying to understand her. He listened carefully.

Much to his surprise, he heard Mea Culpa cry out, "Throw a coin into the slot!" He stared at her, his mouth opened in disbelief. She uttered a single word, "Please..."

All was quiet as if the fairground had been deserted. He took out a ten cent piece. Carefully he dropped it into the slot. The wooden box began to shake, White heard the sound of turning cogwheels and the unwinding of a spring. Mea Culpa opened her mouth wide. A loud cry broke the glass, the wooden panels of the box burst apart.

Mea's curled up body rolled through the fragments of glass, splinters, and metal parts. She stretched her arms and legs and started crying. White Dirk vomited in his hat and left the booth, leaning over, running with fast, uncertain strides. Only after he arrived at the Ferris wheel and looked in disgust at the contents of his hat, did he realized he should call for help. Ten minutes later he entered the booth for the second time, accompanied by a police officer.

There were two empty chairs and a crystal ball sitting in the middle of a little table. There were no fragments of glass, no wooden splinters, or metal parts on the carpet. There was no one present. Mea Culpa had left the fairground. She never came back.

❀ ❀ ❀

Free interpretation of an article from the archives of The Society of Tamfana.

Place: Gelre, the present Dutch province Gelderland.
Time: Around 1200.

Hallucinating with hunger and thirst, a young knight sat down leaning against a big beech tree. His jerkin was torn, tufts of wool and horsehair stuck out from between the linen. The thick garment made it easier to bear the weight of a heavy coat of mail. His coat of mail, his shield, and helmet were missing. He didn't even have a horse. His only valuable possession was his sword; he had driven it into the ground next to him. Clotted blood from a head wound had colored his blond hair red.

A figure loomed in front of him, a man dressed in a long coat, carrying a leather shoulder bag. He had the utmost trouble raising his hand far enough to make it look like a greeting.

"My name is Alwin," the knight mumbled, after which he licked his tongue past his dry lips. "I am a very sorry traveler, but I have no food to share nor drop of water to..."

He fell silent when the man raised a hand – not to greet him but to interrupt him. "I carry no weapons and I have something to eat and drink with me," the deep voice intoned. "You had plenty of time to rise to your feet, grab your sword, and take what you needed."

The night shook his head slowly. "My sword protects the helpless only; that is what it is made for."

The man sank down on his knees and placed the leather bag between them om the ground. "Those are fine words, the right words. And I do believe you. There was something I had to do in Reurle after which I walked past farmland and went through the woods, trying to find a place to sleep. Then I saw you sitting here with your back against that tree – an exhausted knight errant, I gather?"

"How did you know..."

The man raised his hand for the second time. Not a word was spoken between them. The man opened his bag and took out a little stone jar. He carefully brought it to Alwin's lips and let him take a few sips. Soon Alwin started to feel better eating eagerly of the bread and ham the man offered him.

Alwin felt a strange pressure in his ears. He felt the wind stroking past his cheeks, but could not hear the rustle of countless beech leaves above him. The man's voice echoed in his head while his lips remained closed. The words made images appear in his mind's eye, he saw himself as a boy in and around his father's castle, always surrounded by others. The building changed into a huge ant-heap and he could not find his way back home between all those identical, swarming insects. Endless numbers of ants went toward the heap, carrying richly varied booty with them, dead beetles, wings of butterflies, parts of grasshoppers, and the abdomen of a wasp. A single ant walked the opposite direction getting further and further away from the anthill. The tiny insect reached the base of a gigantic beech and started to climb up...

"Do you understand?" sounded in Alwin's head. He nodded. "You are the ant that had to leave the nest. You had five elder brothers. Two of them passed away at a young age. The three remaining brothers can't wait to take over from your father. Fratricide is a possibility we can't rule out. There is no place for you there, young nobleman... You took your horse and left, facing an uncertain future, a knight with noble intentions. You drew your sword to defend others and you placed justice above power. But where has it taken you in a world full of oppression? You are too tired to climb up, you are about to fall down."

Alwin got up slowly, staggering on his feet. Turning his face toward the beech, he looked up along the trunk. A tiny insect fell; the ant crawled between his feet and disappeared into the moss. He turned towards the man who had also risen to his feet. "I feel strong, even rested, I have drunk and my stomach is filled. Is there anything I can do for you?"

"Pull your sword out of the ground and throw it as far as you can."

It sounded like an order so Alwin reacted immediately. He caught hold of the hilt with both hands and flung his weapon through the air with all his might. It whizzed past the beech, past other trees, turning round and round and the sharp point disappeared deep into the earth.

"Your future begins where the sword is, go there! You will outlive all your brothers and learn to value life. Someone like you deserves prosperity and luck and that is what you shall have."

Alwin started walking noticing how self-confident and determined his steps were. His weariness had left him. He became intensely aware of himself and felt a blessed solidarity with his surroundings as if he realized he was destined to be here and everything should go better from now on. He pulled on the sword. Grass, moss, and soil disappeared, a hole appeared. At the bottom lay a stone jar, much bigger than the one the man had brought to Alwin's lips. It had been broken into two almost equal parts by the sword. A great number of centuries-old Roman gold coins lay exposed. Alwin stooped, there were too many coins to pick up with one hand. He quickly stood up and turned around. The man had taken his bag and walked away from the beech.

"Do you want to share?" Alwin shouted.

Without turning his head, the man waved goodbye.

"Your name!" shouted Alwin. "At least tell me your name!"

"...Nimbus!" The man boomed, disappearing between the trees.

Alwin was alone again. His astonishment grew as he took more and more gold coins from the pit. Prosperity and luck?

Chapter 2

THE READING MAN

After a turbulent night, mild Sunday morning sun shone down on the Witte de Withstraat in Rotterdam; the soft light had driven drunk darkness away and temporarily tamed nightlife's chaos. Behind closed doors, the restaurants, pubs, coffee houses, galleries, and shops were getting prepared for another hectic day.

Rein Vulpes had taken a stroll through the awakening inner city. Stopping at the Witte de Withstraat, he looked for a seat at a terrace. Sitting down, he looked around, a smile passed over his face; he was alone in the long street with hundreds of empty chairs on either side.

A man in his mid-thirties with light brown hair and light brown, lively eyes, he always made use of his stage name, derived from Vulpes vulpes, the Latin name for a red fox. His first name was real and he felt a strong affinity to Reinaert, the fox from medieval Europe portrayed in adventurous animal stories as a very sly rascal who is always one step ahead of the others. Rein always managed to push things his way, he knew how to lead everyone up the garden path, how to set a trap for other animals, from cat to dog, from badger to hare and even the strong wolf, the bear, and the royal lion. He knew many lines from poems about the fox and every now and then when the situation asked for it, he recited:

"Then hear me, noble gentlemen, I will be happy to inform you how I, innocent like the hares, came to my first tricks and snares..."

Rein Vulpes was given to laughter, he was pliable, but was not to be trifled with and he was used to going his own way. He lived from day-to-day with the illusion that he owned the town; he diminished all people around him to mere walkers-on in a play that was especially written for him.

"And when the curtain falls, when I breathe my last, it is all over and done – then nothing exists anymore."

Rein thanked his cheerful character because he was always able to see things from two sides. He understood the problems of a bank manager just as well as those of the poor devil who couldn't get a loan; the motivation of a criminal was just as clear to him as the lament of someone who got robbed. When two people disagreed with each other he could side with each of them and come up with solid arguments to prove they were both right. But most of all he preferred to mind his own business.

He was a man of many talents, specializing in painting. After many successful efforts, he considered himself a master forger. When he delved into the life of a painter and studied his oeuvre – whether the artist concerned was alive or already dead for ages – there came a moment when he identified himself so well with the said artist that he was able to imitate his style perfectly. Rein Vulpes knew how to put himself in someone else's shoes.

A man turned up the street, looked around searchingly, and walked straight to Rein, recognizing him immediately. A stout man but small in stature, he laboriously sat down next to Rein, blowing his cheeks up and breathing out loudly.

"Rein! Finally, someone who won't let me down, thank you for that. It's good to see you. I had a dozen appointments yesterday and no one turned up. And I really need some money. Have you been able to sell that watch?"

"You know you can always count on me, Brink, the man gave me four hundred euro."

Brink's small eyes bulged slightly. "That is good, very good indeed...' he stammered. "As you know, I had thought it worth about seven hundred and fifty but it was rather damaged."

Rein took twenty twenty-euro notes from his pocket and gave them to Brink who, in his turn, gave six back.

"Thirty percent for you was the agreement."

"That was the agreement, repeated Rein.

Brink was a cowardly swindler who did not dare sell what he had stolen. He had built a network of people who did that for him, keeping himself out of harm's way; he'd already spent one year in prison and he didn't want to go through that a second time. Still, he woke often bathed in perspiration from claustrophobic dreams wherein he broke down the walls of his cell with a sledgehammer.

"Perhaps you've gotten more than four hundred euro, doesn't matter. You can keep the rest for yourself." He screwed up his little eyes and leered at Rein. Because Rein did not react, he hastened to go on, "Thank you, thank you very much. I hope to arrange something for another time."

A few days ago Rein had taken a streetcar to Schiedam entering a jewelry shop in the old center; the proprietor bought gold, silver, and watches from individuals. "Inherited from an uncle, I would like to know if it is worthwhile to get the glass repaired."

The owner took the watch to his little office, Rein wondered if the man would take time to see if the watch had been stolen.

"It seems wise to me to have it fixed," said the man, when he returned. "It is a Swiss watch and it is a collector's item."

Rein shrugged his shoulders nonchalantly. "It is not worth much, is it?"

"You should replace the glass and the clockwork has to be cleaned and repaired. I could sell it for five thousand euros right away. If it does not mean too much to you, I would love to buy it from you for three thousand. That might seem to be a lot less, but the replacement, cleaning and repairing cost a lot of money too. And of course, I want to make some profit."

"Sure, I understand," Rein knew for certain the watch was worth much more because he heard it in the man's voice and knew it was so just by looking at his face – hints like that seldom escaped his notice. "We'd both like to make a bit of money. Alright then, let's do it. I have no special memories of the watch... nor of my uncle either." He produced a fake ID and put it on the counter.

Now as he had paid Brink and received his share from him, he smiled, the short ride to Schiedam had enriched him by twenty-seven hundred and twenty euro. "Sure, you can always count on me when you have something you want me to sell for you."

Brink nodded, and all of a sudden he seemed in a hurry. He slid down from the chair and knocked against the table, it was big enough for twenty people or more.

"They will start tapping beer in a couple of hours, Fox, but I will not wait for that. See you later."

He tottered away, stopping suddenly as his hand slipped into the inner pocket of his jacket.

"Wait a minute," he said as he turned around and came back, "someone's looking for you. I don't know his name, but he addressed me in a pub on the Oude Binnenweg. He had heard from someone that you were an extremely good painter. Here is his number. I didn't want to give him your number because I didn't know if that was okay with you. Give him a call. Or don't. You'll have to decide that for yourself, of course..."

Rein took a little piece of paper from him. Brink walked away, this time he didn't come back.

Rein raised his head up to the sun and felt satisfied as more people entered the street. After some time he took his smartphone and dialed the number written on the piece of paper.

"Hello?"

"My name is Rein Vulpes, you mentioned me to an acquaintance, Brink by name, in a pub here in Rotterdam. He gave me your number."

"Nice to hear from you, Rein. I understand you make use of a stage name. Well, everyone calls me Argus because I seldom trust anyone..."

He started laughing so loud, Rein held his phone a couple of inches from his ear. He did not react nor did he laugh along with the man. Argus told him the name of the pub and asked if Rein knew it. "There are not many pubs in Rotterdam I don't know about."

"How about meeting there, in a while, let's say between a quarter past twelve and half-past twelve? I don't know who you are, but I'll be wearing a worn, checkered jacket, I have light blue, skittish Argus eyes..."

He burst out laughing again. Rein's reaction was short, "I'll be there around that time. See you then."

❀ ❀ ❀

Behind the Art Nouveau façade of the pub on the Oude Binnenweg, time had held its breath; anyone drinking with half-closed eyes could make himself believe he'd just tasted beer from early 1900. The last time Rein had been here, a noisy regular had dragged everyone further back in time with a story about jenever.

"At the end of the seventeenth century, England had a Dutch king, William III," said the man. "British soldiers had been in our country already to help fight against Spanish domination. They drank jenever to quash their fears, they called it Dutch courage. During that time jenever was spelled with a g: genever. William III of Orange imported it. When the English started to make it, they called it gin." He pointed at a stained-glass window, "There only a stone's throw, lies Schiedam –

and no gin in the world tastes better than the jenever distilled in that town!"

Rein sat at a small table in the pub. He asked for a tulip glass of jenever to taste to see if the man had been right and also a glass of beer to enjoy with half-closed eyes; two orders, so he wouldn't have to choose.

He watched as the man in the worn, checkered jacket entered and looked around nervously.

Rein raised his hand. Argus sat down opposite him. "Hello, Rein! It's still early, but I'll have the same. Then it will automatically become a lazy Sunday and I'll take a nap before dinner. Listen, I'm only a messenger, a middleman. All you need to know has been written down."

He took a folded piece of snow-white paper from the inner jacket pocket and gave it to him. Rein unfolded it, taking the time to read it.

"A middleman, one who doesn't know his client can never let his tongue run away with him," continued Argus. "That makes me reliable–follow me?"

"Of course," Rein mumbled, without looking up from the paper.

The letter was addressed, "Dear Mr. R. Vulpes..." The unknown writer came to the point immediately offering a fantastic amount of money for a painting, followed by a detailed description of what he had to paint, a painting that appeared to originate from the

Dutch Golden Age, the time of Rembrandt van Rijn, Johannes Vermeer and Frans Hals. "Canvas, frame, and paint will be delivered to you; use this paint only." He was asked to paint a middle-aged man sitting at a table-turning a page in a thick book. On the floor, there was another thick book, on which his right foot rested. On the spine of that book he had to paint a name in big letters: Nicolaes Nimbus. The instructions were short and clear; the letter ended with two questions, Do you agreed to the proposal and When will the painting be ready? Someone would come and collect it and pay him in cash on that day. After that, he should forget that he had ever made it. The painting should be hard to distinguish from real works of art of the seventeenth century; the unknown client knew techniques used to age the paint, among other things, the craquelure process. Rein was no expert where that was concerned, but he knew it was possible to make a new painting look old, heating was used as well as different types of special varnish.

In the meantime, Argus had gone to the bar and came back with a little tulip glass of jenever and a glass of beer. "Well?" he asked.

"I'll do it." Rein folded the paper and put it in his pocket. "As soon as I receive the material, I will start. Someone can come and collect it two weeks from now, on Sunday or the Monday after that. Do you have my address?"

"Everything will be alright," was all that Argus had to say to this.

Both men were silent, sitting opposite each other, sipping their strong jenever and cooling their throats with beer. There were not many customers in the pub and now and then it was so quiet one could hear the tap water running in the buffet's rinsing tub. It took Rein no more than a few seconds to sink away into a mental state, allowing him to daydream. He had no desire to look upon the skittish rolling light-blue eyes of Argus and felt relaxed, safe, and satisfied in his own fantasy world; he often compared his physical body and his invisible figments to that of a tangible mushroom and the huge, underground network of fungal hyphae.

Argus brought him back to the real world, "All success with your painting." Argus stood up, walked to the door, opened it, and disappeared.

Rein remained seated for almost an hour then he paid his bar tab and went home. He lived in the center, a side street of the Kruiskade. He rented an apartment there – a spacious atelier with a small bedroom, a bathroom, and a kitchen off to the side.

That afternoon he read the instructions again, cleared his atelier, and rifled through a number of books about Dutch painters from the Golden Age.

On Monday morning a courier brought a big parcel. There was no name or logo on the courier's van.

Rein didn't have to sign for the parcel; the name of the sender was nowhere to be found on the package.

The parcel contained one stretched canvas, a frame, several brushes, and a large number of glass paint pots. Rein noticed the canvas and the frame were old and the structure of the paint was quite different from what he often used in tubes.

He grinned knowing what this meant – when experts examined his painting, they would conclude that it most likely was made in the seventeenth century. That required incredible craftsmanship, patience, and devotion, three qualities he had at his disposal. He placed the blank canvas, took a few steps back, and filled the emptiness with different projections of his fantasy.

An art forger had to be an art connoisseur. Rein had studied many unsigned paintings from the Golden Age – splendid works of unknown artists. There were portraits full of character among them he could use as examples for his own middle-aged, reading man. He was also thinking of works from less known masters, Abraham Bloemaert from Utrecht, Adriaen van der Werff, and Arent Diepraam, both from Rotterdam. Rein used his imagination to project changing images on the canvas and finally decided what he should paint.

He left his apartment and walked to the Kruiskade to buy food for the entire week so he could work continuously. Most of the time he cooked extensive meals, but during this time pizza, noodle soup, eggs, and bread would be sufficient. While he walked to different shops, he thought about the contents of the parcel. The frame and the canvas were old, without being valuable. But if the paint was actually made according to the traditions of the seventeenth century, the contents of the glass pots were unique; it must have cost a lot of money to have it made. He knew how difficult it was to mix the right ingredients in the right proportions. Linseed oil, lead, cobalt oxide, iron oxide, dried and ground scaled insects, burnt animal bones, glass crushed into powder, clay, and sand, wheat flour...

The creation of such a piece of art was a three-part process, starting with the so-called dead-coloring – applying a thin coat of paint quickly giving everything its place, where all the colors were determined. After that everything was brought to life by applying new coats, Next time for the refinement, the detailing and highlighting.

Rein returned home with a bag full of food, his head filled with ideas. He locked the door, determined to work till late that night.

✿ ✿ ✿

Only after Rein stood right in front of the canvas did he notice it had been carefully cleaned. This aroused his interest. His client wanted to have a painting of a reading man so badly that he had sacrificed a centuries-old work of art for it.

Rein had a huge collection of secondhand books about the art of painting but he didn't exactly handle them with care – he tore out pages of images he could use and pinned them up on the wallpaper to the left of the easel. Different portraits of men hung there, including a self-portrait of Rembrandt and a number of reproductions showing mostly furniture from the seventeenth century, he had plenty of examples for a table and a chair. He began with full conviction that he would not make any mistakes. He had found a picture of a painting from Pieter Elinga Janssens, The Reading Woman. He used the chair on which she sat, but he painted it in another position – giving it a quarter turn. The table was painted looking exactly like one he'd found from an unsigned still life. He had countless examples of candlesticks, mugs, vases, clothing, footwear, and of course books to choose from.

For the head of the man, he studied Matthew and The Angel from Jan van Bijlert and a work by Barent Pietersz Fabritius, while he looked constantly at the techniques Rembrandt used.

A hazy figure came into being, surrounded by vague forms and light tones. Rein didn't allow himself much sleep, got up early, and worked till late at night. The Reading Man was given character, not by magic did his eyes sparkle or his skin appear true-to-life – it was all a matter of true craftsmanship. Rein Vulpes was a painter of the highest level. At four steps, it looked as if one was able to count the man's hairs, two steps forward, his beard changed into a grey illusion of paint.

The paint was special and every now and then Rein smelled unknown scents when he opened one of the glass pots. He used a particular, smooth-spreading gold to paint the name on the spine of the book that lay on the floor and on which the foot of the man rested... Nicolaes Nimbus.

A few days later he framed the painting. The four parts fit together without a problem, fastening them with thin, little wooden laths.

Rein expected Angus to collect the painting, but he never saw him again.

On a rainy Monday morning, exactly two weeks after the parcel had been delivered, a man rang the doorbell. He had a flat cardboard box with him that would be perfect for the transportation of the painting. The man handed Rein an envelope without uttering a word.

Now standing in the atelier, the man hardly looked at the work of art, lifted it from the easel, packed it very carefully in bubble wrap and covered the four corners with cardboard shock absorbers. Rein rushed to his little bedroom to check the contents of the envelope. He found the promised amount of money within it but no thank you note. He hid the money and walked into the atelier.

"The painting is not ready in its current condition; one should remove the frame. Actually, I didn't need the frame at all."

The man wore a black suit and a white shirt. Rein thought he might be a chauffeur by trade. "I am not allowed to say much about it," the man shrugged his shoulders as he continued, "and I don't know much about it either. Everything came from somewhere in The Netherlands. Now I have to take it abroad..." The painting was now packed in the cardboard box. "I have a long way to go," said the man, while he reached out his hand. "I'm off..."

Rein shook hands with him and opened the door. "Abroad... What do you mean, Belgium? France? Germany?"

The man didn't look back, walking in the direction of the Kruiskade, where he turned to the left. Rein thought he might be on his way to a parking garage to collect his car. Perhaps the man lied about a long boat trip; boat, plane...

Rein felt tired but hungry. He had worked till late every night, living on only pizza, noodle soup, eggs, and bread. After shopping and eating a big lunch he went to bed and slept for six hours.

He practiced the art of lucid dreaming, honing it to perfection. The Dutch author and psychiatrist, Frederik van Eeden, had coined the term in an article published in 1913. Lucid dreaming is a state of being where the dreamer is aware of the fact that he is dreaming, able to guide his dreams in a certain direction; Rein was able to dream what he wanted; more than often he was the sly, unsurpassed fox who played tricks on the other animals, or the human variant able to get everything he longed for.

To Freud, dreams were so complicated that only a psychoanalyst was able to unravel them, later adversaries said the opposite by suggesting dreams had no secret disguises; they are just what they are and nothing more. Rein was certain the brain of a sleeping individual could fantasize in unlimited ways, that it is possible to interfere, creating images and subjects as one pleases. Even in broad daylight, he was able to let himself sink into a dream state wherein he was the director of a film that he saw in his mind's eye, and of course, he always played the leading role. The last time was in the pub on the Oude Binnenweg, as he sat opposite Argus. He knew he would have a pleasant time if he ever got placed in an isolation cell.

But this Monday afternoon his dreams were disturbing. Pleasant images had evolved and he had immediately provided them with a storyline that took him to a universe without limits. Descending from a star-spangled sky, he ended up in a street full of bars, nightclubs, and gambling houses. A porter dressed in a bright red uniform beckoned him with his left hand and opened a door with his right hand, "Come in on! Come in! No wish remains unfulfilled. And everything is free, so there is nothing to lose and much to win..."

He stepped inside and much to his surprise he saw the room he had recently painted. The reading man looked up from his book, annoyed by his presence. Rein ran outside opening the door of another establishment. The same man sat reading his book. Rein made the surroundings change and floated over a flat landscape, following the windings of a river. The moment he stood on the ground again, he saw a table and a chair on a grassy field; the man sat there reading his book. Rein was no longer able to control his dream, when he finally woke up he could only think of the man he had painted.

"Nicolaes Nimbus," he thought aloud as he pictured the golden letters on the spine of the book while walking via the Kruiskade toward the Westersingel.

Feeling richer with new geld in his pocket, he sat in a restaurant and ordered a bottle of wine. Studying the menu, he could not choose between one of two dishes. If he had been bigger and fatter, he undoubtedly would have ordered both at the same time. Often when he was undecided, he made use of a die. "Even numbers for steak, uneven for fish..." He rolled the die across the bright white tablecloth. "Three. So fish it will be."

Rein ordered, waited, and drank, sinking into a daydream once again confronted by the reading man. Often he was given orders to imitate an artist or copy a famous work of art in detail, promising he would never tell anyone he was the one who painted it.

This time it was different as if the scent of that particular paint had influenced him as if the paint had penetrated his brain so that he had to paint the reading man in his head with imaginary brushes over and over.

His fish was served and he started eating. The first bite reminded him that, despite his extensive lunch, he was still very hungry and probably able to dispatch a second meal as well.

While he ate and drank, he decided to locate the painting come Hell or high water. Why was I asked to paint it and who was the client? Perhaps I'll find it on the net.

He left the restaurant, walking back home with his hands in his pockets. After drinking that bottle of white wine he didn't feel like going to a pub. He refused to look back, he had a strange feeling someone was walking right behind him.

The man he had just painted made him think of the oldest bronze statue in The Netherlands – a standing, reading Desiderius Erasmus; the residents of Rotterdam said it was accredited with magical powers. The statue stood on the Grotekerkplein. People believed Erasmus turned a page each time the St. Laurens Church clock struck the hour.

Rein started walking faster, imagining Erasmus doing his utmost to keep pace with him, with his book under his arm, a hand on his bonnet to prevent him from losing his headgear, the wide sleeves of his gown swinging to-and-fro at every hasty step.

Chapter 3

Dieter Brunn left early that morning from Friedrichshafen for a hundred and twenty-five mile trip to Munich. The pitch-black Mercedes rode at a moderated speed on the busy highway. Dieter listened to music, making certain he was unavailable to anyone. Safe, inside his comfortable metal cocoon, with no drivers on the road other than himself, he had time to think.

Together with the business associate of his deceased father, Antomius Heck, he had built an imposing conglomerate in Germany, Austria, and Switzerland, so many corporations that he has lost count long ago. The companies, listed as Holdings Brunnheck, developed specialized equipment concentrating mainly on perfecting satellites, guarding them against cyber-attacks, robotization in all possible fields, and the creation of artificial intelligence.

Technique and innovation worked hand-in-hand in Bavaria and Dieter felt at home there. He was a well-to-do man of influence and in certain ways, he was happy as well but he worried about the future. But he was not alone where that was concerned. A group of important entrepreneurs in the fields of technical sciences, biotechnology, artificial intelligence, philosophy, and psychiatry shared his concerns working closely to monitor changes before they became uncontrollable.

Dieter Brunn was on his way to a meeting with this group of men and women.

His personal opinion about business and the possibilities of the future: "If you don't do it, someone else will."

Practice had shown him this way of thinking would go far to advance the human race. He had memorized his verbal itinerary and refreshed his memory while driving.

Do you want to start a company that produces implantable equipment that links people to computers to make them more intelligent? Do you want to develop a system that makes billions of people dependent on the blessings of artificial intelligence? Do you want to make it possible for expectant parents to have a child that has at their disposal all the qualities they consider appropriate? Do you want to bring humanity to a higher level, using artificial intervention?

If you don't do it, someone else will and after the train has left the station and the brakes don't work, it will become a wild ride. It is not an old-fashioned locomotive; it is a wonder of technology with a robot as the engineer, loaded with everything that will change the world in the most drastic way. Perhaps the trail will end at the abyss, dragging us all into damnation, "...or the robot that is smarter than us will tell us the ultimate joke, so that we will literary laugh ourselves to death..."

Halfway through the trip, Dieter stopped at a roadhouse for a cup of coffee, black, no sugar, as he searched for a seat at a window with a view of the parking lot. He sat there wearing jeans, a leather jacket, and white sports shoes – no one would ever suspect he was enormously rich and influential. He looked like a common man in his thirties, just an inconspicuous traveler attracting little or no attention.

Despite his age, Dieter looked at the world with a certain melancholy, something had been lost never to return, a stable youth with pleasant college days fondly remembered. Scientific developments tended to change everything at a fast pace and he had taken part in it.

He wanted to stay involved in that process, hoping to live for a hundred years at least, perhaps one hundred and twenty was a hundred and fifty impossible. Worldwide people searched for ways to eliminate disease and strengthen the body. It was one of the most important items on the agenda and for some of the members it was a matter of urgency, they were in the winter of their lives. They pumped millions into companies that searched for the solution to near immortality. It would be so sad to die today while it might be possible tomorrow to postpone the unavoidable.

Fort Web took up the entire top floor of Gabi Stein's office buildings. Gabi was an entrepreneur who, despite her age, still managed her CompuStein Hightech enterprises. The group, Das Web, was expected to meet there later.

Dieter drank his coffee, enjoying his anonymity, surrounded by so many people. Everyone left him alone; no one asked him even one question.

The newest scientific conclusions were considered hard-as-nails fact. Blind evolution had created man and man, no more than a collection of natural parts, without a soul that would continue to exist after death – life, registered by the human brain, was a bizarre illusion.

Most of the time, Dieter was satisfied with that illusion, but he wondered often why a human being could be so painfully aware of his own uselessness. It was not for nothing that Das Web had admitted a philosopher in its ranks, Carsten von Haller, he had the gift to change uselessness into a benefit.

❋ ❋ ❋

Dieter parked his car in front of the building and got out. The CompuStein Hightech logo looked like a screen carved in a rock as if a genius from the stone age had come up with a sensational invention. It was as a huge, artificial design on the roof of the building, under it he saw the dark windows of Fort Web.

The big glass doors flew open for him. He was recognized by unseen equipment. Someone waved at him from a counter and several people said hello. He greeted them as he walked through the enormous hall to the elevators. He was also recognized in a special single elevator that whizzed up through a transparent shaft to the top floor, unreachable by everyone who had nothing to do there.

The curved glass door glided to one side. He stepped out and walked via a hall and a corridor to an immense space, the Fort Web living room. Gabi ran up to him and embraced him, kissing him on both cheeks and stepping back so she could look him over.

"Dieter Brunn, don't you ever get a day older? You are blessed with eternal youth!"

She had a smooth face and a beautiful, slender figure, only her eyes gave it away, she was no longer a young woman. times She had talked about that with Folco Andermann, an old friend, a giant in the pharmaceutical industry. She had asked him to search for a way to make her eyes sparkle like those of a person of twenty.

Carsten von Haller, the philosopher, had meddled in, "The eyes reflect the state of the mind. Your eyes can lie about everything, Gabi, except for your age."

Gabi stepped forward, putting a hand on Dieter's shoulder. She whispered in his ear, "Thodor Baron is acting strange. He mentions the same point in time constantly. Twelve o'clock. For the rest of the time, he keeps silent and he seems rather confused. We have no idea what to do with him."

It was half-past ten. "I am curious," was his only comment.

The furnishing seemed antique and the walls were hung with paintings that had the look of Cézanne, Manet, and Renoir, but everything was an imitation and of recent vintage. The classical music piped softly from invisible loudspeakers, was composed by a computer program developed by one of Gabi's companies.

The gatherings were always informal. On certain days, like this one, every member tried to get there to exchange information, to conduct some business, and brainstorm new ideas.

People stood up to shake hands with Dieter. Rosa Linge, a young woman who owned a number of high-tech companies, like Gabi, was happy to see him, "I have some interesting things for you to look at, Dieter!"

Folco Andermann, a giant in the pharmaceutical industry, greeted him cordially. Lucas Montaigne, a designer of advanced hardware for hospitals and the army, said he needed his help to perfect a complicated project.

Carsten von Haller, the philosopher, looked at him from under thick, grey, bushy eyebrows and remarked, "You really look terrific! The secret is solved, all you have to do is – just like you have – buy yourself a house on Lake Constance. It's good to see you, Dieter."

He talked with many men and women as he walked, with a big mug of black coffee in his hand, to the meeting room and the library. The complex was huge with a dining room, a fitness center; there were bedrooms as luxurious as the most expensive hotel rooms, bathrooms, and a kitchen. Members spent the night here often when they had much to discuss and the day was too short. The kitchen was seldom used because food and drinks could be ordered by the restaurant on the grounds and be delivered directly to their rooms.

Thodor Baron was seated in the library; he had a broad, balding forehead, the few hairs he still had hung down in long, thin wisps behind his prominent ears. He sat there on the edge of a chair with his hands on his knees moving back-and-forth to a rhythm that did not correspond with that of the classical music everyone else heard.

Dieter came in and stood in front of him. "Hello, Thodor. We haven't seen each other in a long time... How are you doing?"

"Twelve o'clock," Thodor mumbled, without looking up at him.

"What?"

"Twelve o'clock," Thodor repeated, still moving his upper body to-and-fro.

Thodor was one of the first members of the group, introduced by Folco Andermann. The old Folco had always consulted fortune-tellers before he made important decisions or signed contracts. He and Thodor had become good friends.

"There are a thousand ways to convince me fortune-tellers are useless and there is no reason to believe in what they do," Folco always said to skeptics. "But they know things that can be very useful, they see things that remain invisible to me and it has always been wise for me to listen to their advice."

Thodor soon became friends with everyone. He had been in dozens of labs to undergo tests; the workings of his brain were examined countless times. Slowly but surely more and more members began to ask the fortune-teller for his advice when they had to make an important choice and most of the time the advice turned out to be wise. It remained a mystery how Thodor was able to look into the future and still he was invited to come to a laboratory for another thorough examination. Thodor had no problems with that at all, he was very co-operative and left all the suspicious scientists in despair. Everyone liked him, for many members he had become a confidential friend who took time to listen and was always willing to give advice. Thodor was a phenomenon, a mystery, an impossibility, or maybe the exception to the rule; his predictions remained confusing but turned out to be very lucrative.

"Very well then," said Dieter, "twelve o'clock, Thodor..."

Dieter walked along with some other members and entered the meeting room, where identical thrones stood around a large ornate table. The elaborate chairs were designed to make everyone feel important and attention-worthy.

He remained standing; his back against a wall, he crossed his arms and smiled.

Carsten von Haller, the philosopher, stood by the table while two of the thrones were occupied by new members, Herta and Rolf Wallis, owners of the Wallis Biotech group of companies. Carsten, a conceited person who loved to hear himself talk, was considered the group's conscience. Now that he had found two willing victims after welcoming them cordially, he explained his plea for consciousness to them. Dieter had heard it often, but it still fascinated him so he listened in again.

"Life isn't something you can grasp and hold, life is happening and you are a part of it. In Germany we have always done our utmost to explain our place on Earth, I don't have to tell you how many philosophers have tried to come up with answers to the important questions of life."

But he will do it anyway. Dieter was thinking and he was proven right immediately.

"Fichte, Kant, Schopenhauer, Schelling, Hegel, Nietzsche, Heidegger..."

And of course, he will mention himself as well, to make himself feel important.

Carsten von Haller mentioned more names and said, "Very carefully I bring up the rear in order not to disturb all these men of consequence... Everything turns on what makes us human beings so unique – and that is our sublime, and up to now, inexplicable consciousness. Let me be clear about one of Das Web's most important stands: If we find ourselves sitting on top of a mountain somewhere to enjoy the view of the beautiful valley in front of us, we would not have any trouble with a robot sitting next to us interpreting the same landscape with its artificial consciousness."

Carsten stood between the two thrones, put his hands to the left and the right, and leaned forward, "I know as well as you that artificial intelligence has no consciousness. You even know that better than I, because you, like so many others, are searching for artificial intelligence, using of tricks beyond my comprehension to make all kinds of devices constantly more intelligent. What engages our attention is the speed at which scientific breakthroughs are made. We're always right on top of it, but we realize at the same time that we might reach a point where we ourselves are of no use as the tech we created takes over. How do we keep genetic manipulation under control; how will we behave when we realize everything we think and feel is registered and saved; what will all those working people do after they have been superseded by technical miracles; will they ever find a job again? While all these questions keep us busy, we put the pedal to the metal to stay ahead of our competitors. Outside of Fort Web, everyone fights his own battle, here we concentrate on everything that can help us make individuals live as long as possible, away from that valley of tears, to the green meadows where a human life never ends... That is why we invest so much time and money, that is why we set up new companies. And we are successful. Of course, we want to benefit ourselves as much as possible. Everything is at the service of the man with his unique consciousness. We need to be on our guard constantly for anything that might damage or change our consciousness forever."

He shook his head compassionately. "Future generations will benefit from the work you do. And there's still a lot to be done. We have not been able to construct a living, self-dividing cell, not to mention a snail created by a scientist that climbs up slowly along lab walls. For the time being, we cannot comprehend that something originates from nothing or that the universe can grow like a balloon while nothing exists behind the final frontiers. And all that we make up in-between we call science..."

Rolf Wallis raised his hand ready to object. His wife, Herta, beat him to the punch, "That sounds too simplistic to me, these days we all know that..."

Carsten didn't listen, he continued imperturbably, "We must exploit every opportunity to make our lives as pleasant as possible, without having to change ourselves into manipulative machines. Happiness, long life, and a clear consciousness, they are what we strive for."

Carsten went on about ethical implications as it pertains to the human body. "Although I must admit that I would love to have another body," he grinned, "my brain would best remain the way it is."

He continued talking, even when Herta and Rolf Wallis stood up and walked to the door; he pushed her past Dieter, still talking and gesticulating.

"How human are we," Dieter heard him say, "After our DNA is manipulated, our bodies stuffed with electronics as armies of nano-bots race through our veins? Will we still feel anything after we've changed that much? A long healthy life, that is what we are striving for, but at what price? Let me be the human watchdog..."

Dieter walked on and sat down on one of the thrones. The only other person present was old Folco Andermann, the tycoon who had built his pharmaceutical mecca.

"Yes, Dieter," he said with a sigh, "future generations will benefit from the work we do, that is the most meaningful thing our philosopher said. The decay of the human body is a sad process; all you need is a mirror to witness it."

He banged the tabletop with his fist when Gabi Stein and Rosa Linge entered the room, followed by Lucas Montaigne.

"Never mind, we have a lot to discuss now..."It was a quarter to twelve.

Gabi drew Folco's attention to his financial obligations concerning a laboratory in which he was part owner. Gabi hoped that Dieter would be interested. She got right to the point, "We can take over the Nanofacto from Gaul & Graf Technics. Your knowledge will be very useful, Dieter. If Rosa, Folco, and Lucas join in, we can do it, the five of us, twenty percent share each."

"Yes, I am in," was Dieter's spontaneous reaction.

"I'm in too," said Lucas, "no matter what it will cost me."

It was ten to twelve.

Gabi talked about Nanofacto, about the number of employees needed and about their special research into the possibilities of nanotechnology. And then she mentioned loads of money, but no one batted an eye.

It was five to twelve.

Thodor Baron entered the room. Without saying a word he sat down on a throne. Clasping the armrests, he started moving. His mouth was open and his eyes were open wide as if he was shocked by something only he could see.

"Freeda should see this," said Gabi, while she pushed her chair back with force.

Within half a minute she was back with Freeda Olbers, a psychologist and neurologist who was closely involved in many undertakings of Das Web, at her side. Gabi took her seat again. Freeda, a brunette in her mid-forties with unsmiling thin lips and a constantly worried look in her dark eyes, sat down next to her, opposite Thodor. She loved extravagant clothes and drove a canary-yellow Porsche. She preferred to be transient, spending her nights in hotels near the research centers where she worked temporarily, renting bungalows at holiday resorts, or staying in the bedrooms at Fort Web.

Everyone was quiet as they kept an eye on the time; it was noon, twelve sharp.

Thodor Baron burst into laughter, it was a forced laugh; the look in his eyes remained serious. He shook his head fiercely as long, thin wisps of hair fanned out to all sides. Then the laughter stopped as suddenly as it had begun. He placed his hands flat on the table and stared through the window between Gabi and Freeda at the view of Munich. His voice sounded flat, without emotion.

"Fortune-telling is a particular phenomenon. Through the ages, people have tried to catch a glimpse of the future. Seers always had much influence and they were treated with respect. Not so long ago one claimed that fortune-telling had been overtaken by science, but after that researchers began to understand time is something special, it can be interpreted in different ways. If absolute time does not exist, it creates unknown possibilities…"

Thodor swallowed two or three times as he screwed up his eyes. When he started talking again, his voice sounded strange, hollow and deep, "Time is the fourth dimension. Time spins, time runs, time jumps to all sides and won't allow itself to be caught or tamed. Don't you understand what I'm talking about; are you all just a bunch of idiots?"

Freeda tilted her head and raised an eyebrow, Gabi sat up straight bumping her head against the back of her throne.

The color drained from Thodor's face, within seconds he looked pale as death. "When the rain has soaked the bark and makes tree trunks shine when the drops run down the leaves, there is rest and satisfaction in the forest..."

"What do you mean by that, Thodor?" Dieter inquired.

Again Thodor shook his head fiercely looking around as if he had just woken from a deep sleep, not immediately realizing where he was, "I have to make a confession."

He grabbed the edge of the table and while he rocked his upper body to-and-fro, looking through the window, he continued, "Clairvoyance does exist and only very special people can master the art of prediction, they are the true experts. Unfortunately, I am not so special... my gifts mean nothing at all. I confess to you that I am nothing but a swindler."

Folco Andermann started laughing. "If that was so, we would have discovered it long ago. Thodor, you have given me the best advice more often than not. I am very grateful. We cannot precisely determine whether someone is clairvoyant or not, but I believe your brain is used to the max when you concentrate or go into a trance – so many brain cells start communicating, someone once compared you to a network of highways packed with vehicles winding around a metropolis with their countless headlights blinking at night in every direction..."

Freeda Olbers did not agree. "That is something you can see often, Folco, fierce emotions! That certainly doesn't make him unique."

Thodor started to make hissing sounds as he closed his eyes and talked with his jaw clenched, "Leave me alone!"

Freeda reacted immediately, "Thodor... is someone forcing you to tell us certain things?"

Thodor let go of the table, folded his hands, and bowed his head as if he was going to pray. "Please forgive me. I am nothing more than a swindler, a conjurer with knowledge of the human character, and an insatiable hunger for money. Yes, Folco Andermann, you believed in me. It was never difficult to guess what you were looking for; I anticipated your wishes."

Folco coughed in his fist as he avoided looking at the others.

"Others were confident in me as well," continued Thodor, "so I was admitted into your midst, I became a member of Das Web. Soon many of you agreed I worked wonders, I gave plenty of good advice and you paid me generously. But I made even more money elsewhere. Competitors put me on their payrolls and I informed them of your businesses and plans... I heard more than enough interesting things to satisfy them..."

Lucas Montaigne began to swear wholeheartedly when he realized how much he had entrusted to Thodor.

"Predicting the future was very easy for me," Thodor continued imperturbably. "All I had to do was confer with different people so I could tell you how certain affairs would develop. And every now and then things were arranged so that my prophecy would turn out to be right."

"I have no idea what this is all supposed to mean," said Lucas Montaigne, who seemed to be under control now. "This is all rather vague to me. You haven't come up with specific examples."

Thodor continued in an emotionless voice, "Silicon Valley, California, you wanted to know if it was wise to bid for Vinata Enterprises. I said it would a wise investment, that you could get Vinata for three million less if you waited for one week. Erwin Dawson, a Vinata exec, had arranged that beforehand. The same goes for your deal with Superi Techno Inc. when you asked me to..."

"Enough!" roared Lucas. "That is correct. You are a swindler indeed."

Thodor rose to his feet and walked to one of the windows. He remained standing there with his back toward the table and the thrones staring out at the city, the double-domed towers of the Frauenkirche, the tower of the Rathaus on the Marienplatz and the countless roofs that shone in the light of the sun. He rattled off a few more examples to prove he had lied constantly, that he had been informed beforehand and that he had sold confidential information to their competitors. And then, all of a sudden, he fell silent and stood stock-still.

Dieter Brunn, Gabi Stein, Rosa Linge, Folco Andermann, Lucas Montaigne, and Freeda Olbers were baffled. Everyone tried to calculate their losses thanks to Thodor Baron. Then Dieter remembered what Gabi had said, "Thodor... are you being forced to tell us certain things?" He had not reacted to that. Dieter asked him now, "Who is forcing you to tell us about this, Thodor?"

Thodor turned round slowly, tears running down his cheeks. His voice sounded amazingly deep, "Mandragora officinarum... the mandrake, family of the nightshade. The root grows in the shape of a little man, a magical little man with special qualities. Pull him out of the ground and you'll hear a horrid yell that chills you to the bone. At least, that is what people say about it..."

Lucas Montaigne, a big, broad-shouldered man, slammed his fist flat and on the table and cried out, "The truth, Thodor! No deceiving nonsense! Answer Dieter's question – why have you decided to tell us this now?"

Again Thodor seemed as if he was waking from a dream. He wiped his tears away staring at the six people in surprise as if he'd just seen them for the first time in his life. He spread his arms wide, looked up at the ceiling and said in a loud voice,

"Nicolaes Nimbus has taken me in! Nicolaes Nimbus forces me to say and do things. He has punished me because I broke the rules of the game of fortune-telling. After all, I have been cheating... There is nothing I can do against it, I cannot defend myself; I am no longer my self... Oh, I beg you, forgive me!"

Dieter stood and walked toward Thodor. In a split-second the pitiable Thodor became an aggressive person; he bumped against Dieter and stormed with clenched fists toward the table.

Dieter almost fell to the floor, tottered sideways, and had trouble restoring his balance. What he was seeing did not correspond with what he was thinking.

He was disoriented, feeling that he was standing outside, looking in. Didn't I just kiss my wife goodbye? At the same time, he witnessed Thodor lashing out at Rosa Linge. His fist hit her square on the side of the face. Never in her life did Rosa have to deal with violence. She closed her eyes and slumped down on her throne.

Dieter looked on as Lucas Montaigne recovered and started to fight with Thodor. Old Folco stepped in; both the fortune-teller and Lucas beat him up.

Dieter was lost. I had stopped at the roadhouse for a cup of black coffee without sugar and in the meantime, he looked on as Lucas punched out the old man and fell upon the fortune-teller. Rosa sat up straight and started to cry when she noticed she could not move her jaw. Gabi Stein stood up and walked toward Freeda. Freeda wore a long, multi-colored shawl. Gabi took the shawl, wound it three or four times around Freeda's neck, and started yanking. Freeda almost choked, caught herself by the throat, and pressed her long nails into her skin. She began to bleed.

Dieter just stood there musing, looking out the window of the roadhouse. Suddenly Lucas Montaigne stood in front of him and raised his hands in despair, "Why don't you do something?" Lucas shouted.

"Why won't anyone come to help us?" Dieter shouted back. "There is a slew of people in the other rooms, but..."

He did not finish his sentence. Lucas hit him with both fists and he fell to the floor.

The coffee tastes funny. Where is my car? Am I on my way to Munich, to Das web!

"...My car!" Dieter mumbled while he scrambled to his feet.

His head was clear. He touched his face and felt no pain.

Five people sat down at the big table – Gabi Stein, Rosa Linge, Folco Andermann, Lucas Montaigne, and Freeda Olbers. Rose exaggeratedly moved her jaw; Freeda held her shawl in her hands and began to fold it carefully. There was no blood. Folco looked himself over expecting to see massive bruising, stood up, and sat down again. He felt relieved; he was perfectly fine.

"Well... here we are again – back in the meeting room," philosopher Carsten von Haller intoned. He stepped aside, accompanied by Herta and Rolf Wallis.

"As I've already said, we have what it takes to invest in small, innovative businesses and we can buy out creative scientists."

Dieter stopped him. "Carsten, you will have to go elsewhere. We have a number of important things to discuss now. Perhaps you might order lunch for the three of you."

"Come with me, we'll get us something to eat... what a good idea, thank you, Dieter Brunn..." He let Herta and Rolf go first as he closed the door behind him.

Dieter took a seat now and noticed Thodor Baron sitting quite a distance away from the others.

"I just had the most bizarre experience ..." he started. "All of a sudden everyone was fighting. While I was thinking of other things, I watched you going after each other with fists raised."

The others chimed in, they had experienced the same. While they also thought of something they had done earlier that day, they had watched everyone fighting with each other.

"It felt so real," sighed Folco, "and then, just like that, it was over."

Freeda tapped her fingertips against her neck, inspecting them carefully.

"How on Earth..." she sighed, "I thought for sure I had torn my skin open with these sharp nails of mine... And you, Gaby, tried to strangle me with my own shawl. But you know what's worse, what frustrates me the most? I have no explanation for this behavior..."

Everyone stared at Thodor Baron sitting at the opposite side of the table by himself.

He hissed, shook his head fiercely, and made defending gestures trying to convey to them that he had gotten annoyed when one person looked at him. He shoved his throne back quickly and leaned forward. He started to bang his head on the table so hard that everyone was afraid he might split his skull.

Dieter stood up and ran toward him. He grabbed the fortune-teller by an arm and dragged him away from the table, pushed him on the floor, pressed his right knee to his chest, and clasped his hands around his wrists. Next Thodor banged his head on the floor, till Dieter managed to shove his left shoe under it.

"He's gone round the bend!" Dieter yelled.

Freeda approached them. "Thodor must be admitted to a psychiatric institution, I have connections at one of the best clinics, not far from Munich. As soon as he has calmed down a bit, we will take him there. I will call the clinic and explain the situation letting them know we will be on our way soon."

Chapter 4

Freeda Olbers asked Gabi to call a doctor immediately. As a psychologist and a neurologist, she had no authority to examine someone in a situation like this without the assistance of a doctor. Gabi contacted a doctor and went to the elevator to wait for him.

Lucas helped Dieter to keep the fortune-teller under control. Thodor had stopped banging his head on the floor and Dieter, who still held him by his wrists, was relieved as Thodor tried to relax.

When the doctor arrived, Thodor behaved passively. He did not overreact to questions and did not protest when the doctor listened to the rhythm of his heart and measured his pulse rate. Thodor stood up and rocked to-and-fro as if he was standing on legs made of rubber.

Freeda explained Thodor's recent bizarre behavior to the doctor. Then, all of a sudden, Thodor started to spit and pushed the doctor away.

"An angry planet is the cause of many disasters!" Thodor cried out. "Don't try to fathom the secret motives of a heavenly body if you are not initiated in the right way!" He spits again and slapped himself in the face with both hands.

Dieter and Lucas caught hold of him as the doctor gave him a sedative. "What is his situation at home? Is he married? Do we have to inform his wife?"

Folco knew Thodor best. "He is a bachelor. His parents passed away. He was their only son. As far as I know, he has no family. He has never mentioned any relatives to me."

The fortune-teller sat down on a throne and kept quiet. The doctor conferred with Freeda and agreed with her, "Yes, a complete examination is best in this situation. The staff will decide if they want to admit him and for how long. The Triton Clinic seems like an excellent choice to me. He is physically sound, so there is nothing more I can do. Anyone that attempts to crush his own skull needs professional help as soon as possible."

"I already called them," said Freeda. "Dieter and I can leave right away, so we know for sure he will remain calm."

The doctor smiled. "No need to worry about that for the next couple of hours. I think he will fall asleep as soon as he is seated in the car."

※ ※ ※

Freeda's canary- yellow Porsche was too small for even three passengers and she didn't dare get behind the wheel with the fortune-teller sitting in the passenger seat. Dieter suggested they drive to the Triton Clinic in his car.

The doctor accompanied them to the parking lot and tried to communicate with Thodor. He supported the fortune-teller, who moved as if he was as drunk and helped him to sit in the backseat of the car. Thodor did not answer a single question and as soon as he sat down he sunk to one side with his cheek pressed against the side window and closed his eyes.

Dieter started the car and drove away. Freeda pointed out the window in front of her– her nails were polished, each one was a different color – her long nail almost touched the windshield. "That is Thodor's Volvo. Gabi's security people will keep an eye on it."

Next, she pointed out in the direction they had to go, till they reached the highway that led them away from Munich, "Just stay on this road for the time being."

They started talking about the events in the meeting room. CompuStein was well-protected and there were cameras everywhere. But Gabi required complete privacy in Fort Web so cameras were not installed in the big room.

No one understood what had happened in the meeting room and there was no film to record how everyone had behaved there.

Dieter looked in the rear-view and suspected Thodor was sleeping. "It is so bizarre to think that we believed in him all the time. Anyhow, we have given him the benefit of the doubt. Folco Andermann has always said he had special talents at his disposal."

"Thodor has given us the proof of his swindling," said Freeda. "It remains a mystery to me. What confuses me most, however, is my own behavior, or my memory of my aggressive attitude. It was an orgy of violence and we all took part in it. Was it a collective hallucination? It makes me nervous when I cannot explain someone's way of acting but now I cannot even explain what I have done myself."

It was quiet on the road. Dieter drove eighty miles per hour. In the side mirror, he saw a silver-grey Audi coming up on his tail. The Audi was doing ninety. After passing, the car swerved a bit too early to the right so Dieter slowed down to give him more space.

"Are you going to shrug that off just like that?" asked Freeda.

"What do you mean?"

"That man just cut you off. You have to stand up for yourself. Go after him!"

"And then what?"

"Ram his car, or don't you have the guts to do it?"

"Of course I have the guts!" Dieter's voice sounded loud and incensed. "You are right, I'll teach that guy a lesson, just you wait and see!"

"Step on the gas!" Freeda screamed.

The Audi was moving along at a faster pace and Dieter set off in pursuit. He grasped the steering wheel and immediately felt as if he was driving in the Indy 500. Freeda leaned on the dashboard and stared outside, mesmerized.

"You should kill that bastard, Dieter. Crash into his car so hard that it somersaults twenty times before it comes to a standstill against a tree."

"I'll check to see if he's really dead. I will kick his windows in if they are not already shattered, drag him outside, and roll him in the gasoline flowing from the smashed gas tank."

"And then you'll set him on fire!"

Thodor Baron was sitting on the edge of the backseat holding on to the front seat's head restraints. He leaned forward; Dieter and Freeda could see his grinning face between them.

"Yes! Yes!" Thodor cried out in a hoarse voice, "he's all yours, Dieter; he's yours, go for it!"

Dieter felt drops of sweat trickling down his forehead. The distance between the Mercedes and the Audi had not diminished. He looked at the speedometer assuming he was driving more than one hundred and twenty-five miles an hour. He shook his head when he noticed he was still only doing eighty.

"You let him escape!" Freeda yelled. "That's not good! You should tear him apart, you hear me?"

"Tear him apart! Tear him apart!" Thodor chorused, as he banged his fists against the back of the head restraints. "Come on! "Tear him apart! Tear him apart!"

"Tear him apart!" Dieter echoed.

He switched the radio on and increased the volume. Screaming guitars joined a forced, hoarse, devilish voice.

The road was straight as an arrow. Dieter moved the steering wheel back-and-forth with the rhythm of the music as the car swerved from one side to the next.

"He's heading for that parking lot!" Freeda yelled. "Look, he's sticking his arm out of the open window and now he's gesturing. He wants you to follow him. Has he gone mad? Now we got him, he's digging his own grave!"

Dieter put the pedal to the metal, driving as fast as he could. "I hope I don't blow the motor! But if we make it, I will tear him a new asshole!"

"Tear him apart!" Thodor yelled again.

He was almost there... The silver-grey Audi veered to the right and slammed on the brakes. Dieter stopped at the curbside just behind the Audi in the deserted parking lot. There was a meadow with picnic tables alongside it.

"...Murder!" Dieter screamed as he opened his door.

"...Murder!" Freeda said while she stepped out.

"Murder... murder...," loudly from the backseat.

Dieter felt a breeze stroking his sweaty face as he exited his car. He felt as though he had just sobered up after a wild binge. Freeda walked up to him, "This is impossible, Dieter, this just cannot be... The doctor gave Thodor a sedative to put him to sleep..." Dieter raised his eyebrows. "He should be unconscious, but he's banging his fists against the head restraints and..."

She fell silent as the door of the Audi swung open. A man in a triple-breasted suit stepped out, walked up to them, and immediately started talking, "I saw your car swerve. You must have a flat tire, didn't you notice it? That is why I gestured for you to follow me and..."

He did not finish his sentence. He took off his sunglasses and looked at them searchingly. Dieter stood still with sweat visibly on his brow. Frida was extravagantly dressed, as usual, the colors of her long shawl clashed with her short purple dress. She had put yellow pumps on this morning because she thought they went so perfectly well with her Porsche. Her dark brown curls were held together by a gold-colored ribbon; her thin lips were blood red.

"Oh..." the man said as he turned around quickly and walked back to his car. "I'm so sorry; I won't bother the two of you any longer." He walked back to his can, got in, started the motor, and drove away.

"The car swerved dangerously? He thought we, that I..." Freeda got into the car and closed the door.

Dieter heaved a deep sigh, opened his door and slid behind the wheel. As soon as he had closed the door, Freeda leaned over and put her arm around his neck, moving her fingers through his hair.

"And why not?" she laughed.

"Right," was all that Dieter muttered.

She kissed him on the mouth stroking his leg with her right hand. His left hand slid over her purple dress, to the hem, then lower. Her legs feel so smooth, so warm. Heavy-metal blasted from the speakers.

Thodor mumbled softly from the backseat, "That's the way to do it, Dieter. Your wife, Katja, doesn't have to know anything about this ... And of course, this is very smart of you, Freeda. Dieter is about ten years younger than you..."

Dieter moved to the left and Freeda moved to the right. He switched the music off and started the Mercedes. Driving away from the parking lot, they were back on the highway in a flash. In the rear-view he saw Thodor sprawled on the backseat, eyes closed.

"Do you already have plans for the holiday?" Freeda asked. Dieter didn't find it strange that she had launched into a new topic.

"We will combine it, work and play, along with the usual trip to several of my companies. Katja and I will go to our chalet in Switzerland and to our house in Austria. Katja has become very enthusiastic about a house on Lake Come in Lombardy, Italy. It should be very beautiful there; many celebrities have bought houses there. I already know this will cost me a fortune."

"But Katha is worth a fortune, isn't she?" Freeda chuckled.

"Of course she is. You are right about that. We will look anyway. First Switzerland, then Lake Como and finally to one of my other companies in Austria. We recently bought a house there not far from Innsbruck, but we also plan to stay in a splendid hotel in Vienna."

"You have to leave the highway in a couple of minutes. And then it's only five minutes to Triton Clinic."

❋ ❋ ❋

Thodor Baron was drowsy, acting confused when he found himself in the clinic sitting in a chair in a big, functionally furnished consulting room. He looked around with sleepy eyes, his hands on his knees as he rocked in a steady rhythm; now and then he muttered a few words, "Toad doctor... Please... Prophecies... Saint's Day... Providence... Talisman...!"

Dieter let Freeda do the talking. Freeda explained the situation to Annemarie Weiher, a psychiatrist who had become a dear friend to her when they studied together at the Ludwig Maxililians Universität Fakultät für Psychologie und Pädagogik in Munich. Annemarie said the doctor who had examined Thodor in Gabi's

CompuStein Hightech had called te Triton Clinic and explained that a new patient was on his way.

A big, strong male nurse had to intervene when Thodor stood up cursing and waving his fists. The male nurse grabbed him and pushed him back in his seat.

"He is barely able to resist," said the male nurse, "his muscles are weak, but his mind is strong."

"In the car, he was half asleep during the trip here," explained Freeda, "and then, all of a sudden, he became aggressive." Freeda and Annemarie looked at each other in surprise.

"The doctor told me he was given a proper injection," said Annemarie, "a combination of haloperidol and..."

"Promethazine," Freeda filled in. "Yes, I know. I was there. The male nurse is right. Physically he is relaxed, but mentally he's on the warpath. And that should not be possible at all; it should have curbed his fury almost a hundred percent."

Thodor remained seated and when Annemarie started to ask him several questions, he answered in a calm voice. He realized psychiatric help was needed and would gladly admit himself into the clinic.

"Someone needs to bring you clothes, someone has to arrange several things for you."

Thodor took a bunch of keys from his pocket. "Freeda knows where I live. There are pans of food on the stove and everything will rot if you don't throw it away. There's a big leather trunk on the bottom of a big closet in my bedroom. Just select some clothes for me; I am too confused to think about what I might like to wear." He had more requests and Freeda hoped she was able to remember everything.

❀ ❀ ❀

Dieter drove fast on his way back to Munich again. He felt uncomfortable now that he was alone with Freeda. He concentrated on the road listening to the instructions on the navigation system taking them to the district of Glockenbach. Freeda kept the conversation superficial telling him she had been in Glockenbach to visit Thodor.

"Of course I made use of his gift of prophecy as well. Thodor had always been sociable; he invited me for a drink in one of Glockenbach's countless pubs several times. In the summer we even sat on the grass of the Gärtnerplatz. Later we had dinner on a sun-drenched terrace. He owns a big apartment there. I hope you can park your car there, that street is very busy..."

Dieter found a space. Freeda found the right key for the front door as they went up the staircase to the apartment. Once inside, she did not know what to do with the pans on the stove. She'd never cooked meals herself; she'd always had breakfast, lunch, and dinner in restaurants, bistros, and pubs. Dieter threw the food into a garbage can, cleaned the pans, put them in their proper place, also found the brown leather trunk, and filled it with clothes. When he carried the trunk from the bedroom to the living room, he saw Freeda standing in front of a big table.

"Look at this, I found a notepad. I picked it up to leaf through it, it is full of notes, seems to me he uses it as a diary."

"That is private; we shouldn't read it. It would not be prudent if we did..."

"...And Thodor is not here to permit us."

They looked at each other and burst out laughing. It sounded loud and hysterical. Dieter remained standing there with his mouth wide open; he moved his head in her direction as if he was intending to bite her. She pulled her multi-colored shawl away and showed him her bare neck. Dieter growled and finally managed to close his mouth again. "There is something odd here..." he hissed. "Do you feel it, too?"

"Bad air perhaps," she whispered. "I have a feeling that something is watching us, something so old it finally started to decay... Do you also feel a strange pressure on your eardrums?"

They kept quiet, listening. They could not hear the sounds that came from the street, except for the impatient blaring of a horn.

"Invasive eyes," whispered Freeda. "Shrunken, soon they'll roll like hard marbles from their sockets..." She took a deep breath and continued in surprise: "Why am I talking nonsense? The diary! It is all about the diary!"

She opened it and started reading. Slowly she turned one page after another. Thodor Baron had written in detail what he had done every day, where he had been and who he had met. They found out that he was a swindler indeed. The information he received from important employees and owners of companies from Europe and the USA that he received, he used the next day to make people like old Folco Andermann believe that he really had the gifts of prophecy. It was all written in very small script, there was even enough space to note at what time he had got up and at what time he had gone to sleep, what the weather had been, and what the stock exchange had done with his shares. But his last note was written in huge caps, Nicolaes Nimbus. From the last, he had drawn a line that went down to the bottom of the page.

Dieter moved his finger past it, all the way down: "Looks as if Thodor sunk back, the ballpoint slid across the paper..."

"I am scared to death," Freeda said while she closed the diary. "I'm terrified. Are we finished here?"

"I have to do a few more things."

"Well, hurry up then. Here are the keys. I will wait in the street. I can't stand being here any longer." Standing in the doorway she also said, "Better open a window, maybe something evil will escape then! Do you hear me?"

One second later Dieter was alone in the apartment. It felt bizarre having to admit he felt safer when they were together as if the Freeda could have made the difference between life and death if they had been attacked by something unknown, something terrible.

As quick as possible he did the things Thodor had asked for – he put fish food in the automatic dispenser of an aquarium, his fingers trembled so much he spilled a lot of it. He grabbed food from the refrigerator and put it in the freezer, checked an alarm system and switched off several appliances that were on stand-by, took the keys, and the brown leather trunk and walked to the door. Feeling helpless, he put the trunk on the floor and walked up to the table. The moment he reached out to pick up the diary, he got the strange feeling he was being observed. He turned around fast, the dead silence seemed ominous, as if at any moment he expected something would scare the hell out of him. Suddenly he did not dare pick up the diary or open it to look at the name in big capital letters and the long, downward slash of ink. He snatched up the trunk and left the apartment. With a sigh of relief, he locked the door and ran down the stairs.

Freeda stood there waiting for him in the busy street. She took him by his free hand and started to drag him along with her.

"There are so many pubs and bistros here!" she said in a hurried voice.

"Are you hungry?"

"Of course not, I'm thirsty. What I need is a stiff drink! I love cool white wine, but now I'm in the mood for something stronger."

Not much later they sat down in a big pub and Freeda ordered two glasses of Asbach Uralt. "I don't want anything to drink," Dieter remarked. "I have to drive, first to Fort Web and then all the way back to Friedrichshafen."

"I know, I know, they're both for myself, and the moment I've finished them I'll order two more. Fortunately, I can always count on a bedroom in Fort Web – I even have a closet full of clothes and other necessities there."

As soon as the Asbach Uralt was served, Freeda emptied her glass in one gulp and shoved it across the little table toward Dieter, after which she reached for the next full glass.

"Freeda Olbers..." she said with a deep sigh, "psychologist, neurologist, a woman with deep insight who often has deep discussions with philosophers like Carsten von Haller. Now I find myself to be raving mad, I'm seriously considering admission to the Triton Clinic. Lacking haloperidol and promethazine, I am trying to anesthetize myself with brandy!"

She emptied the second glass in two seconds.

"That's better, back to normal. I know I am not suffering from delusions. This is not a case of hysteria caused by anyone involved in whatever's happening. I don't have a logical explanation for everything that has happened today, but I know we are dealing with an external entity. Something we don't understand has exerted a certain influence upon us. Knowing that sets my mind slightly at ease. And it seems to be temporary – a temporary change of behavior. Where does that come from?"

"While we were at Fort Web I was thinking perhaps it might be collective insanity."

Freeda shrugged her shoulders... "Yes, you might describe it that way, Dieter, but it gets us no closer to the cause – it might originate from ourselves, or perhaps it is being forced upon us; I am leaning toward the second possibility."

Dieter wanted to eat something even though he wasn't really hungry. He ordered an apfelstrudel with whipped cream and vanilla ice cream. Freeda ordered two more glasses of brandy.

"A fight amongst us that turns out to be real, Dieter, blood lust, fear, no, perhaps the agony of terror... and excitement. I will not deny it, I have had fantasies about how it would feel to kiss you, but in your car, I would have gone a lot further if Thodor hadn't stuck his head between our chairs all of a sudden and started to encourage us... My impulses were triggered by an outside source, just like you need a transmitter to fly a drone."

Dieter had to assist Freeda when they left the pub thirty minutes later. In the car, she was too drowsy to help out so Dieter made use of the GPS while driving back to the Triton Clinic to deliver the trunk. He used it again driving back to CompuStein.

He parked his car next to Baron's Volvo and woke Freeda. She held on to him when they entered the building... one glass of wine too many apparently.

More members had come to Fort Web, small groups of people were conferring everywhere and all the seats in the meeting room were occupied. Freeda retired to the bedroom she had used before. She took a shower and gathered other clothes from a locked ceiling-high closet.

Dieter entered the meeting room. Gabi explained how she and Rosa Linge had come up with an additional sum of money that Fort Web could invest in new enterprises. She wanted to keep part of the money in reserve, but there were millions still available for interesting ideas.

"Any new plans?" she asked.

Five men and women raised their hands. She pointed to Herta Wallis, "You first, Herta. You and Rolf are new here, we are all curious, what is your opinion?"

While Herta started talking, Gabi looked at Dieter. She excused herself, pushed her chair back, rose to her feet, and walked over to Dieter.

"How did things go?" she asked in a soft voice.

Dieter told her Thodor had been admitted to Triton Clinic. He told her about chasing after the silver-grey Audi, the horrifying atmosphere in Thodor's apartment, and the name he found in the diary.

"Everything is back to normal, now that Thodor is no longer present. It would seem wise not to get anyone else involved. We must meet here another day, you, Rosa, Folco, Lucas, Freeda, and I. Let's ask Carsten von Haller to join us. First, we must take time to come to terms with everything we've experienced today."

"Right, this is so important that I will make time for it regardless of what I am doing. Please tell me as soon as possible when you want me to come back."

She touched his arm with her fingertips. "I have to get back to my throne now... What do you think, Dieter, I mean about what has happened? It scared me so much, just like it frightened Freeda. Can a person go crazy without any reason, just like that, all of us trying to punch each other when you realize some time later that you haven't been violent at all?"

"No, it seems impossible, but we've all experienced it."

Her eyes grew moist when she looked up at him.

"We've all experienced it," she repeated, after which she turned on her heels and went back to her chair.

"I had to confer with Dieter Brunn about something. Go on, Herta. I will catch up later in case I missed something. Anyway, I am ready to listen again..."

Dieter went to the dining room and ordered a meal. Someone he knew very well sat down with him, during the meal they discussed different possibilities like forces in interesting Das Web projects.

Later he ran into Folco Andermann in one of the corridors. Folco said he didn't want to talk about anything, that he was too tired, that he needed time to find out for himself what had happened.

Dieter decided to go home. Getting into his car, he stared at the Volvo parked to the left of him. So much has happened in the last few hours and I never panicked? I have no explanation for what has happened to us but it's as if I am on the other side looking through a mirror. Even Frieda can't explain it and still, I feel so detached.

❀ ❀ ❀

He felt inclined to do something before he started the Mercedes and drove to Friedrichshafen. Slowly he leaned forward, opened his mouth, and bit into the leather-covered steering wheel. While he bit down as hard as he could, he looked at Thodor's Volvo, as if a silent command had come from its empty seat. Two seconds later he sat up straight and leaned against the back of his chair. He wiped his fingers past his lips and wasn't surprised about what he had just done; he didn't think about it when he left the parking lot. Dieter craved the comfort of his abode.

Chapter 5

A Timeless Phenomenon

Rosa Linge paid a lot of attention to her looks. She was young and rich spending loads on money on plastic surgery striving to have the body of a top model. Her friends had nicknamed her the tooth fairy. Her pearl-white teeth had become an obsession with her. She preferred to be treated by Alrik von Hecht, an ambitious young man with a dental practice in Munich. He always managed to make her feel comfortable. He soon found out that she was a bright businesswoman who owned several high-tech companies. Rosa knew he was on the payroll and dreamt of his own practice, that he was in debt thanks to investments that were less than forthcoming and lived in grand style. Aside from his shortcomings, he was an absolute professional who always aimed at perfection.

The anesthesia and the bright light made her drowsy, but she did her best to listen to Alrik as attentively as possible as he explained everything he was doing in detail.

After drilling into her second molar in the upper right quadrant, he worked with tiny files and made her wash her mouth out with a diluted chlorine solution to eliminate bacteria. Then the molar had to be refilled with a special material, "Guttapercha," said Alrik, "rubber from an Indonesian tree. We're almost done with your root canal."

"I need more of it please."

Rosa could not understand what the assistant said, perhaps she was too far away from her. Then she heard Alrik's voice again, "Yes, molars are quite large..."

Rosa closed her eyes. She imagined a complete set of teeth, the most beautiful implants; thirty -two teeth with enough space to contain a gigantic arsenal of micro apparatus to bring the human body to perfection, all as easily replaceable as an old-fashioned light bulb. There were countless possibilities. Everything necessary to upgrade the human body, the brain included, could be installed into strong artificial teeth. She thought of many things at the same time, from an external memory that was connected to a chip within the brain to a minuscule safety system that constantly monitored the condition of the body, from a home-base of millions of nano-robots in the future to inducers that guaranteed sleep with the most beautiful, outrageous dreams. She was so engrossed with her thoughts that she did not notice what happened around her till she felt someone pushing against her shoulder.

"Rosa, did you fall asleep?"

Alrik made her hydraulic chair rise and held a mirror up to her. Rosa looked at her face and wiped her long, blonde curls aside, opened her mouth, and lifted her head to see the molar in her upper jaw. It looked perfect.

In the meantime, she was thinking about patents, about possibilities, about working with her good friend Gabi Stein and about a meeting with a large number of Das Web members.

"Perfect as always, Alrik. Could I talk with you in private in a moment?" As soon as the assistant left, Rosa stood up and said, "Listen, Alrik, what would you say if I paid off all your debts and gave you your own practice as a present?"

He looked at her in surprise. Then he burst out laughing and shook his head. "My debts, that's a lot of money. And a practice of my own would cost a fortune."

"I understand that," was her short reaction.

"Are you serious? And what are you expecting from me in return?"

"I need you; you're a damn good dentist, an implantologist, a creative thinker... I am seriously thinking of paying your debts and as soon as that is done we'll never mention it anymore. You'll have your own practice and you can take on people to get things rolling. You should concentrate on the design of special implants. Later I'll give you all the details. Oh, by the way, I almost forgot to tell you it will make you a rich man in a short time..." She reached out her hand. "What do you say?"

"That sounds very tempting, Rosa, so of course I will say yes."

Rosa settled her affairs. Gabi Stein became her business associate in a new adventure and many members of Das Web were interested enough to join and support her financially. Alrik von Hecht's dental practice became a small but important part of a big, new laboratory. For Rosa, it was just a matter of investing and experimenting for the future.

Alrik was debt-free and his creative contribution brought in a lot of money. He worked closely with scientists from the laboratory. His clinic attracted many wealthy people from the business world and the German movie industry; its reputation was spotless.

From that time Rosa was called a tooth fairy more often. To someone like Gabi Stein that was a well-deserved name for a young friend and colleague who proved that she was able to think and act creatively. To many others, it was a nickname for someone who invested a lot of money in a wild idea.

Folco Andermann, the tycoon from the pharmaceutical industry, had this to say, "I have put money in a totally different business that has to do with human teeth. We are searching for a way to make teeth regenerate themselves. Imagine having beautiful teeth forever."

Rosa did not worry about criticism. "I have seen too many movies and cartoons about people who have become half robot," she said. "Steel skulls, telescopic eyes, fingers functioning like deadly guns, a breastplate filled with gizmos – it has nothing to do with the beauty of the body..." And then she moved her hands past her gorgeous body acting robot-like and continued, "Because no one will fall in love with a partially synthetic woman, it seems wise to me for the time being to remain completely human on the outside. Is there anyone who would want to see me totally different?"

She laughed to show off her perfect teeth. Rosa had fallen in love with a man of flesh and blood, Alrik von Hecht. Soon she and Alrik were inseparable, preferring to stay in her big house on Lake Starnberg, southwest of Munich.

Rosa left Fort Web and was at home in thirty minutes. By this hour of the day, the cleaners had already left and couriers had delivered food, drinks, and parcels.

Alrik was home and busy in the big kitchen. He didn't have to do much, everything was already prepared by a professional chef.

The moment Rosa kissed him, Alrik knew there was something wrong. "What has happened?" he asked concerned.

"First, I'll take a shower, later, during dinner I will tell you all about it. Prepare yourself for things that seem impossible. Know that everything I'm going to tell you is the truth, nothing but the truth!"

Twenty minutes later she sat down at the table. She told Alrik about the sensational confession of Thodor Baron, about his madness and the bizarre fight in the meeting room.

"Thodor hit me. That is how it started. He hit me so hard in the fact that I lost consciousness while sitting on one of those gigantic thrones. Not much later I regained consciousness and sat up. I could not move my jaw. I was crying. Everyone was fighting each other. Then, suddenly, it was as if a spell was broken and we were all astonished, nothing had really happened... My face didn't hurt and I could move my jaw as usual. This should have been totally impossible, isn't that so, Alrik? What exactly did happen to us? If only someone could explain that to me! And I already know you will say I have gone mad. You are going to tell me I am stressed because I have worked too much lately."

"No, no, not at all," was Alrik's direct reaction.

"So you do believe me?"

She noticed how he stared at her with big eyes and moved his knife and fork impatiently between his fingers. He held the knife more firmly and pointed with it in her direction.

"Your experience brings back memories. Yes, I believe you. But that doesn't make it more understandable, it makes it more frightening."

They both sat still and forgot to eat. "This happened long ago. I lived in Bremen and went to high school there. I fell in love with a girl, Regina Thule. I often went to her home. Her mother was a very nice woman, but her father..." He shook his head. "Regina said he had been big and strong. When I met him, he was a thin man, passing his time by sitting on an old chair by a window. He sat staring outside and he never spoke a word while I was there. I remember very well how he often clasped the armrests and moved his upper body back-and-forth in a steady rhythm. He ate and drank in that chair and now and then he even spent the night there, refusing to allow his wife to help him get upstairs to the bedroom. Of course, I asked Regina what was wrong with him. He was a fortune-teller, someone of great reputation; he was even referred to as the Oracle of Bremen.

Only now did Rosa begin to find his story interesting. "Go on..." she urged.

"The family lived in a big house. At the back of the garden, there was a stone building. Regina's father worked there. He was a bookkeeper and a tax consultant and a fortune-teller, of course. His customers visited him there to have their fortunes told. One day he didn't come to the house for lunch so his wife went to take a look because he didn't answer the telephone either. She found him sitting behind his desk in his office; he looked the way he would always look from then on... confused, terrified... as if he was able to see something that no one else could see, something horrible... I still remember Regina telling me everything in great detail as if it were only yesterday. Her father always made notes on large sheets of paper. One of those sheets lay in front of him on his desk. He had used a thick marker and had written a name on it; I still remember it because Regina had mentioned it so many times."

"Let me guess," Rosa said in a hurried tone, "Nicolaes Nimbus?"

Alrik nodded and repeated the name, "Nicolaes Nimbus."

"Is there more to the story? Do you know anything else about this name? But that is something we should do as well, find out as much as we can about him."

"Regina told me about the situation time after time because it meant so much to her. She had seen her father change from a big bear into a thin wreck of a man. He was not able to express himself, not even to speak one sensible word. Doctors and psychiatrists did their utmost to help him talk again but in vain. Regina told me he had made piles of money via his prophecies. He told her once that he didn't always tell the truth, he made things up. As far as that is concerned, his story is similar to that of Thodor Baron. Finally, Regina and her mother inquired on their own. I don't know much about that, but I believe they managed to find enough information that led them to The Netherlands. Nicolaes Nimbus was probably born there. Wait a minute, she once remarked and I thought that rather strange. Nicolaes Nimbus was a timeless phenomenon. She said it just that way – a timeless phenomenon. I don't remember asking her to explain it to me. Or maybe I forgot about it. Anyway, Regina's father and your Thodor Baron dealt with the same person. And they both ended up going absolutely bonkers."

Rosa shivered. While Alrik talked she thought about what had happened to her and the others in Fort Web. She could not understand how she might have watched something happen that hadn't taken place, that she had felt real pain from a punch she had never received.

After dinner, while Alrik made several phone calls, she went to the big fitness room on the first story of the house to work out. She used the treadmill, worked with dumbbells, and did push-ups; there were mirrors everywhere so she could admire herself constantly. Rosa was horrified by the thought of getting older; she did everything possible to stay the way she was for as long as possible.

Every time she found herself sitting opposite Gabi Stein or Folco Andermann, she realized what time did to others. Time was a murderer, the pendulum of a clock was like a wrecking ball on a chain.

To stay the way you are, that is the point, we have to study all the possibilities... She lay down in front of a mirror. With her hands folded behind her head, she breathed in as deep as possible, sat up straight slowly, let her breath escape through her nostrils, and looked at herself. She wanted to laugh at her image, but didn't dare; she saw a stiff face and read fear in her blue eyes. She repeated this exercise for several minutes, this time with her eyes closed.

One week later Gabi Stein invited a select group to join her, Fort Web remained closed for everyone else. It was noon as Gabi had received everyone in the kitchen for an extended lunch. The kitchen looked like the taproom of an old inn, it had a wooden bar and a fireplace, but the food was brought up via an ultramodern elevator system.

Rosa Linge and Alrik von Hecht, Folco Andermann, Lucas Montaigne, Dieter Brunn, Freeda Olbers, Carsten von Haller and Gabi sat round a big solid oak table.

Alrik was not an official member of Das Web and he had never been there before. Rosa insisted that he come with her so that he could tell everyone about his former experiences in Bremen.

Carsten von Haller, the little, corpulent philosopher, was Gabi's confidant and a walking encyclopedia for all members of Das Web – he had been informed about everything that had happened after the fortune-teller had made his confession. He had become curious immediately. Therefore he agreed when Gabi asked him to be present. As Rosa was the personification of the tooth fairy, one considered Carsten Das Web's mascot, the wise man who was asked for advice by everyone.

All eight people present loved the combination of conversing and good food. There were different salads, hot pies, caviar, cheese dishes, many sorts of new breads, fresh meat and fish, even cooled champagne.

"Welcome everyone, I am always happy to see you again, but now I also feel very relieved. I was the first one present, as usual. Mostly I walk around and step inside different rooms. Or I just stand around musing by a window, while I enjoy the view of my beloved Munich. This morning I didn't feel at ease at all in my own building! I entered the meeting room and in less than two or three seconds I was back in the corridor shaking all over. I know everyone has thought about the bizarre events that started with Thodor Baron's confession ..."

Her guests nodded while she took a sip of her coffee. "Alright," she continued, "and I am sure we have all have searched the internet for that strange name – Nicolaes Nimbus. That's what I did, of course, and the result was very disappointing. Dieter has something to tell us about this and my dear friend Rosa has Alrik with her, he has news for us as well. Welcome, welcome, Alrik. But I suggest we listen to Freeda first..."

Freeda put her champagne glass gently on the tabletop as if she was afraid the thin crystal would break. She wore a dress that matched her Porsche perfectly, adorned with countless multi-colored little feathers; it made her look like a giant yellow bird. "Let me try to explain what happened on the strangest trip ever," she began. "Together with Dieter, we took Thodor Baron to the Triton Clinic. We went there in Dieter's car. Of course, we were confused because we did not understand – just like you – what had happened in the meeting room. Who could have predicted that I would urge Dieter to kill someone... Except for Thodor Baron who was acting very weird in the backseat..."

She had caught everyone's attention and she did her utmost not to forget a single detail as she told her story. "I woke up in one of the big spare rooms in Fort Web," pointing behind her, "with a huge hangover and an even bigger feeling of fear. I can imagine how Gabi felt this morning when she was here all by herself. By the time I got out of bed, it was late and of course, everyone had left. I have enjoyed the absolute silence on the upper story. I love to sit in the big living room or stand, just like Gabi, by a window looking at the lights of Munich. Panicking, I remembered locking the door and sitting down on the bed. Of course, it would have been wiser to get dressed and ask a security guard to walk to my car with me. In all honesty, I hadn't the guts for that. For no money in the world would I walk through the empty corridors past empty rooms to reach the elevator. I died a thousand deaths that night. Believe me, as a psychologist I would rather have unraveled someone else's feelings of fear than be confronted with my own."

"What you and Dieter experienced is horrendous," said Gabi, "of course you've already told me about it during our telephone conversations. Now we all know about it and it should give us food for thought. Before we go deeper into this, I suggest we listen to what Dieter has to say."

Dieter started in immediately, "My wife Katja found everything I had to tell her that night hard to believe. It is very hard to imagine something like that if you were not there yourself. Katja has a very good memory. She hardly forgets anything; she even remembers things that seem to be of no importance. She couldn't get the name Nicolaes Nimbus out of her head. We sat down in our living room and all of a sudden she jumped up and walked away. I heard her going upstairs. Not much later she came back with a file in her hands."

He took some time to take a bite and a swig. "That particular file had everything to do with our house on Lake Constance. When we bought it, there was a lot of renovating to do because it was an old house, even much older than a little stone building on the other side of the garden. We wanted to use it as a storage shed but it needed some renovation as well. I inspected the little building; the wood from the roof was rotted. I could stab through it with a screwdriver. About a hundred and fifty years ago, as we found out later – the original owners had inserted an insulation layer of newspapers between the wood and the tiles. I remember throwing away the newspapers that had become wet. But there were dry pages as well and I started to collect them. Katja and I studied the pages. The articles were printed in gothic lettering. We didn't find the name of the newspaper. Later I searched the internet, looking on the website of the Bavarian State Library, but without a result. Most of what we had gathered finally disappeared into a wastebasket. Katja put some little pieces in a file as a curiosity, together with old black and white pictures of the house that were given to us by the former owners. Yesterday I framed a piece of a newspaper page so that it wouldn't get lost. It is unbelievable, Katja remembered that name after so much time..."

He leaned to one side and took something from a briefcase that he had placed against a leg of his chair. It was a black photo frame and behind the glass a little piece of browned paper was visible. The frame was passed hand to hand. Everyone had trouble reading the print but at the bottom right was a headline that was a lot easier to read: Das Rätsel Nicolaes Nimbus (The Nicolaes Nimbus Mystery). Beneath it, a small part of the first line of the article was visible.

"As I already said," Dieter went on, "I could not find out the name of the newspaper. But we do know the pages we threw away were printed more than a hundred and fifty years ago. We found several dates. Now we have the name, in black and white, or black and browned to be exact."

"Rosa Linge reacted, "A timeless phenomenon." The others nodded. "Those are not my words," she continued, "Alrik can tell you more about that."

Everyone looked at Alrik and he made use of the attention by starting in, "That is what a girlfriend from high school once said to me. It was in Bremen, where I lived. Her father went through something similar to what happened to our Thodor Baron." He constructed his sentences carefully and he ended with the same words he had used at home with Rosa, "So Regina's father and your Thodor Baron dealt with the same person. And they both ended up living in a world of their own making, standing on a corner where the buses don't run, waiting for one to come that will never bring them back home."

"Your girlfriend and her mother found a thread that led to The Netherlands," remarked Lucas Montaigne immediately, "I believe that to be extremely important and interesting. You may not know much about it, but it is a fact that this girlfriend of yours – Regina, am I right? –talked about a timeless phenomenon. Someone must have told her something and I would love to know what that was!"

Gabi, a born chairwoman, summarized what had been said,

"Thodor and Regina's father were both fortune-tellers and they got caught cheating. When Thodor went crazy, we all started to act like that as if his state also influenced us. We don't know if Regina and her mother had a similar experience. Anyway, the name, Nicolas Nimbus, turns up in both cases. And Dieter has found the name on a fragment of a newspaper page."

"After that improbable fight between all of us in the meeting room, it became quiet here. But Dieter and I did some most idiotic things. We must have still been under that odd influence. Thodor was with us in the car and later we had gone to his apartment where, as he had told us, the confrontation with Nicolaes Nimbus had taken place."

"That is true," said Gabi, "from the moment you left with Thodor and the doctor, nothing unusual happened here."

Carsten von Haller raised his eyebrows. "We have no idea what we are talking about. There is a slight impossibility, one hundred and fifty years at least between a name in a newspaper and the present, do you realize that?"

Before anyone could answer, the sound of a door slamming interrupted their thoughts. For almost a minute, everyone sat rigid with fear at the table, as if held captive within a colored picture.

"Other than us, no one is here..." Gabi whispered.

Lucas Montaigne rose to his feet. His breast swelled as he breathed in deeply. "I'll go and have a look," he said as when he walked up to the open door. "I believe the sound came from our left."

"Wait for me, I'll come with you." Alrik jumped up to help.

It remained quiet at the table as they listened for any other odd noises. Dieter lost his patience and stood up intending to search the entire floor when Lucas and Alrik came back.

"Nothing, nothing to report," said Lucas, "no one there. There are no open windows so I have no explanation for a slamming door."

The atmosphere in the big kitchen had changed. Invisible, like the wind, something had streamed inside that had gotten a grip on everyone.

"What frustrates me the most," Freeda said, "is the fact that I have no explanation for what has happened to us. Collective hallucination must have an origin but I cannot put my finger on it. Another possibility might be hypnosis, but that is something Thodor Baron is not able to do. What, for heaven's sake, caused me to see things that actually were not there and do things against my will?"

Folco, who always boasted about the fact that he had made his fortune in the pharmaceutical industry, piped up, "Now come on, Freeda, if you think nothing can change your mental being, you only have to swallow a pill – you know that as well as I, don't you? A pill can free you from your depressive thoughts, help you perform all night long in bed, a pill can kill you, make you hallucinate, you..."

"What is your point, Folco?" Freeda interrupted.

"Maybe we all swallowed something without realizing it. I am sure we all have had coffee that morning, for instance."

"No, not me," said Dieter, "I had coffee in a roadhouse on my way to Fort Web. It is an absurd thought that Thodor could manipulate us in that way. Besides, he ended up in a mental institution, remember? Or was that supposed to be part of his plan, too?"

"I know one thing for sure," said Carsten von Haller, "something or someone managed to confuse us completely. It is exactly as Freeda says, she saw things that were not there and did things against her will. And she is also right when she says something like that is very frustrating, especially when you have no explanation for it."

The discussion went on until they finished their lunch. Only after they had gone to another room and sat down on luxury leather armchairs, did they begin to feel a bit more at ease. Alrik von Hecht came up with an idea, "I could try to get in contact with Regina Thule and ask her if we could meet somewhere. Maybe she still lives in Bremen. She is the only one who might probably be able to give us some more information."

"That would be fantastic, Alrik," said Gabi. "I think I speak on behalf of everyone when I ask you to do so. Can you make time for that?"

Rosa reacted faster than Alrik, "Alrik was born in Bremen and we've been there several times. I'm going to cancel several appointments; we can leave in a couple of days. The distance is about five hundred miles. The weather is good so we might be able to go by motorbike again. We have a new BMW's and we have hardly used them."

Alrik nodded, "We will make arrangements to leave soon."

Sitting close together, with stomachs full and drinks within reach, they managed to relax, discussing subjects that had to do with the most important goals of Das Web – fighting and eliminating diseases, finding ways to make people live longer, the newest developments that might determine the future, research into the secrets of the human brain and its miraculous consciousness.

"You need your brain to think about your brain," said Freeda. "For the time being, we cannot fully explain the mystery of consciousness. Can our dearest mascot, our home philosopher, tell me in one single sentence who I am?"

Carsten von Haller took the time to think it over and enjoy attention from the others. He rubbed his chin with his thumb and forefinger and spoke in an almost solemn voice, "You are one who tries to get a grip on what is going on inside your head."

Freeda nodded and seemed satisfied. "A real head-scratcher, Carsten, thank you very much. You should be considered a timeless phenomenon, exactly like Nicolaes Nimbus."

Lucas Montaigne looked up in surprise. "Yes, Freeda, that is such an interesting thought..."

"You mean you also hope that Carsten will live a long and healthy life?" she asked.

"Yes, of course. But that is not my point. Just imagine that you took the phrase timeless phenomenon literally... that a man mentioned in a newspaper report from one hundred and fifty years ago might be the same person who came to see Thodor Baron and the father of that girl from Bremen!"

Chapter 6

REGINA AND KARINA

It was half-past five when Gabi Stein took leave of her visitors. One after the other, Rosa Linge, Alrik von Hecht, Folco Andermann, Lucas Montaigne, Carsten von Haller, and Dieter Brunn went down the elevator. Only Freeda Olbers was still with her.

"I'll go to the bedroom and pack some clothes; then I'll leave for Munich and have dinner in a good restaurant and after that, I will sleep in a splendid hotel. I wouldn't spend the night here for all the money in the world!"

"I don't blame you!" said Gabi.

When Freeda turned around, she noticed the broad sliding doors of another elevator on the other side of the hall.

"I never noticed that before," she pointed to it.

"Oh, it is mainly used by the cleaning crew. They arrive each evening at a quarter past six and after half an hour or three-quarters of an hour they leave."

"That could explain the slamming door," Freeda wondered aloud, "maybe someone came up to get something when we were sitting in the kitchen."

"No, the elevator is only used by them at that time, my rules. Besides, if they were here at any other time don't you think they'd be real quiet and not slam doors? Fort Web is forbidden territory for outsiders and it's no secret. There is an emergency exit to the staircase, but it is locked from the inside and cannot be opened from the other side unless you have the key…"

"Alright," laughed Freeda, "then we're dealing with a ghost, what do you think?"

They walked past the meeting room. The door stood wide open. The women looked inside. "But we don't believe in ghosts, do we," said Gabi.

"Oh, no, absolutely not, I hope we can agree about that! After the heart has stopped beating and brain activity has stopped, it is over; there is no soul or other being that starts wandering about."

"Still it is strange, we often hesitate every now and then, as if we are uncertain."

"That is not unusual. Superstition is something that disappears just like that and in this case, it has to do with the fear of death. We prefer to think about that as little as possible. And we do our utmost, with our energy and lots and lots of money, to postpone death. We want to stay alive. So it is logical to make something up over time to soften the unavoidable. So there could be life after death, a life without a body. Unfortunately, Gabi, unfortunately..." Suddenly she looked at Gabi. "Wait a minute... why are we still standing here? Did you take my remark seriously, do you really think we have a ghost among us?"

"I was thinking about experimenting, that is to say... if I could muster up enough courage. Look here..."

Gabi produced a smartphone and showed it to Freeda in the flat of her hand. "This is something we worked on; the best technicians of CompuStein were involved. This is an ordinary smartphone, but this one has greater possibilities. Pictures remain sharp, even when you zoom in to the extreme. It can even smell money and drugs, like a trained dog. It also has sharp hearing like that of a dog. If a spirit wanted to make itself heard, this special smartphone will hear it. The softest sound would be recorded, no matter where it comes from."

Freeda stepped away from the door and suddenly she became impatient. "Let's go, I want to pack some clothes and get away from here as quick as possible."

She walked through the corridor; Gabi followed her. In the bedroom, Freeda opened the closet and filled a plastic bag with clothes.

"I don't understand you, Gabi. This is not like you. You are a businesswoman and a scientist, for crying out loud, one of the founders of Das Web and we're standing here in Fort Web, the bulwark of exact science!" Gabi felt embarrassed. Freeda went on in a loud voice, "We tolerated Thodor Baron because Folco Andermann introduced him to us. You are the same age; can it be that insanity is the key here?" Gabi burst into tears and now it was Freeda's turn to look embarrassed. "Oh, I am so sorry, I shouldn't have said that!" Freeda said after a while.

She put the plastic bag on the floor and wrapped her arms around Gabi. Gabi pushed her away. "Come on, we'd better go now."

"If I only had an explanation for my behavior," Freeda sighed, playing with the little feathers on her shoulder. "I am so sorry... this was so low, I am very, very sorry..."

They walked through the corridor. Then they promptly stopped in front of the open door of the meeting room. "Of course, you could give it a try," said Freeda.

"What do you mean?"

"Ask your special phone if someone's here. Turn on your recorder. Maybe we can hear something, a voice perhaps."

"But you just said ..."

"Yes, but that was in the spare room, now we're standing here."

Now it was Gabi who was hesitating. "There is nothing in the meeting room. Besides, nothing happened when we were sitting here after you and Dieter left with Thodor and the doctor."

"Nothing happened then, that is true. I have such a strange feeling... When that door slammed... Something must have come in." Freeda burst out laughing, "Is this really me talking? As if a ghost needs to open a door to get inside anywhere. But still... it might have been a sort of warning. What are we going to do, Gabi?"

"Come..." said Gabi. She wiped her tears away, held her smartphone, and carefully entered the meeting room.

Freeda followed her. "Do you know how it works?"

"All I have to do is push a little icon. The smartphone will receive everything. Sounds we cannot hear will be altered so we can hear them. All I have to do is walk around and ask a simple question every now and then."

Arm in arm the women started to walk past the table and the thrones. Gabi held the smartphone out in front of her. "Is anyone here?" she asked in an uncertain tone.

What am I afraid of? I own the building, the offices, my huge office, the labs and workshops, an army of employees work for me; everything is alright.

"If someone's here," she said in a louder, more self-assured tone, "say something, do something. Can you at least tell me your name?"

She felt Freeda pinching her arm nervously. Together they walked around the table three times. Then Gabi put the smartphone on the table and sat down on her throne. Freeda followed her example and asked some questions, "Tell us who you are. Why are you here? What can we do for you?"

They both listened attentively. The silence seemed alive, immaterial but still moving through the deserted rooms and corridors and finally entering the meeting room. Suddenly there was an unbearable pressure on their ears.

"We must get out of here right away!" screamed Freeda.

She jumped to her feet. Gabi snatched the smartphone from the table. Together they ran to the door and through the corridor. A strange feeling invaded them as if something was pushing between their shoulder blades – a prickling of the nervous system caused by the expectation that something like that could actually happen. Freeda was first to step in the elevator. With the plastic bag held tight to her breast, she stood upright and held her breath. Only after she had reached the ground floor did she dare to breathe.

Gabi was alone. It seemed like forever before the elevator arrived on the ground floor; she had to wait for it to come up again. Please, oh, please... hurry! She was on the edge of panic. She remembered Freeda often telling her, "You cannot tell yourself not to think about something, that's not the way our brain works!" The elevator was not slow, she was just impatient. "It is true that your own thoughts can drive you crazy," was something Freeda had said as well – but now Gabi was thinking of something grotesque, something with supernatural powers that might attack her from behind. She didn't dare look over her shoulder. The elevator came up. She got in. "Down! Down! Away from here!" she said it over and over.

Freeda stood waiting for her on the ground floor. Together they went to the other side of the hall. A man in a white coat waved at Gabi. "Mrs. Stein, could I have a word with you?"

Gabi waved her forefinger erratically. "Not now, not now, I am much too busy." The man nodded. How strange, not like her at all.

Not much later both women were seated in Gabi's big office on the ground floor, at the back of the building. Gabi called her secretary to say she was not to be disturbed, "It's almost the end of the day. Tomorrow I will have time for everything. Thank you."

Then she turned to face Freeda, "Let's listen to the recording." They were sitting next to each other on a couch as Gabi placed the smartphone between them. The silence of Fort Web's meeting room was reproduced as a constant, almost unchanging white noise. Then they heard, "Is anyone here? If someone's here say something, do something. Can you at least tell me your name?"

And then Freeda's voice, "Tell us who you are. Why are you here? What can we do for you?" The white noise swelled. And then the heard Freeda scream, "We must get out of here as soon as possible!" The white noise stopped. Gabi had switched off the recorder.

"Let's go out together," said Gabi, "we'll have dinner in a nice restaurant. We'll take a cab because I don't think you and I can drive right now. After dinner, come to my house."

"What a great idea," sighed Freeda, as she rose to her feet. "Then we can have something to drink as well. I could do with a big goblet of cool Moselle wine."

"But I have an even better idea," said Gabi. "What we need, is a Chip 'n Deal. Oh, that will work wonders for us. This is the best way to make a wonderful Chip 'n Deal: combine 0.90 fl oz Martini Fiero, 0.90 fl oz Dutch gin, 0.90 fl oz lemon juice, 0.90 of honey syrup, one lemon leaf and one mint leaf. Fill a gin and tonic glass with ice. Stir it well and fill it with a soft tonic. Top it off with a slice of red grapefruit."

"Sounds perfect to me, Gabi. Let's go then..."

❈ ❈ ❈

Rosa Ling remembered what Freeda Olbers said, "You need your brain to think about your brain. For the time being, we cannot fully explain the mystery of consciousness," and the words of Carsten von Haller: "You are the one who tries to get a grip on what is happening inside your head."

She drove ninety miles an hour on her new BMW motorcycle and followed Alrik at a distance of sixty feet. A smile spread across her face. Her dear, priceless brain was perfectly protected by an ultramodern helmet that was provided with several gizmos that made it possible for her to listen to music or talk with Alrik.

Freeda had measured the electric activity of Rosa's brain several times and see it on a big screen. It fascinated her every time. Freeda had told her the electroencephalogram was a German invention – by the end of the second decade of the twentieth-century psychiatrist Hans Berger had already conducted the first successful experiment. Meanwhile, she had become familiar with EEG, CT, and MRI scans, but she had never found an explanation for consciousness. And here she was, driving from Munich to Bremen, she felt very aware of herself on several levels, from riding rubber on a smooth road to keeping herself balanced on a two-wheeled vehicle knowing that she loved the man who drove in front of her – Rosa Linge was aware of the fact that she existed and that she was supremely happy at this very moment.

But you couldn't push your luck, happy feelings came spontaneously, only to disappear again and again. Someone should develop a little gadget to continue these feelings of happiness. Perhaps a gadget within a hollow molar, she grinned. We'll work on it... If the meaning of life was just as hard to find as that of the consciousness, a continued feeling of happiness was the perfect start for as many people as possible. As many people as possible... her mind was wandering while she adjusted her speed and followed Alrik to the left lane to pass two cars.

Most members of Das Web agreed on the theories of philosopher and mascot Carsten von Haller. His ideas of the future turned out to be negative for most people and positive for the few, an exclusive group. Rosa recalled Carsten saying, "We're at the dawn of a new era," said Carsten, "now we are going to lend evolution a helping hand. We are going to change ourselves, we are going to improve, to beautify ourselves, yes, we're going to bring ourselves to perfection! We are working on our genes and we will connect ourselves to all kinds of ingenious forms of technique. And in the meantime, that same technique will see to an endless army of unemployed men and women. An exclusive group will benefit to the fullest, countless people will miss the boat."

Rosa totally disagreed. She had replied, "You are forgetting something very important. Market forces, they are two magic words! Finally, everything will become cheaper; finally, everything will become affordable for everyone. Just look at what happened in the past, how much the first car cost, or a fax machine, a video recorder, a wireless telephone... Finally, everything will be available for the public at large, everyone. Eventually, we will all benefit from future innovations."

"How can you be so sure about that?" she remembered someone saying while she was driving.

"To answer that question," she had said, "all I have to do is repeat what our good friend Dieter Brunn always says, 'If you don't do it, someone else will.' There will always be a country, a company, a person convinced of the fact that things can be produced for less and that profit can be made by way of mass production."

Rosa had named her company Noncha. The word was not short for nonchalance, it meant non chaos or no chaos. Noncha created order. Noncha built, among other things, fully automatic distribution centers. Unloading, storing, loading of all kinds of merchandise was done by robotic mechanisms. Rosa's Noncha worked together with Gabi's CompuStein; together they were able to make every project, no matter how big or tough to manufacture, perfect.

And she had a special feeling for searching out new chances, new trends, and innovations. She was happy that Alrik had joined the company and set his own course; while he worked together with different teams from her labs, he managed to give his practice a glamorous image and his clients were the most important businessmen, actors and actresses, and television personalities.

Rosa and Gabi were innovative, seizing every opportunity where the manufacturing and selling of new products were concerned.

She recalled an exchange with Gabi, "We should concentrate on everything that gives people something to do," she often said to Gabi, "Panem et circenses, bread and circuses, the Roman way to make everyone feel satisfied... We have to come up with the right varieties. When countless people don't have to work anymore, boredom will set in. I am not afraid that the world will become one big Bavarian Biergarten or one big gambling hall. In the virtual world, there is room for everyone! And when people are completely absorbed in their fantasy roles and enjoy everything they want, they'll have hardly time for kids. That would solve the biggest problem– overpopulation. Everyone stays inside, nature will get a second chance..."

The road was straight, the weather was good. Thoughts came and went. Rosa drove faster to keep up with Alrik. For a moment she looked up. The blue sky hid the unique universe and spontaneously the next thought crossed her mind. How unique am I in this boundless universe – a human being, a thinking creature with a consciousness, using advanced techniques to move along at high speed on the civilized surface of a planet?

✺ ✺ ✺

It had been easy for Alrik to trace his former high school sweetheart, Regina Thule. He contacted her; she was pleasantly surprised to hear from him again after so many years. She looked forward to meeting him and was also willing to talk about her father and their investigations.

They agreed to meet at the roadhouse near Bremen. They talked about the fun they'd had eating together and talking there. Of course, Alrik knew he could have saved himself the trip by asking Regina questions right away on the phone, but he hoped she would give him more information in person. I think Rosa and I could use a few days' rest in the Netherlands.

Because they had left early and driven quite fast, Regina wasn't there when they arrived at the roadhouse. It was quiet on the sunny terrace as they sat down at a table that gave them a view of the parking lot. Alrik went inside to order two bottles of spring water and rolls, while Rosa made some phone calls.

About twenty minutes later a dark blue Volkswagen Golf parked between a Toyota and a Ford. A young woman with mid-length light brown hair stepped out, shoved her sunglasses up on her nose, and looked around. Alrik waved and when she saw him she recognized him immediately.

"So you've always had a good taste," Rosa said in a soft tone when Regina came walking up to them. "She is very pretty, Alrik."

They greeted each other warmly. Alrik and Regina indulged in reminiscences while Rosa went to get something to drink for the three of them. When she got back, Regina told Rosa about her present situation. She was divorced, worked as a pharmacist's assistant, and lived by herself in one of Bremen's suburbs. Alrik said little about his career and explained how Rosa had built her company instead.

"I am very impressed..." said Regina. "That is quite something."

Alrik started to ask questions about her father. He had passed away a couple of years ago, she informed them.

"...While he was sleeping, just like that. That is how the Oracle of Bremen came to his end. My mother visited him twice a week, despite the fact she was hardly able to communicate with him. She is totally withdrawn now; she has almost no friends or acquaintances and prefers to stay indoors most of the day."

Regina talked about her father predicting the future for rich customers, based on vague facts, making use of a combination of intuition and information he had received beforehand.

"Much later we found out how much money was involved. He had made a fortune. He'd put all the money in the bank and my mother didn't know anything about it. There were no taxes paid at the time. But arrangements were made with the taxman; there was enough left for us to live on, my mother hardly spends any money and now and then she gives me a nice amount."

"Can you tell us what happened after your father changed so suddenly?"

"What do you mean?"

"Did you and your mother start to do strange things, like your father?"

"Now that you mention it..." Regina hesitated, "yes, that was very frightening. There was a certain atmosphere in the house... how can I explain that? There was as odd aggression in the air, my mother and I became mean-spirited – unexpectedly and of course also unwillingly. It was as if we hated each other all of a sudden. We had the feeling that we had gone too far; that would happen to us both at the same time. For example, I tried to strangle her while she was convinced she had planned to murder me. Later, after we had come to our senses, she told me she had stabbed me with a kitchen knife. She had seen my blood flow freely and copiously. Fortunately it never really happened. I never put my hands around her neck and she never skewered me with a kitchen knife. We often said the most terrible thing to each other and we both had the feeling we really hated each other. Yes, now it all comes back to me, I remember it very well. Why did you bring this up, Alrik? You were not there when my mother and I were so mean towards each other."

"We have had similar experiences." "Someone within our circle of friends, a fortune-teller, turned out to be a swindler and he made a statement of his own free will. He went crazy, totally off the wall crazy. We were under some kind of influence – I don't know exactly how to explain that – and we went berserk, slapping, punching and strangling each other, or so we thought at the time. t And our man mentioned the same name as your father, I wrote it down..."

"Yes," said Regina, "you mentioned Nicolas Nimbus while we talked on your cell. That is unusual indeed. And isn't it an odd coincidence?"

"It is! You made inquiries. And you ended up in The Netherlands."

"Yes, that's right. It all started in a strange way. I told all kinds of things to a woman I hardly knew; I thought she would not understand what I was talking about anyway..."

***

Regina visited her father in a psychiatric institution. As usual, he only wanted to talk about insignificant, daily things –what he had for dinner, his hair had been cut, the rain was coming and there were no interesting articles in the morning paper he had found in the communal living room. He refused to discuss personal things and he never asked about home or why her mother didn't come along with her. He lived in his own small world from day to day without ever doing anything special. Sometimes he didn't say a word for over an hour; he just rocked back-and-forth in his chair. That was exactly why Regina came to the institution alone; her mother couldn't stand to see the man she had loved so dearly in such a dreadful state.

Regina got impatient with her father. He hadn't said a word for several minutes so she rose to her feet and walked through the corridors to a backdoor that gave entrance to a big garden. Narrow paths led past flowerbeds and grass fields. She sat down on a bench and raised her head up to the sun, closing her eyes.

Momentarily her vision darkened further as someone passed her. When she opened her eyes she saw a woman sitting next to her. She knew her name. Katrina had been involved in an almost fatal auto accident. Surgeons had saved her life, but they'd also removed a portion of her brain. From that moment on, she was unattainable; no one could guess what was going on inside her head. She was still able to talk and every now and then she said things that surprised her psychiatrists, normal things.

"It is as if other parts of the brain can take over the tasks of the parts that have been removed," a nurse had once remarked. "There are a few moments of brightness and then it is possible to have a good conversation with her. But that never lasts long. After only a few minutes it is over and it is almost impossible to make contact with her again."

Regina said hello to her. Karina did not react. Suddenly Regina started to talk, the same way she talked to her father most of the time. She felt relieved knowing she could say certain things aloud, fantasized that the person sitting next to her understood everything. She talked about her father's hopeless situation, that it was hard for her to see him in this dreadful situation and that her mother found it more and more difficult to come and visit her husband. It was as if Karina understood what she was saying. She knew she had caught her attention so she kept on talking.

Karina nodded and opened her mouth as if she was trying to say something, but could not find the right words. Then she raised two fingers and said, "I have taken three pills this morning."

Regina held up three fingers, "Three pills, Karina, three..."

There was no reaction so Regina started talking again. She talked about the day her father lost his mind and did not skip over the details. She mentioned the stone building at the back of the garden, her father's office, how he sat at his desk with mortal fear in his eyes. She mentioned the big sheet of paper full of thumbnail sketches, words and numbers and a name, written with a thick, black marker:

"Nicolaes Nimbus..."

Unexpectedly Karina laid a hand on her wrist; she felt the strength in her fingers. "...An important name from across the border, he lives in The Netherlands."

Regina was on the alert right away. She pushed Karina's hand away and produced a little notepad she always had with her to write down strings of words her father had spoken so that she could try to find a connection or a meaning. She held her ballpoint in her other hand and said, "Go on, Karina. Please, go on..."

She hoped that Karina would tell her more. And she did, "...The Society of Tamfana," said Karina. "The Netherlands. Elise van Vennen. She knows that name. Nicolaes Nimbus. Yes, Elise knows who he is."

Regina wrote it down in a script that only she was able to read. "Continue..." she repeated.

Karina stood up, clapped her hands, and walked away. The information was sufficient enough for Regina and her mother to begin their investigation into her father's odd behavior.

❋ ❋ ❋

"Karina had been a journalist. She worked for different newspapers and weeklies, including important magazines. I could not find much on the internet. So I went to the offices of different newspapers here in Bremen; that was more successful. Someone gave me a copy of an article written by Karina. I found four important bits of information- The Society of Tamfana, The Netherlands, Twente, and the name Elise van Vennen. Nicolaes Nimbus was not mentioned. Karina had researched old folktales and superstitions. She had gone to The Netherlands and talked to Elise van Vennen about an old society, Tamfana. It was not hard to find Elise so I talked with her on the telephone and later visited her with my mother in Twente. She turned out to be a nice woman and fortunately she was able to speak German. She was also rather strange... How can I best describe her? ...Chaotic and full of fantastic stories. You might say she lives in another world too... Now and then I could not follow her. Tamfana does not exist anymore. Her grandfather had been the chairman of the society. He had built up an extensive archive, files full of historic information, old folktales, myths, and sagas. Elise showed us different articles about Nicolaes Nimbus, the name was already known around the year 1200, but Elise said the person in question was much older and might have been a Germanic seer who lived in Twente about two thousand years ago. Regina laughed as she continued her narrative.

"That is too absurd for words. We had come all the way to Twente for that – just to learn that my father had written down the name of a fantasy figure from old sagas! Karina was talking nonsense... Nicolaes Nimbus could be an immortal seer who can turn up somewhere just like that!" She snapped her fingers and relaxed.

Rosa and Alrik laughed along with her, while they gave each other an understanding nod.

Not much later they followed the Volkswagen Golf to her home. There they would change and the three of them would drive to a good restaurant in Regina's car. Regina lived in a small row house in the district of Habenhausen, in the south of Bremen, at the left bank of the River Weser.

Over a sumptuous dinner, Regina spoke about her father and told them how to get in touch with Elise van Vennen. The restaurant was part of a big hotel, Rosa wanted to book a room for Alrik and herself, but Regina had another idea.

"Your motorcycles are parked in front of my door so you can spend the night with me."

When Rosa woke up the next morning, she found herself lying happily next to Alrik, who was still sleeping deeply. She stretched, turned her head slowly, and looked in the expectant eyes of Regina. It wasn't time to get up yet.

"Where were we?" whispered Regina.

Rosa turned her back to Alrik and slid into Regina's waiting arms.

Chapter 7

THE SOCIETY OF TAMFANA AND VICTOR THE
VISIONARY

Elise van Vennen lived on the edge of a little village not
far from Oldenzaal. Rosa called Elisa on the phone and
told her she needed to know more about The Society
of Tamfana.

"No problem," Elise's hoarse, agitated voice replied,
"few ask about the society and I love to talk about it
because I have a lot of information. I will gladly blow
the dust from my grandfather's archive when we meet."

The moment they parked their motorcycles in front
of the little house, they knew she had to be someone
who lived in a world of fantasy. The garden was full of
little statues of fairies and gnomes, all of them true
pieces of art. The gnomes stood hidden behind low
bushes, some of the fairies hung with spread wings
under the branches of different trees.

The door swung open. Elise stepped outside. Her
dress was so long it almost touched the ground, making
it impossible to judge whether she walked or floated on
air. Rosa and Alrik wouldn't have been surprised if it
was the latter.

There were no wrinkles in her face and she had bright blue eyes. She was a woman whose age was hard to guess, she could be thirty or fifty or maybe even older. After she had greeted her guests with a firm hug, she gestured at the countless little statues and said, in almost perfect German, "My grandfather made these himself. All of them. Don't ask me how he managed to chisel such fragile little wings in stone. Isn't that just pure magic?" She looked so intently at Rosa and Alrik it made them feel shy. Waving a long forefinger to-and-fro, she said, "Don't tell me you don't believe in magic now that you have come to here all the way from Munich. Let's go inside."

The living room was small. The furniture had been damaged by her cats. Elise poured them a bitter-tasting, dark tea and after she sat down she started talking, "Like our stomach needs food often, our brains cannot do without stories. We feed our minds with stories and interpret them by the nature of our character. That is what we do all the time, tell each other stories. I grew up in this house. I lived with my grandparents. My grandfather was a historian, always looking for old stories. He searched for them in places were others seldom looked, in old archives, in monasteries and churches, in private collections. My grandfather told me stories when I was a little girl and when I closed my eyes and listened to him, I was lost in a world full of fantastic events –I still have the feeling that I am not able to leave that world entirely, I always find myself partly here and partly there."

She scribed a circle with her finger and she pointed to her head. Rosa and Alrik looked at her in surprise, eyebrows raised. It did not seem to bother her so she kept on talking. Her grandfather had been mainly interested in regional stories, old sagas and legends from the neighborhood, old German and Celtic traditions, Roman influences, and old medieval poems full of magical meanings. He'd founded a society and named it after the mysterious goddess Tamfana. There was an old rumor that a temple had been built for her near Oldenzaal.

"All the information that my grandfather and the members of his society found was saved. The Old Dutch was translated into modern Dutch; the authors of the tome wrote the most interesting articles. The members of the society came together here and read stories to each other. I loved to sit on the floor, right there near the fireplace, listening with bated breath to the voices of the adults. I can still see it all before me as if the images are being projected on the dark wall opposite me as we speak. I remember glowing eyes in the fireplace and little creatures dancing around me and I never dared to touch them. The Society of Tamfana collected reports of magical events mostly. My grandfather always said life would become boring as soon as magic disappeared. No more sorcerers, no more alchemists searching for miracles, no more fairies and goddesses, no more believing in the supernatural. Well, the old people have passed away and the society no longer exists, but the archives are still there, safe and sound."

She rattled on and on about Tamfana and a golden cup that was recently excavated, about mythical dogs, witches, and other bizarre apparitions.

"The Society of Tamfana aimed to try to preserve the past, the way it was experienced by people and the things they believed in. They bought books from England and France about the heydays of magic and the slow disappearance of it in modern times. Tamfana tried to preserve local beliefs, mostly in Twente, but also in the entire Netherlands and parts of Germany. Borders often changed with the death of a king or a duke and the appointment of a new ruler."

Then, finally, she asked, "What exactly is the reason for your visit? Is it about a certain person from the past? It was not exactly clear to me over the phone..."

"Nicolaes Nimbus," Rosa blurted as quickly as possible.

Elise's reaction was instantaneous, "Ah! The man of all times."

"What does that mean?" asked Alrik. "What is a man of all times supposed to be?"

Koos Verkaik

Elisa smiled. "For some great magicians, age is an unlimited concept. That is to say, as long as you don't get killed in an accident. Men like Nicolaes Nimbus are still around. As long as they don't get hit by a train or a car, as long as they don't fall from a balcony or get stabbed or shot, they will remain among us."

She rose to her feet and beckoned her guests. "Come with me, I'll show you the archives, there we will find everything you'll want to know about him." She led them through the kitchen to the back garden, where a stone shed stood. An army of cold stone gnomes marched through the high grass, little fairies peeked between the leaves of the bushes.

"Everyone lives inside of his own illusion," remarked Elise, as if she was able to read the minds of her guests. She opened the door of the shed and stepped aside to let them in. There was a table with three chairs inside, behind the glass doors of a high closet were rows of old books and there were two metal filing cabinets packed full of important information. Elise slid a finger past several files, took one out, and put it on the table.

"Let's take a seat shall we," she said, while she leaned over to switch on a desk light. She opened the file, started to skim through it, and took out several sheets.

"Now look here... These are all facts; the members of the society composed short articles from them. I will read the most interesting parts to you, my German is good enough to translate the text for you."

Rosa and Alrik sat down next to each other and listened to Elise's mesmerizing voice. The oldest report about Nicolaes Nimbus was from around the year 1200. A young knight was mentioned, who found himself hallucinating due to hunger and thirst in Gelderland, being rewarded with gold by a certain Nimbus. The same Nimbus predicted a bright future for him.

"Nimbus said this and we have recorded it verbatim, 'You will outlive all your brothers and learn to value life. Someone like you deserves prosperity and luck and that is what you will get.'" There was someone in Leiden, around about 1750, he pretended to be Nimbus and was unmasked right away by a true fortune-teller. Elise mentioned a much later incident in North Holland in 1950, wherein a fortune-teller by the name of Mea Culpa was punished for all her lies. More articles mentioned false predictions and appearances of an angry Nimbus.

Elise translated everything very well and seldom stammered. When she finally finished, Alrik looked at her and asked in a surprised voice, "Do you really believe we will have to deal with the same person all the time – Nicolaes Nimbus?"

Elisa answered with a counter-question, "And where does this interest come from?"

"As you know, the father of my friend, Regina Thule, had dealings with Nimbus. In Munich, we witnessed a similar incident. That aroused our interest." He explained everything in detail, much more information than he had let on during their telephone conversation.

It was only then that Elise answered his question, "Yes, it is the same person. I do not doubt that."

"But such a thing is impossible, isn't it?" Rosa interrupted, "no one lives that long."

"Well, I disagree on that point," reacted Elise, "if the end is inevitable for billions of people, it does not mean an individual could not make a deal with the Grim Reaper that magic will keep the organs vital forever."

"How can you know such things?" asked Rosa.

"That is what my grandfather told me. He and the other members of the society made inquiries about that. Experiencing something from close quarters where Nicolaes Nimbus was involved, you must have noticed different things – the changing of the atmosphere, the feeling of his presence, and of course the reaction of the one who was being punished. Alrik told me about your friend, the fortune-teller, who started to act strange."

"That is true, all those stories... It all comes down to the fact that fortune-tellers who trifle with the truth will be punished; but why only fortune-tellers, of all people?"

"I already said we cannot do without stories," explained Elise. "We tell them, we hear them, we interpret them, we share them. The biggest sin is telling the wrong story whenever predictions are involved. The one who does so willingly negatively influences the future. The effects can change everything. Anyone who follows the wrong advice will make the wrong decisions. The true seer has obligations to his friends and his clients. Those who don't fulfill their obligations should be punishment. Nicolaes Nimbus knows how to find people who profit by whispering wrong advice in the ears of the doubtless."

Rosa asked if she could purchase the articles about Nicolaes Nimbus. "Then I will take them with me and get them translated as quickly as possible."

Elise shook her head and laughed. "You're a businesswoman and you know everything is for sale and everything has its price. Now make me an offer..."

Rosa hesitated. What am I supposed to say? If she is willing to sell them to me I hope she won't ask a small fortune. Before she had a chance to say anything, Elise pointed at a corner of the shed and continued, "Look, the solution is right in front of you, an old-fashioned copy machine. I will copy all the pages for you. That will take a while. Investigate the other archives in the meantime, you are certainly allowed to open every file. That will help you see the amount of work the members of The Society of Tamfana put into the project, even though you probably won't be able to read Dutch."

All three of them stood up. Elisa started to copy page after page and Rosa and Alrik opened file after file, rifling through the reports of magical events from the past. There were thousands of pages about the Germanic tribes in Twente and about the middle ages, about fantastic events and especially about magic and superstition. Other files contained stories of events from all parts of The Netherlands, Belgium, Germany and Switzerland, sagas, legends, rituals, incantations, maledictions, and predictions. Their knowledge of Dutch was sufficient to help them understand the meaning of the different stories.

Elise gave Rosa the copies in a big envelope. "You have to keep in mind," she said, "things you don't believe in can still be true after all. After the final displays of magic, several decades ago, this phenomenon disappeared from our society. We have other things to concentrate on and to worry about. But our heads are still programmed to stay sensitive to what we have started to call superstition – we still know that implausible things turn out to be real after all. Nicolaes Nimbus is a brilliant seer. He slips through time, having does not influence his body and mind. That is written in the articles I gave you and you can read all about it after you have gotten them translated. It gives me a good feeling to know there is still interest in these texts from the Society of Tamfana. Stories... as long as they are good are immortal as well..."

They walked back into the little house where they had a long conversation together.

Rosa and Alrik spent the night in a hotel in Denekamp, close to the German border. When they woke up the next morning the voice of Elisa van Vennen was still echoing in their heads and they remembered everything she had told them.

Their conclusion was identical, they both had the same thought, "Imagine, just imagine..." and they said it at the same time. They talked about it at breakfast as they sat down near a window and had bread with boiled eggs, cheese and ham, coffee, and orange juice. Through the window, they saw their motorcycles shining in the sunlight.

"Yes, that's the point," said Rosa, "just imagine that it's all true. Everything in me says it isn't so, but then I remember what happened in Fort Web and what we had to deal with. That makes me hesitate and then I start thinking again, just imagine...what if?"

"Elise van Vennen spoke with conviction," Alrik responded. "Did you see all those old books in the stone shed? Voluminous works about Europe's magical past. Most case studies of supernatural experiences seem amusing to us now until we happen upon something that remains totally inexplicable. Nicolas Nimbus was a seer, a brilliant seer. Elise said that more than once."

"That is what he was and still is, apparently," said Rosa. "The big difference is defined in those two little words... was and is."

"Then and now," Alrik filled in.

Half an hour later they drove back home taking their time. Countless thoughts surfaced in Rosa's head and disappeared on the wind. Clearing one's head was a metaphor and an illusion, thinking never stopped during the daytime and it went on and on in nightly dreams.

Carsten von Haller, the philosopher, was a popular guest at parties hosted by wealthy businesspeople. He had sensible things to say and silence never lasted long when he was present, once he caught anyone's attention he rattled on and on.

Herta and Rolf Wallis, the newest members of Das Web, also appreciated his friendship and had invited him to one of their garden parties. Their company, Wallis Biotech, was in the same business park near Munich where Gabi Stein's CompuStein Hightech was located. They lived in a gigantic house at a few miles from Herrsching am Ammersee. Their property was quite picturesque, especially the two round towers with wooden pointed roofs, giving the impression on misty days that one had built a castle there. There were outbuildings, sheds and a garage. Big, shining cars were parked along the entire front of the house.

Many guests were already present when Carsten arrived. He went up a broad stone staircase to a covered terrace and walked across black flagstones to the open front door. Walking down a long hall, he stepped into a big living room where he was heartily welcomed by Herta and Rolf and was introduced to important people from the business world. He was used to the fact that everyone was a bit taller than himself and he had to look up to make eye contact, but spiritually he walked above the others, far enough above them to compensate for his short stature.

With a glass of wine in hand, he made small talk as he moved slowly but surely in the direction of the French doors that gave entrance to a garden that was surrounded by luscious fruit trees. Finally, he stepped into the garden with other guests. There were tables everywhere, filled with food and drink. Two chefs were busy cooking at an oversized gas cooker/barbeque.

"This is how life should always be," a man said to him, he had introduced himself earlier as Gregor, Rolf Wallis' good friend. "Nice weather, enough food to build a mountain, and enough drink to fill a swimming pool."

He wanted to come back with a profound but humorous remark until he saw someone who immediately attracted his attention. It was an old man, looking even smaller than himself because he had a crooked back and leaned on a cane. He was thin, wearing a suit that seemed a size too big and he shuffled carefully through the garden as he walked along. His head was bald, except for a thin strip of hair that grew from ear to ear along the back of his head and he had strikingly long sideburns. Even more striking were his prying eyes, lackluster eyes rolled to-and-fro from under thick, snowy white eyebrows.

"And then go for a swim with a full stomach," was all he could think of, adding a dull, "and drink till the pool runs dry, of course."

"I see you're watching that old man," said Gregor. "You probably don't know him... He is still a striking personality."

"An eccentric billionaire?" was Carsten's guess.

"Not in the least, not in the least," said Gregor, "although he must have made a lot of money in his lifetime. He's undoubtedly a rich man, but not a billionaire. And now he is old and is growing demented. There is a big possibility that he doesn't even know where he is right now. I think Rolf asked his chauffeur to take him home later. But make no mistake, almost everyone here owes a lot to him."

"Who is he?" Carsten inquired.

"I never knew his family name," Gregor whispered, "I wonder if there's someone here who does. He is known to everyone as Victor the Visionary. Almost all of his predictions came true."

"Victor the Visionary," he said thoughtfully as if pronouncing the name gave him more clarity. "Isn't it a proven fact that predictions seldom turn out to be right?"

"In general, yes," Gregor interjected, "that is certainly true." He pointed toward the gas cooker and continued, "There are also lots of bad chefs, but that doesn't mean there are no top chefs around. Those two work for me; I own twenty-five restaurants."

Carsten thought it strange that Gregor picked this moment to tell him he owned several eateries and employed many top chefs so he ignored the comment. "So Victor the Visionary is the exception to the rule?"

"Exactly, that's the right way to say it. He has proven himself time after time with unsurpassed stock market predictions. When ten out of hundred predictions come true, it is possibly just a matter of coincidence. If ninety-nine out of hundred predictions come true, you have a special gift, one that makes it possible for you to look into the future. That old man had that gift, I swear. But there is nothing he can do anymore, he is growing more addle-brained by the moment. But there was a time when he could make you a wealthy man by whispering something in your ear."

"How...?"

Gregor waved his hand. "Real visionaries are like top chefs, they have their own holy professional secrets. You will never find out what they can exactly do or which ingredients they use." As far as Gregor was concerned, this was the end of the conversation. He walked up to someone else for another chat.

Carsten emptied his glass and walked up to a table jammed with bottles of different wines and champagnes. While he refilled his goblet, he observed Victor. The old man shuffled along. People patted him on the back and shook hands with him. He wanted to have a talk with the man, to get as much information from him as possible, so he had something special to import during the next meeting at Fort Web.

Clouds rolled in from the Ammersee, forming a dark grey mass above, and then it started raining. It was not much more than a constant drizzle, just enough to make everyone leave the garden and head for the big house. One of the attendants quickly covered the barbecue. The tablecloths got soaked. The food and most of the bottles were taken away quick as a wink.

Carsten stood by the French doors discussing the pessimistic works of Arthur Schopenhauer. "A man can do what he will, but not will as he will... That was one of his interesting quotations. Free will, do we have free will or not? Anyhow, he did not believe in goodwill where human beings are concerned about others and we all live together in a valley of tears..." He enjoyed knowing that different people listened attentively to everything he said. "If there is something like free will, where does it come from?" he heard himself asking. "Can we find free will in the left hemisphere of our brains, as some neurologists imply? Or is it in no particular place at all?"

"What is your opinion about this?" a lady in a tight glittery dress asked between two sips of champagne.

"Free will is an illusion we should cherish," he answered. "I consider our consciousness a bonus that evolution accidentally gave us. Who we think we are is the sum of our different brain activities. Therefore we are never able to..."

He looked outside through the open French doors and saw a lonely person sitting in a wooden summerhouse at the back of the garden. It was Victor the Visionary. Carsten did not finish his sentence, pointing at the empty glass in his right hand. He smiled and walked away. Not much later he managed to slip outside unseen. Looking up at the sky, he concluded it wouldn't stop drizzling anytime soon. He still held his glass in his hand as he fetched an opened bottle from the table. He walked through the garden, stepped under the wooden roof of the summerhouse, and sat on a white enameled cast-iron chair next to Victor the Visionary.

"Rain washes our sorrows away," he said with a deep sigh.

Victor did not react. He just tapped his cane on the wooden floor. Carsten found it annoying, there was no rhythm within the tapping. To get him talking, he asked him some questions, told short anecdotes, and made philosophical remarks. He told his funniest jokes and never used aggressive language. Victor didn't open his mouth or even look at him. He didn't dare offer him wine. Maybe the old, fragile man was not allowed to drink any alcohol or perhaps his heart might give in after a few draughts.

Then, unexpectedly, Victor opened his mouth; Carsten looked at him expectantly. "Berlin is far away from here," he said in a hoarse voice.

"What about Berlin?" Carsten asked eagerly. Victor shrugged his shoulders and remained seated, tapping his cane on the floor. Carsten leaned toward him and spoke in a soft tone, "We are brothers, you and I... We are both able to predict the future. That remains among us, of course. Outsiders have nothing to do with that."

Victor nodded and Carsten's hopes grew. "Brothers... Visionaries... Secret science..."

"Billions of people," Victor said in a grating voice. "You know what we have to say then..."

"Of course, but of course," Carsten gambled, "Others don't understand at all."

"And still it is so obvious," Victor's voice sounded louder now. "I mean the comparison."

"That is what we know, you and I and I. It is about the comparison."

"...Billions of people, billions of faces. But no one face is alike. They all differ. The face is only a small part of the body. But there are billions of ways to draw a unique face."

"That is the truth," Carsten whispered, not knowing what the old man meant exactly.

"Lines," said Victor, an interplay of lines. Oh, it is so obvious! The right number of lines in the right place, on a piece of paper, feeds your brain. You look at it and you have power over your own mind."

Carsten put his glass on the floor and leaned backward. This was special information. The old man wasn't aware that he had given secrets away. Carsten urged him to go on. But now the man remained silent.

The drizzle had almost stopped and the layer of clouds had become thinner. Carsten could see the French doors at the other side of the garden. It wouldn't be long before the first guests stepped into the garden and the chefs removed the lid from the barbecue. Time was running out. Carsten burst out laughing and managed to make it sound real. Victor the Visionary looked at him with raised white brows. "We're on the right side, we have nothing to fear. I have recently heard someone else has been caught cheating and was visited by the one and only Nicolaes Nimbus."

Now Victor reacted, "Oh, that hurts, oh yes, that always hurts."

Carsten understood the old man knew who Nicolaes Nimbus was. He asked questions about him, but the answers were not forthcoming. People were walking on the grass, butlers putting food back on the tables, and chefs had turned up again. Carsten rose to his feet and walked away. He left the bottle on the floor.

"Wait!" the hoarse voice of the visionary boomed.

He stopped and turned around.

"You recognize each other by a feeling that you have developed," the old man spoke softly. "That is how it goes and it will always be that way. You recognized me, but I... I had no feeling of recognition when I observed you. Who are you?"

"...A happy philosopher!" Carsten answered spontaneously.

When he walked through the garden he heard the tapping of the cane on the wooden floor. Carsten repeated to himself what he had heard from the man, a man who had become too old to control his intellectual faculties, no longer able to keep a secret.

It was of less import that he had been in Berlin. The remark about billions of different faces was not important as well. But the interplay of lines was important indeed: "The right number of lines in the right place, on a piece of paper, feeds your brain. You look at it and you have power over your own mind." Visionaries recognized each other because they had developed a special feeling for it. And finally, it was obvious that Victor the Visionary knew who Nicolaes Nimbus was – it hurt every time Nicolaes Nimbus turned up to reprimand someone who had broken the law of true divination...

Yes, he was a happy philosopher indeed, someone who had important things to say at the upcoming meeting of Das Web. He showed his best side again and entered into conversation with different people in the garden and the big living room of the house.

An hour later, while standing in line at the barbecue, he saw Victor the Visionary. He was leaning on his cane as a uniformed chauffeur supported him. He shuffled slowly through the garden in the direction of a gate that gave entrance to the front of the house where the cars were parked.

"There goes Victor," he heard a woman behind him say. "He is much too old and unhealthy for a busy party. Herta and Rolf should not have invited him."

A man piped up, "As far as I could see, he didn't have anything to eat or drink and he didn't speak a word to anyone. Poor man..."

Carsten stood in front of the top chef and pointed at a big piece of steak and a couple of hamburgers. "An important philosopher cannot live on clear formulations and deep thoughts alone," he said aloud, counting on the people standing behind him hearing him, "real thinkers fictionalize better with a well-filled stomach..."

Chapter 8

After an extended lunch, most people who had attended a meeting in Fort Web went back home or to their own companies. Seven stayed behind: Gabi Stein, Rosa Linge, Folco Andermann, Lucas Montaigne, Carsten von Haller, Dieter Brunn, and Freeda Olbers.

They went to the meeting room and sat down on their thrones. Everyone had been informed about Carsten von Haller and Victor the Visionary. Rosa had given everyone a translation of the articles from the archives of The Society of Tamfana. Now they could discuss it freely, knowing the walls of Fort Web had no ears.

Gabi asked Rosa to address the meeting. Rosa spoke about the current condition of Thodor Baron. "His situation hasn't changed much. Annemarie Weiher is his regular psychiatrist and she sees him daily. Thodor is indifferent, more into himself, does little more than eat; he drinks and stares out the window all day long. He may get aggressive unexpectedly, then he starts to swear and wave his fists. Extensive examinations have indicated that his brain is undamaged and he should be able to function like any other normal human being. He could revert to his old self at any time. But I honestly don't expect that to happen after hearing how things went with Regina Thule's father in Bremen. I visit Thodor regularly, I was at the Triton Clinic two days ago. Thodor didn't recognize me nor did he speak a word to me. He sat on a chair at the window in a common room, held the armrests with both hands and moved his upper body back-and-forth, nothing else. He never looked at me and of course, I have no idea what was going on in his head."

They reminisced about Thodor Baron, after that they discussed the effect of false advice in business. Everyone agreed that Elise van Vennen was right when she told Rosa and Alrik that anything like that is a great sin.

Carsten von Haller had plenty of time to talk about his meeting at Herta and Rolf Wallis' party. He mentioned Victor's revelations about the interplay of lines that fed the brain and gave someone the power over his own mind, about visionaries who were able to recognize each other and about the fact that Victor knew all about Nicolaes Nimbus.

"Later I talked with people who knew Victor well before he had to deal with dementia," said the philosopher. "Everyone agreed that his gift was close to perfect, especially where stock market predictions are concerned."

"It was a good idea to sit with him when you saw him relaxing in that summerhouse by himself," remarked Freeda.

"I think my own conclusion is spectacular," Carsten beamed. "For I know Victor was a true visionary and I believe someone like him can recognize someone at the same higher level. And if these two facts are true, I am also convinced he really knew who I was talking about when I mentioned Nicolaes Nimbus."

"That interplay of lines makes me think of self-hypnosis," said Freeda. "This sounds interesting, what a far-reaching concept."

"He compared the possibilities of the combining of lines with the faces of the billions of people on Earth – not one is similar to another," the philosopher quipped.

"It is a secret we'll probably never solve," Lucas Montaigne joined in. "A computer can produce an unlimited interplay of lines, but someone has to concentrate on every creation to find out if something happens in his or her brain. It is fascinating to consider that something like that might actually exist..."

"Anyway, I will do some research," remarked Dieter Brunn.

The group talked about the translated articles from the archives of The Society of Tamfana and Rosa spoke in detail about her meeting with Elise van Vennen. They discussed Rosa's treasure for over half an hour and then chairwoman Gabi Stein concluded, "So we agree that Nicolaes Nimbus is a man of flesh and blood. Very well then – the search for a longer, healthier life is a worldwide billion-dollar industry and we will invest a lot of money where that is concerned. When we talk about billions of dollars or euros, the money we need to prove Nicolaes Nimbus is real means totally nothing, of course. If he exists and we find him, we should be able to examine him. Time has no influence over him... we are talking about a timeless phenomenon indeed... Imagine the possibilities!"

"Yes, yes, you are right; just imagine..." said Freeda with a sigh. "As a neurologist, I would like to take the lead in such an examination. What goes on in the brain of someone that old? How will such a brain look anyway? Everything is important, his blood make-up, his DNA, his... If you only had a fingernail, a hair, or the tiniest piece of skin of an immortal; that would already be sensational. But let's be honest about it, this is all too good to be true."

Lucas Montaigne interrupted, "All facts combined plus our own experiences tell us that Nicolaes Nimbus is alive. And if that is so, I can imagine his priceless importance to science in general and to us in particular. Rosa is right. A thorough search doesn't have to be expensive. Does anyone have any ideas, how should we begin?"

"If you don't know where to search for someone, you must try to attract his attention – or set a trap," Folco muttered.

"Right," reacted Dieter, "let's consider that a possibility."

"Let's have a drink," said Rosa. "Why don't we all go to the big living room where we can flop down in comfortable easy chairs. We'll have a drink and discuss different ideas."

All seven went to the kitchen to get bottles and glasses and walked to one of the sitting rooms. As soon as everyone sat down, they brainstormed, throwing out everything they could come up with but their ideas were rejected one after the other.

"It seems an impossible task," sighed Dieter. "How on Earth can you get in contact with someone if you are not even sure he actually exists? Where does he live, where is he right now, where is he going to be one minute from now?"

"It comes down to this," said Freeda, "we have to get his attention. That seems like the most logical first step."

Folco had been silent for a while, just sitting and pondering. After Freeda's remark was uttered he snapped his fingers, "This might work..." he started and when he noticed everyone was looking at him, he explained, "Not so long ago I wanted to expand one of my companies so I bought the entire building complex. On the ground floor, there was a paint lab where they made new sorts of paint and did research on the texture of paint that was used in past centuries. The lab was as good as bankrupt. I was shown around by the last rat to leave the sinking ship and he asked me if I would mind disposing of all the junk and chemicals. Well, I did as he asked but can you guess what I found? Some of the stuff was worth saving. Paints with the exact components of those from the seventeenth century and canvases that really were that old. Original works had been erased from the old canvasses so that one could test the paint. So I have old canvases, old frames and the right paints in my possession. All we have to find now is a good painter."

"What is it exactly that you want, Folco, what do you mean by a good painter?" Gabi wanted to know.

"Don't ask me for details yet," he answered, "the idea just hit me and now we have to develop it. I mean... a painting that looks entirely authentic from the seventeenth century, with a clear reference to Nicolaes Nimbus. A special discovery – we can call in the press, we know how to do it... magazines, television, the internet. Let's blow up a story to absurd proportions. The painting is expensive, very expensive; that is what we'll say, that is what we'll want everyone to believe.

And yes, we might even sell it to the highest bidder. And the highest bidder..."

"...Might be Nicolaes Nimbus," Freeda filled in the blank enthusiastically. "Someone who has lived for such a long time will undoubtedly be very rich, willing to bid as if the sky's the limit. There is a good chance he'll want to buy the painting..."

"Or someone else who is just as interested in Nicolaes Nimbus," said Dieter. "But how do you link the name of Nicolaes to a painting?"

"The name could be visible, the title of a book, for instance," suggested Lucas Montaigne. "On the spine of a bound book, perhaps in gilded letters... And that will also be the name of the painting: Nicolaes Nimbus. It seems a perfect idea to me, Folco."

Folco rose to his feet and raised his glass. The other six followed suit.

"Let's do it," he smiled, "we will develop the plan carefully and during the process, we will come up with new ideas. What shall we drink to? Let's toast to the insanity that probably contains a kernel of truth, how about that?"

"To insanity, that seems sufficient to me," Carsten von Haller seconded as he stood.

"Cheers," everyone repeated. "To insanity!"

Freeda Olbers felt a shiver run down her spine. She looked at Gabi Stein and read fear in her eyes. Dieter

Brunn started coughing. Others tried to smile but only grimaced.

After everyone sat down again, they came up with different suggestions to make the plan perfect.

❋ ❋ ❋

Anyone who drove from Munich toward Freising, if they avoided the highway, hoping not to get lost on the narrow country roads, realized immediately that he or she had discovered something odd as they passed the old, ramshackled house of Remco Castor. Between two little villages, where the landscape was primarily sloping meadows and well-kept farms, there was a rotten spot, like a broken molar in a perfectly good set of teeth. The house and the outbuildings had a stone base. Above it, the walls were of wood, wood that had deteriorated after more than one hundred and fifty years from vivid brown to sad flat black.

Along the entire front, at the side of the road, empty picture frames hung on poles of different heights. Even the most hurried motorists slowed down to observe framed pieces of empty reality. Upon further inspection, anyone curious enough noticed an unimaginable amount of piled up junk that filled the entire garden. Heavily damaged wooden chairs, tables, closets, boxes, and crates filled with crockery and tableware, vases, plant stands, garden statues, and several rusty cars that would never be driven again; all indications of what one might expect to find inside the downtrodden dwelling.

Above the door, a big sign dangled on a rusty nail, in red faded letters, Art Shop Remco Castor.

Castor's mental picture frame had contained changing but always negative images; his world view was as black as the wood of his moldy house.

Folco Andermann parked his brand new Audi opposite the rusty wrecks. He had almost gotten lost, it had been a long time since he had been there. Castor – no one ever addressed him by his first name – and he were cousins of the same age; they had met in their youth, mainly at family parties. He knew Castor was born here, in the house of his parents, and that his great-grandfather had started an art shop– his grandfather had made something big out of it, his father, the brother of Folco's mother, had spent all the money. Castor had started to sell as much rubbish as possible to keep his head above water – it seemed impossible these days to make a living by selling art only.

Castor stepped outside the moment Folco walked up to the door. The men shook hands and embraced.

"Nice to see you again, Castor, you look great!"

"When I unfold my wrinkles, my face grows twice as big. You, with your millions...a big man in the pharmaceutical industry, how many of your own pills do you have to swallow to look as young as you do, cousin?

Wait here. It is hot. Let's stay outside. I'll get us some nice cold beer."

Castor disappeared inside as Folco remained standing by the door looking through the big picture frames to a meadow at the other side of the road, where cows were grazing. He found everything strange, even bizarre, but he knew he was in the right place. Castor came back. Two half-liter bottles of beer dangled between the fingers of one hand while he used the other hand to push two old, wooden chairs up to the wall next to the door.

"Have a seat."

They both took a swig and then Castor began to ramble on about his position in a world where everyone had gone crazy on a raid looking for useless things. He shied away from that, he didn't want anything to do with it. Folco waited patiently till his fury had spent itself. Every now and then a car passed by, slowing for a couple of seconds and accelerating again. No one ever stopped to visit Art Shop Remco Castor.

"The madness is complete in your filthy rich circles," he muttered. "Paint one single letter or a figure on a canvas, mix ten different colors or let a chimpanzee do the work; don't be surprised if it's sold for a couple of million euro. And the true artist has a stomachache due to hunger."

"That's exactly what I want to talk about, Castor, about art."

"Yes, you mentioned a certain plan and said something about needing me when you called. Well, what's in it for me? I could use some money, you know. Not much happens here. That is to say, nothing has happened here for a long, long time. I can be honest about that with you, can't I, Folco?"

"Of course but you are always mad with everything and at everyone. How about playing a nasty trick on the world and making some money at the same time?"

"How much do you have in mind?" Suddenly Castor's voice perked up.

"I'm going to ask you to exhibit one painting for sale and play a sly game in the process."

Castor prattled on as if he hadn't heard him and went on about money, "I don't have any debts. The house costs me nothing. If this is about a bit of cash, that is just what I need. And you can help me with that, you say?"

Folco had an idea that Castor was flat broke at the moment.

"Before I leave I will give you a little something. That is no problem at all."

"That would be nice, Folco, very nice indeed. Life is beautiful when you can sit down in an old chair and have a beer, knowing you can easily buy yourself a few more bottles. What sort of painting are you talking about, for heaven's sake?"

"If you have the patience to listen, I will tell you all about it."

"Wait, I'll get us some more beer."

"Not for me, thanks, I have to drive."

Castor stood up and went inside. Soon he was back with a new bottle in tow. "I'm all ears."

"We will clear up this mess thoroughly," started Folco. "Away with all that rotten wood, away with those broken chairs and tables and rusty car wrecks. If you want visitors to come around everything has to look tidier."

"Who do you think might visit me? And what you call rotten wood and rusty iron is my merchandise."

"You'll get paid, don't worry about that. The story goes like this... you started cleaning that big house of yours and you opened doors that had been locked for a very long time. You were astonished when you discovered an old painting your father or your grandfather had put away. It was standing in a corner somewhere, in one of the many rooms upstairs. What a discovery, a masterpiece from the seventeenth century, almost certainly from The Netherlands! It will be sold to the highest bidder and all the money will be yours."

Castor took a swig. Then he said, "Maybe you thought I wasn't listening a little while ago, but I heard you say clearly that you expect me to play a sly game. Ha! Why not? It will not be difficult for me to convince someone that I found a masterful painting in the caverns of this old den. Which painting are you talking about and what is your intention exactly?"

"Let me put it this way, I am only interested in the person who comes up with the highest bid. And don't think this is only about thousands of euro's, Castor. It wouldn't surprise me if someone was willing to pay a couple of million for it."

"Are you kidding? And it would all be mine?"

"...All yours, exactly. I don't need it, you see. What counts for me is the result. Listen, I am talking about a very old canvas, an old frame, and the right paint. Still, someone might find out that it is a recent work because the painting will probably look rather new. But there are certain methods..."

Castor raised his free hand. "Ho, ho! Wait a minute. The trick to making a new painting look old is due to the fact that it is handed down from father to son. That is one family secret that I will be very proud of. If what you say is true, if the frame and the canvas are old and the paint looks old, leave it up to me to make the story and the painting look authentic. Folco... a couple of million! For that money, I would show anyone proof that your smartphone was made in the seventeenth century by a brilliant clockmaker! Now tell me, honestly, is there a snake in the grass? Is there a chance I will not get any money at all?"

"You just play your role. That is all. I guarantee you will end up a rich man. Count on two-hundred-thousand and keep in mind it might eventually be a million, maybe two million. It's as simple as that."

"I feel dizzy, Folco. What kind of painting are you talking about, what does it look like?"

"It has yet to be painted..."

"Give me a few details about the painting and about the role I am supposed to play."

Folco told Castor what he needed to know. Later, after Folco slipped his cousin a couple of thousand euros they went into the house. Had they been many years younger, they would probably have made a game out of it, jumping over piles of junk that filled the corridor, the kitchen, and the living room. They finally managed to reach two armchairs, legs stiff as Folco pushed several magazines and books from the cushion to the floor.

"You're not a salesman, Castor; you're a collector of useless junk."

"Alright I concede, but now that you're here everything can be thrown away. I will help with that, the moment you've left I will make a bonfire in the back garden."

Folco explained his plans further. He didn't speak a word about Das Web and made his cousin believe he did everything for personal reasons. Castor was not curious about motives; he realized he would feel much more comfortable living in the angry world when he had a certain amount of money at his disposal. He promised Folco he was more than happy to cooperate.

"Men will come to install little cameras. Everyone who visits the Art Shop Remco Castor will be filmed. Everything that happens here will be registered and a matter of record. The painting will be placed in unbreakable glass. No one will be able to steal it."

After some time Castor took his cousin up to the first story of the house. He opened the door of a small room with a rusty key,

"Take a look inside. This is what the past smells like, I've seldom opened this door and have no idea what's inside. I could have found that painting here."

Folco saw an old desk on a wooden floor with several high mirrors stored behind it. "What do you know, you discovered the painting behind those mirrors, Castor. That seems as good an idea to me as any."

❋ ❋ ❋

As soon as Folco Andermann drove away, Castor started to clean out the big house. He carted everything he didn't want to save to the back garden that bordered an extensive meadow. He smashed broken tables and chairs to pieces with an ax and piled up the wood. Then he set the pile on fire using old newspapers and magazines. It was a calm day as the smoke went straight up.

"This bonfire will burn for many days," he grinned to himself. He brought the things he could still use or sell to one of the outbuildings; it had always been used as a depot of sorts.

Within twenty-four hours the wrecks were towed away and everything in front of the house was cleared; only the poles with the empty picture frames remained standing. Folco had hired professionals who also helped clean out the house.

A team of technicians arrived a few days later to install mini-cams high and low and in every corner of every room. Castor had to climb two sets of stairs to have any privacy. He didn't even pay attention to the cameras; he went his own way thinking constantly about the money that would change his life forever.

❊ ❊ ❊

The Das Web seven did everything they could to reach their common goals. Thanks to Dieter, a Dutch art forger was found who was instructed, through an anonymous middleman, to paint a seventeenth-century work of art. As soon as he agreed, the special paint, the aged canvas, and the frame were delivered to his home wrapped in plain heavy paper. Folco had already found the perfect location and the right man to exhibit the painting, Art Shop Remco Castor. Lucas Montaigne sent men to install the small cameras. Gabi Stein and Rosa Linge found technicians within their own companies who designed a splendid unbreakable glass cover for the painting. Carsten von Haller knew many people in the media world; he approached them to inform them about the painting. Gabi Stein asked her friend, Alrik von Hecht, to do the same – Alrik had received many positive reviews of his deluxe dental practice; he knew he could ask his patients and reviewers for their cooperation.

Freeda Olbers wrote press releases and made use of the internet to spread the word about the newfound work of art, The Reading Man, the agreed-upon name for the painting.

Monitors were installed in a Das Web meeting room; what was happening in and around Castor's home in real-time was now available to the group twenty-four-seven; all images were saved so that it was not necessary to have someone present in the room.

Publicity turned out to be the biggest problem. The discovery of a beautiful painting from the seventeenth century was unique in itself, but if it was not signed and wasn't attributable to a celebrity like Rembrandt or Frans Hals the news would soon be forgotten. Still, the name Nicolaes Nimbus was everywhere and anyone could bid for the painting.

Castor played the role of his life and played it well. He placed a wooden chair next to the front door and sat waiting for his first visitors at first light. He invited people of the press, art collectors, art connoisseurs, and curious others to come inside. The living room was cleaned up and the wooden floors had been scrubbed several times and varnished. Along the walls, there were some chairs, a couch, and a closet.

From nine o'clock in the morning till six at night a broad-shouldered man in a grey uniform was present. He sat almost motionless on one of the chairs and never bothered anyone. Castor did not speak a word with him, but he appreciated his presence. The man was relieved by an almost identical attendant who behaved exactly the same –as if they were acting in a silent movie.

A man who was not present in the room hung around near a van on the other side of the road and noted the license plates of all cars that parked in front of the house; they were also recorded by mini cameras installed outside.

The painting stood in the middle of the room. It was an impressive work of art and exhibited spectacularly as if it had been cast in crystal and stood on a pedestal of black glass. Of course, everyone wanted to know how Castor managed to display his find with such beauty and his answer was, "It is a present from rich friends who want the painting to be completely safe.

You can walk around it and see the backside as well. It is a prototype. They are hoping this might be a better way to exhibit paintings in museums. You can get as close as you wish; you will never damage it. It is very well protected."

Many asked how the painting would be removed from its casing if need be but he was unable to answer the question; he had no idea himself.

"But I do know it has been fastened in some way so that it cannot be pushed over and the glass is unbreakable. Imagine a museum with paintings on pedestals in long rows... perhaps even glass cases hanging down from the ceiling!"

Next to the painting was a white shield. On it was text in black letters: Nicolaes Nimbus. Origin: probably The Netherlands, seventeenth century. Not signed. Reading man of letters or a magician, maybe Nicolas Nimbus (unknown person), with a foot resting on his book.

Castor led his guests upstairs and showed them the small room, "This is where I found the painting. The door had been locked for so long, for so many years, I didn't even know where the key was. Then I found a couple of rusty keys in a little wooden box. I was curious about all those high mirrors. When I removed a couple of them, I discovered the painting. Fortunately, I know a lot about art and I understood immediately that I had found something very special. Perhaps my father had bought it, or maybe my grandfather. I'd never seen it before and no one had ever mentioned it."

Of course, he didn't say anything about the fact that he knew so much about art he was able to make new paintings look old; a complicated procedure of heating, carefully working with a special, secret mix of ingredients that penetrated the paint without damaging it and heating it again to make the paint appear hard and cracked. It had been a tough job but there was always a chance of damaging the work of art. A special oven was necessary to do it properly, but Castor had learned to do it with a simple hairdryer!

"So you want to sell it," a journalist from a Munich newspaper said when she visited him one afternoon. "...To the highest bidder. Do you have any idea how much you will get for it?"

"This is the very detailed work of a master painter who knew what he was doing," he answered. "Perhaps we may yet find out who painted it. And then the name, Nicolaes Nimbus, is the title on the book, but who is he? That is a mystery to me. It is an intriguing piece of art so I expect it will be sold for a record price. I will not speculate about it now. But I know it is worth a lot of money."

The tiny cameras filmed everything and sensitive microphones recorded every word the visitors said. An ingenious computer system was put into place and the results were shown in the room at Fort Web: pictures of faces with all the information that goes with it, names, ages, and professions. Every word that was uttered could be a clue to someone's identity and Castor had been instructed to ask the right questions.

The journalist from Munich was still present when a peculiar man entered; he walked around the painting and pressed his nose to the glass to see everything as well as possible.

"I would like to buy this," he said. "Can I make a bid?"

"Of course," said Castor, while he shook hands with the man. "What is your name? Where do you come from?"

"Ten thousand euro," he said while ignoring Castor's questions.

Castor shook his head and just smiled.

"Yes, yes, I thought so," the man hastened to say. "But at least I gave it a shot, right? What if I multiply my price by ten? I am willing to pay one hundred thousand euro for it."

"I will take down your name and address. I expect the painting will fetch a much higher price."

"I am flexible; I might come up with a better offer shortly..." The man wore a dark grey suit and had a narrow, pale friendly face and bright blue eyes. Three striking accents made him look eccentric; a wide-brimmed straw hat that was probably older than he was, a long shawl instead of a tie that was knotted in six nooses, and shoes made of small, square pieces of white and black painted leather.

The journalist became curious. She introduced herself to him and immediately asked a question, "You go from ten thousand euro to a hundred thousand right away. Is it possible that you know more about the painting or the name on the spine of the book?"

"I know nothing at all, but I do know it is a very beautiful work of art..."

Castor asked him for his business card. "Better to give me yours," was the reaction, "I can always contact you later."

The computer system worked well, somewhere in cyberspace some useful information was found. His picture was large and vivid in the room at Fort Web, together with his name and profession. He turned out to be a fortune teller who had come from Ingolstadt to see the painting. A conclusion was rapidly decided, in line with what Victor the Visionary had said, Nicolaes Nimbus was a well-known name among certain circles ...

Chapter 9

Rein Vulpes had bought an old Toyota with more than two-hundred-thousand miles on the speedometer, filled the trunk with clothes, and drove to Germany early in the morning.

Without warning the name he had painted in gold had turned up everywhere on the internet, Nicolaes Nimbus. He knew the painting was being exhibited in a house or a shop somewhere along a country road between Munich and Freising. It was for sale and naturally, anyone could bid on it. Curiosity and a preference to get as much variety in his life as possible led to the spontaneous buying of the car and his decision to hit the road.

The indestructible motor growled with delight when he put the pedal to the floor. Rein knew the people who had asked him to create the painting didn't want anything to do with him, but he didn't care. He was used to doing as he pleased and would rather let himself be influenced by a rolling of the dice rather than by people he didn't even know; he had put his heart and soul into the painting and he was eager to know what had happened to it and where it was being exhibited.

His adventurous spirit led him to shy away from long, straight highways; his only navigation system was his sense of direction. He had money in his pocket, was in a good mood, loved to drive, and was constantly curious about what he was about to experience around every new turn.

It always gave him a good feeling to be going to places he had never been before. The fastest route was about five hundred miles. There was a good chance he would drive a couple of hundred miles more. He stopped often just to look around, have something to eat and drink, tank up, or take a break.

By later that evening he found himself somewhere between Karlsruhe and Heilbronn so he parked his Toyota in front of a hotel. He had a good meal in the dining room of the restaurant, drank a few nice cold beers at the bar, and went to sleep early in a room nearby.

True to his restless nature, he jumped out of bed the moment he opened his eyes and after a quick breakfast, he was behind the wheel again and driving away. After a short quiet ride, he ended up in a little village close to the house where his painting was exhibited. He parked the car in front of Restaurant Etzel, a white building with a large door that stood invitingly open.

He asked a friendly man behind a pinewood bar about the painting; he knew immediately what he was talking about. "Only a few days ago many people came here asking for directions to Art Shop Remco Castor. I decided to walk over there and see it for myself. One man told me the painting was very special. As far as that is concerned, I was not disappointed, it is truly splendid; it is old and very intriguing. What a great discovery! It has been a hot item around here. People have come from all around to see it. How about you? You speak German very well, but I think I can hear your Dutch accent... Well, you're almost there, only two thousand feet to go, head toward Munich." He pointed to the right.

"Maybe it'll be easier to find after I've had a glass of beer."

"I think so too," the man quipped.

Rein drank more than one glass and when he left the restaurant, he decided to walk instead. After he passed several big farms, he saw an old house and some outbuildings. A van was parked on the other side of the road; a man in a grey uniform was leaning against it. An old man was sitting on a wooden chair next to the door. Rein saw poles of different lengths with an empty picture frame at the top of each one situated along the roadside. He could not restrain himself as he walked up to the highest thickest pole and climbed up to the top, sitting with legs dangling on the lower part of the rusted frame. As he looked over his shoulder, he spied sloping meadows and when he turned his head, he saw the old man jump up from his chair.

"Why has no one else come up with that idea?" the man remarked. "Wait right there, don't move, I'll take a picture of you." He took a smartphone from the pocket of his corduroy trousers and took a few steps forward. Holding the smartphone up, he said, "The frame fills the little screen perfectly, you sitting there with a green background and blue sky above you. Who are you? I don't think we've met before." The man walked toward the pole.

"I'm the only fox able to climb this pole," Rein answered.

"Not a German fox, I think. Are you a smart fox?"

"But of course! I even won a fight with a wolf."

"Impressive and how did you manage to do that?"

While Rein climbed down, he said, "I got some good advice and smeared myself with butter. That way I was too slippery for the wolf and besides, I flung sand in his eyes with my tail when I pretended to be scared and fled right away." Then he reached out his hand, "Rein Vulpes is my name; I am from The Netherlands..."

"Remco Castor, everyone around here calls me Castor. Did the fox leave his hole to admire a work of art?"

"Even the lion, the king of the jungle, shivers when it is made known that I have left my hole," said Rein. "And I only care about art as long it isn't about a daub; far too many painters use their brushes as if they are conducting an orchestra!"

"Have I finally met someone who understands the world is nothing more than a rotten apple, that you best mind your own business lest you become as mad as the rest?"

Rein put a hand on his shoulder and spoke in his best German, "Your no good world is the scenery for my play, Castor, and I think you will be the perfect person for a supporting role."

"Fortunately it is quiet for now. There have been many visitors this morning, the last two just left. Come, let's go inside, I'll show you The Reading Man. For that is why you are here, right, to see The Reading Man?"

The sun shone on the wall of the ground floor with the almost black wood above it. Rein spotted the sparkling of two tiny lenses and wondered why bigger cameras hadn't been installed. He knew what to look for, he discovered identical little lenses in well-chosen places in the corridor and in the big room where Castor was taking him. He had an eye for the tiniest details, especially since they shouldn't be there.

Rein nodded to a sitting attendant in a grey uniform and the man nodded back at him in silence.

"Here it is, my discovery!" Castor almost yelled in an enthusiastic voice, as if Rein was his very first visitor. "I found this amazing old painting in a room that had been locked for decades, hidden behind several full-length, antique mirrors."

"And the fox is right again, he's just an actor in my play."

But he didn't say anything. Where mini-cameras were installed, undoubtedly very little microphones were nearby as well.

His work of art surprised him. Soft light shone down on it from the ceiling. The glass casing was non-reflective. The black glass pedestal brought the painting to just the right height. The craquelure and an almost invisible haze that could only have come into being by the factor of time gave it a just-right ancient radiation.

"Do you want to bid as well?" asked Castor. "Suddenly the bidding is going very fast, especially by phone. A certain group of people is interested; the last bid was over a million euros. What is your profession? I mean, even foxes must eat..."

Rein answered promptly, "The fox was lazy from the start, when no one looked he stole his part."

"That sounds exciting," laughed Castor. "And what do you think of the painting?"

Rein walked around it, leaning a bit forward with his hands clasped behind his back. "Impressive." Both men turned their heads when they heard the sound of two car doors closing.

Two men and two women entered the room. Not much later three men waltzed in as well. Castor started to tell them about his discovery and of course he took everyone upstairs to show them the small room with the antique mirrors. He mentioned the last bid of one million, no one seemed to bat an eye. A woman wanted to know how many times she could bid if she wanted to bid more. One of the men said that he was willing to pay one million one-hundred-thousand euro.

Rein watched as Castor asked just the right questions to find out who the visitors were and what they did for a living. Rein gathered they all had impressive business careers. Castor took their business cards and made appointments. Everyone went downstairs again. After they walked around the painting a couple of times, they took their leave and went back to their cars. Rein decided to leave too. He hadn't said very much, he just listened.

Castor would not let him go, saying, "Where are you going? You came all the way from The Netherlands. Stay awhile."

"My car is parked just down the road, in front of Restaurant Etzel. They have good beer there so that is where I'm headed."

Castor looked at his watch. "Their kitchen is already open. Are you hungry, or just thirsty? My treat! I

haven't left the house for days; it is high time I got out...
How about it, Mister Fox?"

"I think that's a good idea."

"We're going to Etzel," the attendant nodded.

They left the house and started to walk toward the
restaurant. "You have been rather silent, fox," Castor
began.

"That's right; I prefer to keep my mouth shut when
there are as many hidden microphones as there are
hidden cameras."

"How..."

"I have an eye for things like that."

"Hmmm, you know, Rein, I've wandered this rotten
globe for many years. I only have to look someone in
the eye to know who I am dealing with, be he a
swindler, an egoist, a liar, a hypocrite, or just a fool. I
think you are okay. No, actually I'm very sure about
that. But that does not mean I will explain the cameras
and microphones to you."

"Do as you please, can I trust you as much as you
trust me?"

"...Of course, of course!" Castor said spontaneously.

Rein saw no reason to keep the truth from the old
man. It seemed in his best interest to confront him with
it.

"The painting you found behind the high mirrors...?"

"What about it?"

They walked past a farm. Rein put his hands in his pockets and shrugged his shoulders. "It is from The Netherlands."

"Yes, I know."

"I painted it myself not that long ago."

Castor stopped, closed his eyes, took a deep breath, and groped about as if he needed support. Rein grabbed him by the arm. "You're not going to faint, are you? Relax, it's no big deal. I have come here out of curiosity, certainly not with evil intent."

Castor started panting. It took more than two minutes before he recovered. He looked at Rein with sad eyes. "If anyone finds out it's a recent work of art, certain people I have dealt with will not like it at all. Well, to be honest, that doesn't really bother me. But personally, it would be traumatic to me. Do you know what one of my visitors was willing to pay for the painting? ...One-million one-hundred-thousand euro. That would all be mine, fox, I wouldn't have to share a single euro with anyone else."

"You know we can trust each other, right? This must stay among us. That is to say, at least until you have gotten your money. I have no interest in running this up the flagpole; there is no reason why I should begrudge you such a large sum of money."

"Do you want a piece of the action?"

"You invited me for a beer and a meal. That is enough for me, more than enough." Castor sighed with relief. "Thank you so much for that. Let's go on then but let's walk a bit faster now – I need something stronger than a glass of beer."

They walked on in silence. Castor started talking again when they sat down at a table in the restaurant.

"Suddenly, life can be so fascinating! Nothing is always alright and no one is honest in this world, then someone climbs up a pole and sits inside one of my picture frames – someone I believe when he says he will be happy for me when I get that money. And what you said about painters using their brushes like a conductor, that has become much clearer to me now. You are a true artist, you are on equal par with the old masters from your own country!"

"Someone has seen to it that it looks really old."

"I did that myself," said Castor, proudly straightening his back. They both burst out laughing. And they even laughed louder after Castor added, "You need a huge oven for that. But I did it with an old, noisy hairdryer!"

A waitress who had come up to their table stood with a smile on her face, waiting till the men finally stopped laughing. "It's been a long time, Castor, we don't see you here often. And finally in a good mood! Welcome. What are you having?"

"Two beers and two cold Bommerlunders," Castor added. "And we want something to eat as well."

"Congratulations on your great discovery. You're becoming famous in your old age, Victor. The drinks are on the house – if you only knew how much money a film crew had spent here recently. They were on their way to see you and had lunch here. We get a lot more customers these days. ...Thanks to you!"

Several people came up to Castor to have a chat with him; only after dinner was served did they leave him to eat in peace.

"Enjoy your meal, fox, I hope you don't mind if I keep some information to myself. To be honest, I don't know what's going on, but someone approached me with a certain proposal – but I don't want to mention his name..."

"I understand, that's no problem at all."

"Okay, let's talk about other things. How about art that isn't real art, people with a lot of money and no taste, to begin with? Let's talk about the unimaginative, the rotten world in general, and the wickedness that mankind has in common?"

"That seems a terrific beginning to me. " Rein ate, drank, and listened. The old man mixed his dark pessimism with sufficient humor and enough subtle sarcasm to keep him interested. Nothing about his worldview was positive, but there was no talk of hate or revenge.

"It would have been better if we had remained ignorant like the animals," Castor concluded. "Now we are saddled with a consciousness that is not big enough to comprehend what everything around us means exactly. Knowing a lot, but not knowing everything, that drives you to the edge of insanity. All we need are the last little pieces of the big puzzle. Someone has thrown them away and we cannot find them anymore."

New customers entered the restaurant and they put an end to their dialogue – everyone wanted to talk to him, take pictures with Castor and offer him a drink. Within minutes he told them about The Reading Man and toasted with a glass of beer or an ice-cold Bommerlunder.

When Rein and Castor left the restaurant, they had to support each other; they could hardly walk. It took Rein more than ten minutes to get some clothes from the trunk of his Toyota and put them in a linen bag. Together they went back to Castor's house, now and then they stumbled through the grass, they fell over a couple of times and scrambled to their feet again, swaying from left to right and agreed that everyone in this world was heartless, except for themselves...

Lights came on as soon as Castor knocked on his door and his attendants left right after they set foot inside the premises. Castor bumped against the walls of the corridor and fell inside the big room through the open door. He hoisted himself on the attendant's chair and produced another key.

"Here you go. Don't lose it. You can spend the night in the biggest outbuilding. You'll find plenty of rooms on the second floor."

Rein took the key. Castor sprawled on his chair, closed his eyes, and seemed to doze off. Rein had no option but to go outside, close the front door and search for the biggest outbuilding without a flashlight to guide him. It was not very late and he wasn't sleepy. After a lengthy search, he found the right building. The key made a grating sound when he unlocked the door. He stared into total darkness while searching for a light switch. A dozen ceiling lights shone, the huge space was in unbelievable chaos. Pieces of furniture were stacked up high; there were mountains of car parts and shelves full of junk. More than likely no one had been there for a long time, he had to shove things aside to reach the stairs. He flung chairs and stools through the air and had to exert himself to shove a heavy oak table aside. Even the steps were full of boxes, books, and magazines. He crawled up them on all fours. He found two switches at the top of the stairs, one to turn off the lights on the ground level and one to light up the second story. The long corridor and most of the rooms were used to store countless objects.

Rein found an old-fashioned bathroom. There was no hot water. The cold water hadn't been used for so long, brown-colored water came out when he turned it on. After a minute the water became clearer. One bedroom had fewer boxes and crates than the others. There was a musty smell so he opened a window to let fresh air circulate.

A hard, solid bed without sheets occupied one corner. He found a blanket and lay down.

Although he couldn't say it felt comfortable, he preferred this above a luxury hotel room even though there was no pillow.

The countless objects in the outbuilding formed a common scent of the past and faded memories, the walls breathed an atmosphere that could inspire a sensitive spirit like that of Rein Vulpes. He lay on his back, hands folded under his head, staring up at a moist ceiling and a burning lightbulb that was probably older than himself. A day full of new impressions, a copious meal, beer, and Bommerlunders formed the ideal combination for a night of deep sleep. His thoughts changed imperceptibly into colorful dreams.

❋ ❋ ❋

It was still night, but an invisible sun sent a soft light from just beyond the horizon. Castor opened his eyes and sat up quickly. He knew where he was, in his own bed. A short time after the visitor from The Netherlands had closed the front door, he had stood up, locked the door, and went upstairs. He heard something. He knew all the sounds of the house – from a flapping shutter in a storm to the creaking of old ceiling beams –they never disturbed him in his sleep. But now he heard it again. He knew where it came from and what it was immediately. It came from downstairs, from the big room. The wooden floor creaked under the weight of moving feet, something that remained unnoticed during the day, but sounded a warning at night to wakeful ears; Castor was a light sleeper. There was someone below. *No, it can't be Rein; he's asleep in the big outbuilding. How could he have come inside, without a key to the front door?* Again he heard sounds. He rolled to one side and felt under the bed, feeling for his club, the round leg of an old chair. He stood up and slipped out of the room. It was easy for him to go down the stairs two at a time in his bare feet without making a sound. As a child he would lean on the massive hardwood banisters and let himself slide down, his toes hardly touched the steps.

He reached the ground level and saw a light shining through the open door of the big room. Holding the club in both hands, he started to walk carefully through the corridor.

No one was used to the scent of the past better than him. The unknown amount of old objects he had stored in this house and the outbuildings had a special odor all their own. He smelled it, it was stronger than ever; moist, rotting wood and fungus, but this time it was mixed with – something very peculiar– something that was alive perhaps; it seemed to stimulate the spirit to think of an old, elusive phenomenon. Castor could not describe it exactly and had no time to consider it either, but when he snuck into the room he had a strange feeling that he had stepped back in time.

In the first instance, he thought it was a burning candle, but then he decided it had to be an oil lamp with a burning wick. The lantern was being held up to the painting and there was no reflection of the light on the special glass that covered The Reading Man. It was impossible to see who was holding the lamp. All he saw was a silhouette, one that was even blacker than the surrounding darkness.

Castor took three steps and knew the floor would creak if he went on. The Reading Man seemed so real, it wouldn't have surprised him if he suddenly saw the man in the painting look up from his book.

The oil lamp moved. "Who are you?" said Castor in a loud voice. "Tell me your name! What are you doing here?"

The lamp swayed to the right, the beam of light shone into Castor's face. Castor didn't hesitate for a second, jumped forward and lashed out as hard as he could with his club. He hit something and heard someone gasp. Then he was hit by an invisible fist and tumbled backward. The club fell on the floor along with himself. Castor groped around in the dark hoping to find his weapon. A foot hit him hard in the stomach. He automatically curled up in a fetal position, uncoiled his body, rolled over, and felt the club with his shoulder. He grabbed it as fast as he could and jumped to his feet. He rushed in the direction of the dangling lamp and lashed out with his club. Again he hit something. There was a sound of running feet. The lamp was on the floor. The ink-black silhouette was no longer nearby. He heard footsteps all around him as he turned round and round, swinging his club.

The open door formed a grey rectangle in the blackness as he rushed up to it, intending to turn on a light. He was almost there when he received a hard blow to the temple. He lost consciousness right away. Castor fell hard and remained on the floor lying motionless. The lamp ran out of fuel as the sun emerged above the horizon.

❀ ❀ ❀

Rein Vulpes woke up and smelled something burning. He didn't take the time to stretch or collect his thoughts as he jumped out of bed. He opened the curtains and looked outside through the open window. Flames were leaking from the black wood at the outside of the big house; they had already reached the roof. He had fallen asleep with his clothes on and his head was pounding from yesterday's liquid overdose. He stumbled over books and boxes as he stumbled down the stairs. Scrambling to his feet, he tried to find his way in the darkness wading through piles of junk, bumping up against massive pieces of furniture and stumbling again. When he finally managed to get outside, he felt completely sober thanks to the clean cold morning air. He ran up to the burning building. If Castor was still inside, he would need help urgently. The wood of the solid front door glowed as if it had been scorched by a flamethrower. Above the stone ground level, the fire crackled and columns of smoke rose high in the air. Rein kicked as hard as he could against a burning window hatch. Splinters and sparks flew to all sides. He kicked again and again and finally, the hatch let loose from its hinges and fell to the ground. He broke the glass with a jab of his elbow. Rein coughed, inhaling smoke that sought freedom. He picked up Castor's chair and used the legs to knock sharp fragments of glass from the casing. Next, he put the chair down, climbed on top of it, and slipped inside through the window. Finding himself in a side room, smaller flames danced across the walls. *What kind of bizarre fire is this? Fire here in this small, closed room?* He opened the door to the corridor, smoke got the best of him again. The fire was burning furiously and the smoke made him cough again. Rein covered his nose and mouth with his hand. When he reached the big room, he searched for the light switch.

Castor lay on the floor, now conscious and leaning on his elbow. His lips tried to form a word without the benefit of his voice as he coughed and gagged on overpowering smoke. His eyes grew big with fear as he tried to speak.

Flames were all around; even the floor was beginning to catch on fire. Rein ran up to Castor, stood behind him, bent down and shoved his hands under his armpits.

"Yes!" Castor whispered in a hoarse voice. "I can't get up … Away from here, fox, away from here! Help me!"

Rein felt no pain or disorientation at this moment and he was surprised by his strength when he lifted the man and held him in his arms like a baby. Holding his breath, he started to walk slowly, desperately hoping he could handle Castor's weight until they reached fresh air. In the light that shone through the open door, he could see the corridor filling with smoke. As soon as they passed the stairs, Rein glanced upward; the second story was ablaze like a mad dragon spitting huge red-yellow flames. Rein managed to reach the side room still cradling Castor. …The broken window!

He managed to lift Castor up and through the window as he took a moment to take a deep breath of real clean air. The fire was right behind him and the heat was almost unbearable. Outside it was raining sparks and ash. He could hear the roof collapsing as heavy beams fell. Suddenly there was bright light in the corridor. Jets of flame flashed through the doorway scorching Rein's back and his hair. He climbed out the window while hitting the back of his head because he was afraid his hair had caught on fire.

Castor lay in front of him on the ground. He lifted him for the second time and dragged him far enough away from the burning inferno. They both watched as flames shot up from the burning roof, now all four sides of the house were engulfed.

Castor leaned heavily on Rein, bewildered, wondering how everything that had been dear to him and his family for generations could simply burn to the ground.

A police car arrived, followed by the fire brigade, people from farms and nearby villages began crowding the property. The firemen were not able to save the house; all they could do was to keep the outbuildings wet as they were bombarded by sparks and gray ash.

"You poor man," someone said to Castor, "I smelled fire through the open window of my bedroom and decided to have a look. At first, I thought you were still burning all kinds of stuff in your back garden like you did the other day. What happened? How can anything burn so fiercely all of a sudden? I called the police and the fire brigade right away...!" It was impossible to get inside. Everything Castor possessed all his fond memories, up in flames.

It was already light when the house collapsed completely and the fireman started dampening it down. All that remained were the broken walls of the ground level. The police said it was impossible that any smoldering fire in the back garden could have caused the inferno. Perhaps sparks could have blown toward the house, but that didn't explain how the huge fire had raged on all four sides of the house. They knew Castor hadn't doused his house with gasoline to make money out of it – they found out he didn't even have fire insurance.

Castor assured them that Rein Vulpes, the strange visitor from The Netherlands, had nothing to do with it, "He saved my life. Without him, I would have choked, passed out, and probably burnt to death!" He did not tell them about the blacker than black shadow in the big room.

When the firemen started to pack up their equipment, a miracle was discovered. In the middle of the ink-black remains of the house. The Reading Man was still standing on a solid floor! Its glass covering was clean and the black pedestal still looked new.

People walked through the broad opening where the door had been, waded through the wet, black dirt, and remained standing in an almost respectful way in front of the painting – now and then someone even made a bow. The Reading Man was filmed and photographed by many.

"The Wonder of Castor," someone said. "This is impossible... still, it is real!"

Chapter 10

Old man Castor was shocked, he trembled all over but he refused to stray too far from the painting. Rein took two chairs from an outbuilding so they could sit down together. The fire brigade left. The police asked lots of questions and Castor answered them; he was short and to the point, his voice trembling. The people on the premises went back to their homes to prepare for the day ahead. Now and then a car passed by, it slowed down or even stopped and finally accelerated again just like they did before the fire. Now everything was quiet, Castor told Rein what had happened in the house. "This must stay between you and me. Don't say anything to the police. I was warned, something would happen to me if I talked...he said"

"Warned?" Rein interrupted him. "...By whom?"

Castor waved his remark away with a trembling hand and continued, "I woke up; I'd heard a sound downstairs," he went on, "Oh, everything is gone now, everything is lost! It had always been as if this house were alive, you know, and all the sounds it made were recognizable, every creak, every rattling window. Armed with a club I snuck downstairs. Someone was there near the painting. An oil lamp was swinging to-and-fro. The wick burnt behind the glass. The lamp was held by..."

He fell silent, his whole body shook when he took a deep breath. Rein waited patiently. Finally, Castor went on, "I cannot precisely describe the person I stumbled upon in the big room. It was pitch-black but he was real and certainly not an apparition. I hit him with my club. My arm went numb for a moment." Castor searched for the right words. "Human for sure," he said then, "human but still different. Not like you and me. I don't know how to explain it any other way; I can only hope you understand what I mean."

"More or less," said Rein, "I have a great imagination; I'm trying to picture it..."

"The fire," Castor sighed. "Oh, the fire was all around me, all at the same time. Downstairs, upstairs, in all rooms, outside... the walls, the roof... How could that even happen like that?"

They sat next to each other in the early, moist morning and looked at what was left of the house – wet, black dirt, partly burnt beams, and the broken wall of the ground floor. Castor put his arm on Rein's shoulder. "Please, fox, stay with me for the time being. Seldom have I had to deal with fear. Now everything I grew up with has been taken away from me; please believe me when I say I am scared, terrified... I've told you before that I know I can trust you. I cannot bear to be alone now. Do you understand what I am going through?"

"Don't worry about that, I'm going nowhere at all."

A van stopped at the other side of the road. The attendees looked out their window and two minutes later the van turned and drove away.

A film crew arrived to shoot the scene for the evening news. A nearby doctor arrived to examine Castor. He wanted to prescribe sedatives, but Castor said it was not necessary. Curious people jumped over broken beams and walked through black pools to have their pictures taken standing next to The Reading Man. And all that time Castor and Rein sat together, without having anything to eat or drink. They let themselves be warmed by the morning sun. The old man wiped away tears with the sleeve of his worn jacket and now and then he sobbed softly.

The van returned, followed by Folco Andermann's big Audi. The attendants, silent twins in their identical grey uniforms, went to take a look at the house, or what was left of it, while Folco walked up to Castor.

"Good heavens, Castor, what happened here?"

Instead of answering, Castor pointed at the young man next to him and said, "This is Rein Vulpes, a friend of mine from The Netherlands. We don't have to keep anything secret from him. When he leaves, I will panic, that's for sure. He is allowed to hear everything you and I have to discuss."

Folco raised his eyebrows. For a moment he didn't pay attention to the chaos or the ruins where the old house had stood.

"What is that supposed to mean, did you tell him about anything we discussed?"

"He knows nothing, he knows nothing at all."

From where Folco stood he could see the painting, the high door had burnt completely, just ashes on the ground.

"This... this is impossible..." he muttered, while he walked over to it.

Castor and Rein rose to their feet and followed him. The attendants passed them by, not even glancing their way.

"This is very special," said Folco, when he stood in front of the painting and touched the glass carefully as if it had become fragile suddenly.

"People are already calling it the Wonder of Castor," Rein said in his best German.

"Is there a place where we can have a quiet talk? The men are here to guard the painting." Castor gestured toward a large building.

Not much later they were standing next to each other by a dirty open window on the second floor of one of the biggest outbuildings. A police car had arrived and a fire truck was parked at the roadside. Police and fire brigade staff surveyed the burnt-down house once again.

"I have no explanation for that raging fire. The flames were all around. My vocabulary is stunted and my imagination is too dulled to give a full description of the person I hit with my club. I told Rein I believe the man in the big room was human – but different, I mean, not like you and I... Now everything has been taken away from me and I am terrified. I am too old to deal with this by myself; I want Rein Vulpes to stay with me for the time being."

They walked away from the open window and sat down on rickety chairs. Folco felt uneasy because Rein was involved. He had to choose his words carefully. "The insurance..." he started to say.

"There is no insurance, Folco. I never had fire insurance. I could not afford it."

"I will see to it that the painting is taken away from here as soon as possible. The bids are quite high now. All the money will be yours. You can build a new house and then there will still be enough money left over to live a good life. I am so sorry for you. What has happened here is unfathomable."

"Where will the painting be housed?"

"...A business park at the edge of Munich, CompuStein, the office building of my friend, Gabi stein. It will remain there until we have accepted the highest bid. I hope you will feel less fearful soon, Castor. Hold on and stay strong. You will be a rich man before long. But of course, I realize this won't bring back all your personal possessions."

"There was not much of value in the house anyway," said Castor in a soft tone, while he shook his head slowly. "...Simple, tiny memories of my parents and grandparents... Albums full of old photographs. The sounds of the old house, the familiar atmosphere, it has all gone up in smoke. Ashes can never be mended."

The conversation went on laboriously. Then, all of a sudden, Castor started to wave his arms; the old chair creaked under the movements of his body. Not much later he sat there frozen and he spoke in a soft voice, "I have a strange feeling. About what I have done..."

"What do you mean, cousin?"

Now Rein knew Castor and Folco were cousins.

"What have I done..." Castor said almost to himself. "...With my chair leg, my club. I have lashed out hard; I have roused someone's or something's anger. Rage! It is unstoppable and it will turn itself against me, against us!"

The moment he fell silent, they heard noises coming from the ground level at the other end of the building, the sounds of furniture moving, the creaking and banging of high piles of junk toppling over. The burnt-out building shook. Charred boxes and books fell down the stairs. Rein jumped to his feet, placing his feet far apart as if he was standing on the deck of a sinking ship. Folco stood up as well and leaned against a window. Only Castor remained sitting motionless.

"Soon this ramshackle building will collapse!" Folco cried out. "What is happening here?"

But then it was already quiet again. A door swung open and someone shouted, "Police! Who's inside?"

Castor took a deep breath. "I'm here, Remco Castor and two friends. We are coming downstairs!"

Castor was the first to leave the room. Close to the stairs he stopped and turned toward Rein. He looked at Rein and asked in surprise, "Why do I say things like that? Why do I have such thoughts? About unstoppable rage, I mean..."

It was as if someone had cleaned all the steps with a broom; at the bottom of the stairs lay a huge pile of boxes and books. Everything on the ground floor had been thrown about and many pieces of furniture were heavily damaged. Closet doors had fallen off their hinges, the legs of tables and chairs were broken, tabletops were gouged with deep cracks.

Two policemen stood still in amazement. "Castor, Castor..." said one of them, "what the hell is going on here?"

"Some of the piles have come down, that's all, Helmut," said Castor, who knew the police officer very well. "That makes a lot of noise, doesn't it? Everything here will be junked soon enough."

Helmut nodded. "A raging fire and an outbuilding that almost collapses," he said. "One would almost think it is the work of a poltergeist. But what do they always say about poltergeists, most of the time it has to do with the mixed-up brain of an adolescent, right? Someone of your age wouldn't have anything to do with that anymore..."

While Castor and Folco talked with the police officers, Rein looked at the havoc. He also had no explanation for it, he understood very little about the fire and the fight the old man had in the big room. *...I wonder what my painting has to do with all of this?... Puzzles for a smart fox, to keep my eyes open, time to prick up my ears.*

The police officers left. Folco asked Castor if he needed money. Castor shook his head. "I still have money in my pocket. It's okay, maybe later."

"Very well then, I will see to it that someone comes to collect the painting. And I will make sure the property is thoroughly cleared of debris. You'll have nothing to worry about, I guarantee it."

Gabi Stein, Rosa Linge, and Folco Andermann found themselves in the specially equipped room at Fort Web where they watched dark images on a big screen. All they saw was a burning oil lamp. Now and then there were low sounds they could not place and then the voice of Remco Castor was heard saying, "Who are you? Tell me your name! What are you doing here?"

They saw someone lash out with some kind of weapon and hit someone or something. There was a shuffling noise, followed by a loud thump. The oil lamp never moved and after some time the wick went out.

They watched closely, trying to see every little thing in the darkness. It remained silent for a long time. Then, all of a sudden, there were flames slithering across the walls of the room. Even the floor was on fire and not far from the painting a motionless figure lay. It was frightening to see how long the man – they realized it was Castor – was lying there while the flames closed in around him. Then the light was switched on and a young man came to the rescue, the man from The Netherlands.

"Yes!" they heard Castor say in a hoarse voice. "I can't get up ... Away from here, fox, away from here! Help me!"

Gabi switched off the computer that was connected to the screen and gestured at the other equipment in the room. "How stupid can we be? We assumed we only needed recordings during the day when people came to see the painting and put in their bids. We forgot to install night vision cameras. Now we will never know what has happened exactly."

"It was Nicolaes Nimbus," said Folco decidedly. "...Whoever he is. Castor hit him severely and now he is afraid he has unleashed something horrible."

"If that is true, our plan has worked," sighed Rosa. "Nicolaes Nimbus was challenged; he became curious and wanted to see the painting with his own eyes. True, we have not taken into account that something might happen at night. The right cameras would have provided us with the most interesting images."

"It looks like the fire started everywhere at the same time," said Folco. "...In all rooms and on the outside and across all four walls. If the Dutchman hadn't been there, my cousin would have choked on the smoke and been burnt to death. I already told you what happened in the biggest outbuilding. We found ourselves on the second story and downstairs all hell broke loose. The building started to shake off its own accord."

"Has the Dutchman something to do with it, do you think?" Rosa wondered aloud.

"No, Castor is certain about that. He sees him as a friend, someone who will support him now that he has become so confused and terrified. It was the Dutchman who saved him. We have seen that for ourselves."

Gabi rose to her feet. "All this equipment can be removed, the house we were observing no longer exists. We have to discuss what to do now. We were able to trap him, maybe we will be able to do that a second time."

"Let's build a big trap," Folco voiced, "with a steel door that slams shut immediately."

"Then he'll be ours," grinned Rosa, "he'll have to sacrifice his life to science!" Gabi and Folco laughed along with her as they left the room.

The Reading Man was placed in the big meeting room. The attendants had put it in the van, transported it to CompuStein, and brought it up to Fort Web via the big elevator.

They stepped inside the meeting room and stood in front of the glass-covered work of art.

"The press doesn't know it is here," said Folco. "No one knows. It will go to the highest bidder and I know for certain it will be someone who knows all about fortune-telling. I don't think we will be able to trap Nicolaes Nimbus with it again."

"I wonder," Rosa chimed in, "is he real and not an apparition, he might know more than we think. Maybe he knows where the painting has been taken."

"Then we should destroy the painting!" Gabi cried out. Suddenly she seemed very scared. "Imagine what will happen to us if he comes here. Remember, he has already been here before, Rosa. Haven't we all felt his presence?"

Rosa dragged her feet along the corridor and Folco followed them as fast as he could. "Rosa is right," he said.

"What do you mean?" asked Gabi. "...That he has been here before?"

"No," answered Folco, "that we should sacrifice him to science. We'll turn him inside out and lift the crown of his skull like the lid of a pan, so we can have a look at his ancient brain..."

All three of them laughed as they walked up to the elevator.

❋ ❋ ❋

Rein and Castor had dinner at Restaurant Etzel every evening after the big fire. Everyone who saw them came up to their table for a chat. The fire was big news and the Wonder of Castor filled the people with a certain pride –it had happened right there and nowhere else.

Folco had kept his word, arranging for the wreckage of the burnt house to be cleared away. What remained was a rectangular section of brown earth with a green garden behind it, where a new house could be built. Castor was still frightened and nervous, a weak, fragile impression of his real self.

After a good meal Rein and Castor remained sitting and ordered something to drink. It was already late, the kitchen had closed and there were not many customers lingering about. The door opened and someone stepped inside; Castor had seen him before but he had refused to identify himself.

The eccentric man wore his old, wide-brimmed straw hat, a long shawl knotted in six nooses and his shoes of small, square pieces of white and black painted leather. Now he also sported a cane of dark brown wood with a copper knob in his hand. As soon as he saw Castor sitting at the table he took off his hat to greet him as he walked up to him. This time he did introduce himself:

"Good evening, my name is Mars Kronacher; we have met before. I have come from Ingolstadt searching for you. May I take a seat?"

"But of course," Castor reacted, welcoming any form of diversion.

Mars Kronacher sat down, placed his cane against the armrest, and put his hat on his knee. His bald head shone in the lamplight.

"First let me get us something to drink," he said, "all three of us..." he looked at Rein, eyebrows raised.

Castor hastened to say, "This is Rein Vulpes, a friend of mine from The Netherlands."

As soon as the drinks were served, Mars Kronacher took over the conversation, "I have heard the news about the fire. Of course, I drove past it to take a look and all I saw was a big charred area with a garden behind it. I am very well-off; my gift of prophecy has brought in a lot of money, Mr., eh..."

"Call me Castor, everyone does."

"Good, good, please call me by my first name– Mars. What I would like to say to you is this, I have enough money for you to build yourself a new house. I have searched for you everywhere. Finally, I ran across someone in the village who told me you often dine at Restaurant Etzel. Fortunately, I found you here. Now tell me, Castor, is the painting already sold?"

"Uh, perhaps yes, no, that is to say, almost. I remember you bid one-hundred-thousand euro. In the meantime, someone has bid one-million two-hundred-thousand, but the painting is worth more and additional bidders are expected to name their price."

"I want it," said Mars. "How about I give you one-and-a-half million?"

Rein couldn't believe his ears. Again the fox was one too many for all the greedy animals. He dipped his tail in paint and created a work of art that everyone wanted to have.

Castor shook his head. "Not enough, Mars."

Mars Kronacher just smiled. "I have looked into the future, Castor. And I know I am not mistaken, that's for sure. I saw the painting standing in my living room. Yes, right, standing, covered in that splendid glass, high upon the black pedestal."

Rein knew he should keep out of this hoping fervently that Castor would ask Mars why the painting was so important to him. Much to his surprise, it was

Mars Kronacher himself who came up with an explanation. "It is of no importance to me whether The Reading Man was painted in the seventeenth century or only a few months ago. I have only been able to see it behind glass; I did not call in an expert to determine its exact age or the quality of the painting. In my circles, it is an important work of art and everyone wants it. A name is painted on it and I know that if it is recognized by the right person..." That sounded very mysteriously to Rein, but he understood it was about Nicolaes Nimbus. Mars Kronacher finished his thought, "The painting has something extra, something that is not visible to the naked eye. It is something you must be able to feel. To me, with my special talents, it is an understanding, something has crept under the paint, it seems to be the best way to explain it to you. No, wait, wait... let me say it another way. The man in the painting will never move. But still, Castor, he is alive, in his own inimitable way." Castor's frown conveyed a lack of understanding but the next thing Mars said, he understood very well, "To beat my rivals, I'll give you a better bid right now. I am prepared to pay you two million euros for The Reading Man."

That was exactly the amount Castor wanted to hear. He reached out his hand. His fingers trembled. "It's a deal, as far as I am concerned. I will pass this along, I would love to see the painting become yours. For the time being let's assume the bargain is sealed."

"Let's drink to that," Mars said with satisfaction. And the fox himself was happily surprised when he found out his painting tail had yielded a fortune.

❋ ❋ ❋

Nine thrones were moved into the meeting room at Fort Web. Gabi Stein, Rosa Linge and her friend Alrik von Hecht, Folco Andermann, Lucas Montaigne, Carsten von Haller, Dieter Brunn and Freeda Olbers waited for the arrival of the man from Ingolstadt, Mars Kronacher.

The information they received from Castor was interesting. Mars was prepared to pay two million for the painting and he had made it clear why he wanted to have it so badly.

"A name is painted on it and I know that if it is recognized by the right person... In my circles, it is an important work of art and everyone wants it... Something has crept under the paint... To beat my rivals..."

"We should put pressure on him," said Gabi. "This is our only chance to learn more about those who are very interested in the painting. He knows more about Nicolaes Nimbus, which seems obvious now. Thanks to Carsten, we already know a bit more because he talked to Victor the Visionary. Now we will ask Mars

Kronacher some questions and we will make it clear to him that we won't sell him the painting if he doesn't come up with the information we seek."

Carsten von Haller grinned. "Yes, even in my free time I am still at the service of Das Web," he boasted, "that goes without saying..." He wished he was the one receiving two million for a painting that had cost so very little to have painted. To all the others it was nothing special, even to Alrik because he lived with the wealthy Rosa.

Gabi got a phone call. "He has arrived; I'll go to the elevator right away." She stood up and left the meeting room. About two minutes later she came back in the company of the man from Ingolstadt. He wore the same straw hat, another shawl, and now blood-red shoes with stars of yellow leather. Freeda Olbers, wearing a multi-colored dress, sporting a different colored nail on each finger, looked him up and down giving him an approving smile.

"Allow me to introduce you to Mars Kronacher from Ingolstadt." The man took off his hat and shook hands with all of them. Then he sat down on a throne, put his cane against the side, and put his hat on the table. He stared at the table, immediately stood up again, walked up to it, and studied it attentively as if he had never seen it before. With a satisfied expression on his face, he went back to his throne. "I have already arranged to have the money deposited in my bank, I can pay for it right away. I will also see to it that someone comes to collect the work of art this very day."

Gabi heaved a sigh of relief. The painting filled her with fear; she was also afraid that a fire would break out in Fort Web, just as it did for Castor. *The sooner this painting is gone the better. I don't want my building to burn to the ground!*

Lucas Montaigne took the helm. He straightened his back, his breast swelled as he took a deep breath. Tall and broad-shouldered, he was an impressive man; the look in his eyes showed self-confidence and authority.

"Don't you worry about a thing, Mars. The painting is yours. Before we settle things though, we would like to ask you some questions."

"But of course!" said Mars in a friendly voice.

"There is much interest in this work of art," said Lucas. "It is unusual but the highest bids have come from a certain segment of society." He pointed to others at the table. "We are scientists but we never realized visionaries made so much money in this day and age. So much that one of them can permit himself to pay two million euros for a painting. And to be honest, we've never had good experiences with seers. We know someone who happened to be a swindler, he made use of foreknowledge; he could tell lies without blinking an eye."

Lucas crossed his arms, leaned back, and looked at Mars defiantly. Mars was not one to be intimidated by words or body language. "Please, one should never underestimate the power of the mind. There are people with the gift of prophecy and..." Mars listened to the soft piano music coming from invisible loudspeakers. "...others have that special talent to compose the most beautiful music."

Everyone chucked. Lucas pointed at Gabi and said, "The music you hear is the work of one of Gabi's computers. No human being was involved in its production and no expensive grand piano was used to generate it."

Mars was a man who was not easily daunted. "Bravo!" he said. "Bravo! We can leave this up to technology. But the origin is and remains human, we must never forget that. Man makes computers. Even computers that make computers have a human past. Can you imagine a time when computers are built without the intervention of the human brain?"

Freeda rose to her feet and laughed, "I will say it too, bravo! So well said, can I get you a cup of coffee, Mars?"

"Please do," the eccentric man voiced, "I like it with a lot of sugar and plenty of milk."

"I'll get coffee for all of us."

"Clairvoyance is a gift," Mars continued. "There has always been an élite who never felt the need to shout from the rooftops that they were present. There is mutual rivalry because everyone wants to be number one, recognized as such in their own circles. The painting will give the owner, me, a certain status, that's for sure. I can afford it and I am very happy to be allowed to buy it."

"I am a philosopher," said Carsten von Haller, "I have learned to look at things from different angles and I can juggle words. But I wonder what I am supposed to think when someone says something has crawled under the paint... I do not understand that entirely."

"Yes, yes, that is what I said," Mars reacted enthusiastically. "You can interpret it as you please." He reached for his cane and held it up. "To science, this is and always will remain a hardwood cane with a copper knob at the top. For the sensitive seer, it is an object with a history, touched by different people in different times. The seer can feel what technical equipment cannot register. Wood is wood, gold is gold. Paint is paint, linen is linen. Only the true seer can know it is more." He placed the cane against the side of his throne again.

Carsten shook his head. "Just words," he said, "metaphors... Something has crawled under the paint... Paint is paint and that is true – paint is paint and nothing more."

The discussion went on. Freeda brought coffee for everyone. Folco Andermann produced a silver pocket watch and held it up to Mars with the flat of his hand. "Many old objects have a special story, can you tell me something about this?"

Mars took the watch without looking at it. He held it in the palm of his left hand and covered it with his right hand so that it became invisible. He closed his eyes and smiled. After a full minute, he opened his eyes again. "I will do this one time only, and only to make it clear that not everything can be explained scientifically. You probably expect me to talk about a family heirloom and give you information about a deceased member of your family." He stood up and reached out his right hand. "Take it back." Folco took it, put it in his pocket, and nodded with satisfaction. "It is what it is, just a pocket watch, nothing more than that."

Mars Kronacher knew everyone was paying attention to him now. His fingers played with the long nooses of his shawl and he smiled again. "Nothing more than that?" he said. "But there is always more. Surely we don't know each other. I was introduced to you just a moment ago and I must say I only have remembered your first name – Folco."

"Folco Andermann. We never met before, that is true."

"That is clear then," said Mars. "Let me tell you something. The pocket watch you gave me which I did not look at was an heirloom from its former owner. You have nothing to do with him. The watch is not of pure silver, it is silver-plated and the clockwork is nothing special. You probably didn't pay much for it. France, Paris... You found it at a flea market in Paris and you were surprised to see how the second hand started running as soon as you wound up the watch. There was someone with you, a woman, your wife perhaps? She didn't like it at all. You often open it. Now, on the backside..."

"This cannot be a trick," Folco was surprised. "Even my friends here in the meeting room have no idea where I bought it. I always have it with me because I admire the simple construction of the tiny cogwheels. When you open the backside, you can see them turn round and round. And yes, eh... I bought it in Paris at a flea market. My wife was with me and she considered it an ugly object. I paid twenty euros for it and she said it was too much..."

"That's exactly what happened," Mars said with a grin on his face.

Everyone started to bombard Mars with questions. Carsten von Haller had his wallet in his hand and took out a photo. Mars raised his hand. "No more tests, the show is over."

That raised their suspicions. Dieter Brunn urged Mars to take a look at the photo from the philosopher.

"One more right answer will change my mind," he said. "I have no idea what Carsten wants to show you. We are all very curious about your reaction."

Mars Kronacher decided to let them have it their way. "Anything for the painting... Give me that photo."

It was a little color photo with damaged edges. Mars looked at it. He saw the face, neck, and shoulders of a young woman in her mid-thirties, with brown eyes and long, light brown hair. Mars touched it carefully with his thumbs while he looked up to the ceiling.

"Have you written a book?" Carsten opened his mouth but wasn't able to speak.

"Yes," said Dieter Brunn, "Philosopher amongst Scientists, we all received a copy."

"An admirer?" wondered Mars. "Yes, without a doubt. You were autographing copies in a bookstore; she turned up and gave you this photo together with her business card so that you had her telephone number."

He gave the photo back. "No one else saw this picture and I never told anyone about it."

"So is his prediction accurate?" Alrik von Hecht wanted to know.

"Yes, it is all true," the philosopher admitted. "He could not have known about this beforehand. But he is correct, every word."

Everyone fired questions and Mars answered them, short and to the point.

Finally, Rosa Linge came up with the most important question,

"What does Nicolaes Nimbus mean to you? Who is he really?"

"There are certain things I'd prefer to keep for myself," was the answer. "The painting intrigues me and I am very grateful to you all for giving me the chance to buy it. I understand you not only act on behalf of Art Shop Remco Castor where the painting is concerned, but you also want me to explain the reason for my high bid. I feel emotionally connected to the painting, that is why I am willing to pay so much for it. Now I would like to pay you. My bank will arrange everything. All you need is my signature."

"We want to know more, I urgently advise you to answer Rosa's question as clearly as possible," warned Folco, "otherwise the deal's off."

"I never expected this!" Mars shot back. "I did an enormous amount and thought everything was okay. Don't put pressure on me now!"

Folco repeated himself, emphasizing every single word, "Answer Rosa's question. "Otherwise the deal's off."

"Nicolaes Nimbus," urged Rosa, "who is he and what does he mean to you – that is what we want to know. A name is painted on it and I know that if it is recognized by the right person... What did you mean by that?"

"Well, Castor told you everything, didn't he? There are certain things I am not allowed to talk about, call it a professional secret."

"Tell us!" said Dieter Brunn. "...Otherwise no painting. Tell us what we want to know now!"

Mars fumbled for the nooses of his shawl and looked skittishly at Dieter. "This is not what we agreed upon..." he muttered.

Dieter banged both fists on the table. "Tell us! Tell us! Tell us!"

The others followed his example. The noise of sixteen fists banging on wood worked as a sounding board, it was deafening. And everyone shouted, "Tell us! Tell us! Tell us!"

Mars Kronacher felt threatened. He raised both hands in the air making it clear that he wanted them to stop. But they didn't. They stood up and started dancing around the table. The eight danced round and round; everyone tapped Mars on the shoulder as they passed by.

"Stop it!" Mars screamed.

Dieter Brunn grabbed the cane and started to swing it around. Dancing around the table, he approached the eccentric man again. Now he raised the cane high, ready to lash out with it, to hit him hard – the cane was identical to that of Tijn Raes, who had used it around

1750 in Leiden to intimidate Ada Reede, another fortune teller.

"Stop it, please, stop it!" Mars said. "I will tell you everything I know."

Immediately everyone sat down again. Beads of perspiration pooled on Mars' brow. He took the cane that Dieter handed him with care.

"Nicolaes Nimbus is the conscience of all visionaries," he said in a soft voice. "It has always been that way. No one knows when he will turn up and no one knows where he is. Most of us know his name. The real visionaries know each other, they are connected. When the future is influenced in the wrong way, the results can be disastrous. Fortune telling is a very serious business and wrong information, especially from the motives of gain, is fundamentally an abomination."

"Is Nicolaes Nimbus a man of flesh and blood like you and me?" asked Gabi.

"That is what everyone who knows him says about him, yes. He must be very special, considering his age."

"How old is he?" Alrik wanted to know.

"Who knows? Many hundreds of years, that's for sure."

"Did you ever see him yourself?" asked Freeda.

"No. Never, but he is important to visionaries. The painting is a status symbol. Every seer wants it. But it is mine. I mean, it is mine, isn't it, as soon as I pay for it?"

Folco Andermann pointed at him and said in a threatening voice, "You have a feeling for this kind of thing, you know how such things work. Tell me what is going on here, how we find ourselves where Nicolaes Nimbus is concerned. After you have explained that to us, we'll seal the deal and The Reading Man will be yours."

Mars closed his eyes, his eyelids fluttered. He put his moist hands on the tabletop, fingers spread. The door that Lucas Montaigne had closed not long ago clicked open. A cool gust of wind caressed the heated faces of the people at the table. From somewhere in Fort Web came a creaking noise, it sounded like a dry branch that had broken under the weight of a heavy foot.

"There is a collision coming," Mars said with his eyes still closed. "The old magic is dying while science makes straight canals out of meandering rivers. Two different approaches can yield the same result. That might apply to eternal life. There are different paths to follow. To answer your question – about what exactly is going on – it is clear... Collision... Struggle. The last form of true magic is concentrated in the personage of Nicolaes Nimbus and now you have joined battle with him. Science wants to conquer magic. You want to grab hold of something that is not easy to catch." He opened his eyes and looked around in fear.

"That is all I can say about it. I have already overstepped the mark, I have said things that I should have kept silent. All I want to do now is pay for the painting."

"Just one more thing," said Freeda. "No, really, just one more thing, you can give us a short answer. Is there something, an interplay of lines, a small piece of art that manipulates the brain in such a way that you can see or experience something that someone else cannot see or cannot experience?"

Mars Kronacher heaved a deep sigh and nodded. "That is correct. This interplay of lines exists."

"Can you show it to us?"

"No, absolutely not, I've only mastered this art partially and I am not allowed to give you a demonstration. That is out of the question."

"Thank you very much, Mars," said Freeda. "Now you may pay us two million euros."

Much to everyone's surprise Mars Kronacher closed his eyes again and after some time he started to talk in a soft voice, "You have provoked something. It must have something to do with the fire in the house where the painting stood, the house of Castor. Something went wrong there. Wood touches bone, and that is what I see, wood on bone. That is not good, no, that is not good at all. I don't know what has happened there, but I am awash with negative feelings." He blinked.

The door opened further. No one would have been surprised if footsteps had sounded in the corridor. But except for the soft piano music, it remained quiet in the meeting room...

Chapter 11

REIN VULPES VISITS FORT WEB

Everything was arranged. Mars Kronacher had become the owner of The Reading Man; he promised someone would come and collect it that very day. He took leave of everyone. Gabi Stein did not accompany him to the elevator. Freeda Olbers went along with him grabbing his hand when they walked through the corridor. They remained standing hand-in-hand as they waited for the elevator to come up.

"You are at least as eccentric as I am," she said to him, "it is always so exciting to meet a kindred spirit." She shoved his wide-brimmed straw hat to the back of his head and kissed him on both cheeks.

"We'll meet again," said Mars, "I am convinced of that!"

❋ ❋ ❋

The painting was still standing in the meeting room when other visitors arrived. Remco Castor brought Rein Vulpes along with him. Folco informed the others about the Dutchman; they decided not to deny him access.

Rein didn't even blink when he entered the meeting room and introduced himself right away, "My name is Rein Vulpes. In the animal world, I am like the fox that steals the chickens, amongst people I usually try to control myself."

No one seemed to find his words unusual. Gabi said he could sit on the throne next to Castor.

Folco handed his cousin several signed documents. Two million euros had been transferred to Castor's bank account as soon as Mars had left the building.

"Congratulations. It is all yours, as agreed. I have also arranged for a bank employee to visit you as soon as possible to discuss financial issues with you. I know you are not used to having so much money; this woman will help you as much as she can. So build yourself a new house and enjoy your life."

Castor was speechless. Of course, he knew he would get all the money as promised. Now that it was all settled, he did not know how to react.

Carsten von Haller made use of the sudden silence, pointing to Rein he said, "You hardly looked at the painting for a second when you entered the room. It automatically attracts everyone's attention. Don't you like it?"

Rein opened his mouth to say something. Folco reacted faster, "He has seen it in Castor's house and he saw it undamaged after the house had completely burnt down."

"Isn't that a miracle, Rein Vulpes?" Rosa wondered aloud.

Rein felt some tension building up in himself. Except for Folco, he knew no one there, all he knew was that they were wealthy business tycoons and he was on the top story of CompuStein Hitech, an office building owned by Gabi Stein, the oldest woman in the company. Maybe it was better to keep silent, but that was not in his nature; he loved to surprise people, to completely sweep them off their feet.

"I am very proud to learn one of my works of art has been sold for two million euros."

Everyone understood what he meant. Rein saw angry faces staring at him. Dieter and Folco rose to their feet, walked to a corner of the big room, and started to talk to each other quietly.

After a couple of minutes they sat down and Dieter decided to take the initiative, "I had consulted different connections and through them, a Dutch art forger was found. His name was never mentioned to me. We conferred with each other and agreed; this man would paint our new old work of art. You received instructions via anonymous middlemen and you also got..."

He fell abruptly silent. Rein was asked a question, "What did you get?"

"Special paint," Rein said with a grin, an old canvas. Even the frame was delivered to my atelier."

"It was absolutely not planned that you should turn up here and you know that only too well!" said Lucas Montaigne in a threatening tone.

Rein's grin grew even wider. "Of course I know that. I am impulsive and I don't care what others think I *should* do. If I had decided to stay at home, I would never have found out my work was sold for such a high price. Now I can tell everyone that..."

"No!" Lucas cried out. "No one is supposed to know you painted The Reading Man! We paid you and you have to keep your mouth shut. Or perhaps you want more money? Is that what you came here for? Well, don't worry, we are prepared to give you a nice additional sum for your silence."

"Oh, I can always use money, more money is always welcome," Rein was surprised. "But that was not my intention at all. I went after the painting like a nosey fox that follows the track of potential prey. Or no, more like a frisky fox. I wandered about because I don't like long, straight roads..."

All of a sudden all eight stood up standing so close together they were able to touch each other. They put their hands on each other's shoulders and started to whisper. Then they lined up, turned around, started to walk, and left the meeting room. Rein and Castor sat still listening to the sound of fading footsteps. "Two million..." said Castor. "Only now do I realize what that means. I've always had financial troubles and now I'm rich. Now I can laugh at the entire godforsaken world."

"You've always done that," Rein said spontaneously. "You have always been a poor devil with a big mouth and now you have become a rich man with an even bigger mouth."

A muttering came from the corridor. The voices grew louder. A woman started to scream. Someone slammed a door shut. They could hear quick footsteps. A sound was heard as if someone had slapped a pane of glass with the flat of his hand. Unintelligible words were coming from somewhere followed by a sudden silence. And then, after several minutes, there were sounds from far away. A door was opened and again there were footsteps heard in the distance.

The eight came back and sat down silently.

"We have made a decision," said Gabi, "about you, Castor, and about your friend, Rein Vulpes."

"You have made a decision about me?" he laughed. "I'm the fox from the free field!"

No one responded to his remark. Gaby continued unabated, "You already know, Castor, that you will get help from a bank employee. We will also hire an architect who will design a house for you that will meet all your needs. And we will rent a nice house for you in Freising where you can live comfortably until your new house is ready. From now on you will lead a life of luxury. Unfortunately, you'll have to take leave of your Dutch friend; he's going to work for us." Rein was too flabbergasted to respond.

Castor shrugged his shoulders. "I welcome anything that makes life more pleasant, I will do as you wish for a while. If I like it, I won't complain. When I have had enough of it I'll send everyone away and go back to the rooms in the outbuilding on my own property, no matter how shabby it might be."

"Good, that is settled," said Gabi. "Now we will tell Rein what we are doing and what we are searching for."

Rein leaned forward. There was an atmosphere of restrained aggression in the room. Rein didn't care about it but he was curious about what would happen next. "You have gotten yourself involved in our affairs by coming to Germany!" said Lucas. "Maybe it would have been better if you had stayed home, but since you're here we might better make use of your talents."

"Gabi said we are to explain to him what we will do, Lucas," said Rosa in a sharp voice. Her friend Alrik made a growling sound.

Carsten von Haller took up the baton, "I am only a tolerated friend here, the group's mascot. Maybe I can explain best what the others are doing. Without the use of philosophical finery, I promise. Everyone here has different companies and is very successful in business. Those businesses include but are not limited to refined technologies, the pharmaceutical industry, new computer possibilities, labs wherein scientists are looking into new scientific possibilities like genetic manipulation, cybernetics, the exploring of the universe, space travel, the elimination of all possible diseases and so on. Everyone present realizes scientific developments are happening faster and faster and that even the very near future will be totally different from the present. One common goal is the extending of our lifetimes. Immortality is what we will finally hope to achieve. But for the time being, it would be great if we could reach an age of two or three hundred ads..."

"Get to the point, man!" Dieter interrupted.

"Why don't you tell him yourself then?" the philosopher snapped back.

"A certain name is whispered amongst fortune tellers," said Dieter. "Nicolaes Nimbus. He is, we think, a man of flesh and blood, someone of all times, an immortal. In the first instance, we were looking for him... but now we are hunting him down!"

"That is exactly what we're doing!" said Folco. "...Exactly! We will hunt him down, we set a trap for him, and finally, he will be ours."

Gabi banged her fist on the table when everyone started to talk at the same time. "Calm down! Calm down!" she cried out. "This is an important moment. Should we declare war on Nicolaes Nimbus?"

The eight rose to their feet. They stared at each other and burst out with nervous laughter. "This is war!" said Freeda Olbers. "We will not rest until we have him."

"Come with me to the kitchen, Freeda," said Gabi. "Let's get something to drink for all of us. This calls for a drink. Yes, it is war, the hunt is on; we will not rest till we have him and divide his limbs among our labs."

It was quiet for a moment as both women left the meeting room. Rein took the opportunity to speak up, "All may be well but what am I supposed to do with this information? What do I have to do with it?"

"You're involved now," said Alrik. "You're here after all. You came of your own free will. We have a special task for you. Just a little more patience, please, you'll see."

"Haven't I always said it?" muttered Castor. "The world is raving mad and people are no good. I don't understand anything that has been discussed here, except for the fact that it is insanity, whatever it is."

Gabi and Freeda came in with champagne and enough glasses for everyone. From that moment on nothing was said to Rein or Castor. Eight men and women stood by the table near the thrones, raised their glasses, and expressed their wishes in a passionate frenzy. Castor and Rein stood but remained indifferent.

"The hunt is on. He will not escape us."

"We have to catch him before someone else finds him."

"...War between us and Nicolaes Nimbus!"

"Let's swear that we will not rest until we've got him in our clutches!" said Folco.

They drank and refilled their glasses. All eight swore their oath. They promised to do their utmost to reach their goal and only rest after they had found Nicolaes Nimbus.

"If he is alive, if he is a man of flesh and blood, he will be ours," they promised each other.

Rein took two glasses and filled them with champagne for Castor and himself, pondering these strange events. *This is so bazaar, but I feel somehow removed at times. Everyone else is acting odd except me and Castor. Perhaps I'll play along. Let's see what happens next. I think I am beginning to like this turn of events.*

The eight stood as if turned into stone between the thrones; they stared with their mouths open as if they were listening to something very closely. Everyone sat down again, slowly and at the same time.

Gabi heaved a deep sigh and took the floor, "So it is settled. Our mission is clear. Now let's talk about Rein Vulpes. Freeda, you will be involved with him the most, so it seems wise for you to tell him what we want from him exactly."

"What we want from him?" Lucas Montaigne voiced. "No, what we demand from him!"

Rein stared at his painting and in the meantime, he listened to what Freeda had to say. "We left the meeting room to talk about you, Rein. We agree that you are a really talented artist. You have done a perfect job. But what brings you here? We are still wondering about that. Was it coincidence or was it predetermined? Anyway, you're here now."

Rein produced his dice and showed them the flat of his hand. "Odd numbers mean coincidence, even numbers mean predestination." He cupped his hand, shook the dice, and released them to bounce across the table. "Double two's, it was predestination."

There was a murmur of approval, Rein noticed Folco, Carsten and Rosa nodding. "We hardly know you, Rein," continued Freeda. "Still we have the feeling that you belong with us. We have plans for you. Your work is sublime yet it attracts attention. It is radiating. No, let me rephrase, it is transmitting something that can reach any sensitive receiver, no matter how far away from the work of art he or she may be. Or am I speaking in riddles, Rein?"

"I understand what you mean," he answered spontaneously.

"He is one of us!" Rosa Linge said; everyone started to applaud for Rein.

Freeda continued, "Rein, I am a neuropsychologist, I dig into the brain like a miner working the deepest shaft. And I have also learned how to hypnotize anyone. I would like to hypnotize you daily, just as long as it takes for you to paint a new painting. This way you will make full use of your emotions, your creativity, and your extraordinary talent to paint a particular person – Nicolaes Nimbus. How about that, are you amenable?"

Rein exploded, "This is the stupidest proposal I have ever heard; it is completely absurd! Therefore, I say yes. I'm in." Everyone applauded– only Castor did not clap.

Not much later the painting was taken away to be transported to Mars Kronacher in Ingolstadt. Two men had come up with the big elevator along with a solid trolley. The glass cover was wrapped in soft material. The cart was pushed through the corridor to the elevator with care.

Suddenly the eight conspirators felt relieved.

"A huge weight has been lifted from my shoulders..." sighed Gabi.

Carsten von Haller said it differently, "I have that feeling one gets when an uninvited guest, a troublesome visitor, finally decides to leave ..."

❋ ❋ ❋

Gabi Stein and Rosa Linge often worked together on big projects. They found several experts who developed a new computer program in a short time, combining all their knowledge about the workings of the human brain creating artificial intelligence that could respond to impulses in hundredths of a second. Images of randomly changing interplays of lines materialized in front of an imaginary eye. Every time this happened, checks were run to see if there was a sudden change in the artificial brain that might indicate sensitivity for a paranormal quality like clairvoyance. That was not an easy task because paranormal qualities were still unproven phenomena. But there was enough data about which parts of the brain fortune tellers used when they claimed to have extrasensory perceptions. This was only part of the big puzzle. Gabi and Rosa had another goal in mind as well, "When we take the view that a human being can extend his or her lifespan, to halt the aging process, how are we able to see that in the brain? Where do we start to set such a simulation in motion?

Dieter Brunn offered his help, "I will talk with Antonius Heck," he promised.

Together with his deceased father, Antonius Heck had set up Brunnheck, a concern that had scores of companies in Germany, Austria, and Switzerland. He had been Dieter's mentor for a long time and he was a brilliant scientist with original and often very playful ideas. He always dared to experiment, specializing in robots, in artificial intelligence, and the utmost refinement dealing with the making of parts for satellites and spacecraft. Although he, as a scientist, always searched for proof and believed mathematics stood as far away from superstition and magic as there was a distance between two stars, he believed two contradictory branches of knowledge could exist independently from one another and could function according to their laws.

He often wondered about the strangest things ...Believe in a curse and you will die, he might say for instance; when he discussed magic, it was, try to find an explanation for that! It happened once so maybe it is still happening.

Antonius still worked for Brunnheck and had a large percentage of shares in his name. But he had also become an old man and often he would take a few days to rest. He sold all his Brunnheck shares to Dieter shortly after he decided to rest more often than work.

"I will never retire," he had told Dieter. "The moment I can do nothing, the moment I can no longer make up or design things, everything stops and there is nothing left for me on our planet."

"I will visit him as soon as I can; he lives closeby," Dieter said to Gabi and Rosa. "If everyone agrees, I will tell him what we are doing, everything. He knows a lot about autosuggestion and the powers of the brain that magicians are supposed to rely on to fool their subjects. Maybe he's crazy enough to develop a computer program that can register such phenomena. I will also ask him what he thinks of self-hypnosis by way of a specific interplay of lines."

Chapter 12

BROKEN GLASS

Before Freeda Olbers could concentrate on hypnotizing Rein Vulpes to enhance his creativity, she had something else to do. An invitation had arrived from Mars Kronacher. He'd decided to throw a party on a Saturday at his house in Ingolstadt to show The Reading Man to everyone. The invitation had been sent to CompuStein requesting the presence of everyone he had met there. Frida said immediately that she wanted to go; the others responded; they couldn't make time for it. She called Mars and asked him if he needed some help. He was by himself and eagerly accepted her offer.

"We'll have some fun together," she had said.

Early in the morning, Freeda started her canary-yellow Porsche. She played with the accelerator, the engine growled; she put into gear and drove away. She'd spent a restless Friday night in a spare room in Gabi's big house in Munich.

Freeda noticed everyone in the group was more irritated than usual so she had a discussion with Gabi that ended in a quarrel. They'd never had a conflict before. The tiff had started because Gabi had made a remark she didn't appreciate –it ended when she had to choose between using her long nails to destroy her face or go to bed. Freeda woke hoping she and Gabi could resolve their differences but that wasn't in the cards. Gabi merrily waved good-bye when Freeda got into her Porsche and drove away as if nothing had happened the night before.

Freeda stepped on the gas when she found herself on the A9 and signaled aggressively at early road-users who didn't get to the right fast enough when she wanted to overtake them. It had been a long time since she had sworn so whole-heartedly. She enjoyed every curse that passed her lips as she gave people the evil eye. It felt good. She let herself go; she did not bother to try to analyze or explain her own behavior, as she usually did; don't think, just do was her mood of the day.

Freeda reached Ingolstadt in record time but she had to concentrate to find Mars' house. He lived on the edge of the city in an expensive district close to the Danube.

Freeda parked her car, stepped out, and went to the door. Her heels were just high enough to prevent her multi-colored, fake fur-trimmed dress from touching the ground. The long feathers in her hair had risen like the tail of a peacock on display as soon as she exited her car. She wrapped her long feathered boa around her neck. Mars opened the door as she approached, looking just as extravagant with his shawl tied into many loops wearing a special red and black checked jacket with a red left sleeve and a black right sleeve. But he looked sad and tired as he gave her a limp handshake.

"I am so happy that you are here, please come in." And then he told her what was worrying him, "I went too far when I visited Das Web to buy the painting. I told you too much, I let my tongue run away with me. That is unforgivable and now I am not feeling well."

But that was not what Freeda had come there for as she grabbed him by his black sleeve and dragged him along with her through a square hall to a broad staircase, "Take me to your bedroom!" she said impatiently.

Mars Kronacher had no idea what this was all about, but once he was lying in bed he turned out to be her perfect match. After one and a half hours they went downstairs again. Freeda was glowing with happiness, she felt satisfied; Mars seemed even sadder than before.

Sitting in his living room, she saw The Reading Man standing next to a white piano, "Now that we know each other much better. Please tell me how the interplay of lines works. Or maybe you can show it to me. Will you do that for me, Mars?"

He raised his hands and stared up at the ceiling. "Oh well! Why not? I have made more than enough mistakes already, so why wouldn't I just show it to you? Alright later today, how about after the party?"

"...Promise?"

"I promise," he confirmed. "How could I refuse you anything after our blissful romp?"

A caterer brought an enormous amount of food and drink. Freeda started to arrange things in the kitchen. *He could never have done this without my expert assistance.* But she was wrong about that. It turned out that Mars took care of himself very well and he knew how to give his guests a festive welcome.

The first guests arrived around lunchtime. Freeda studied everyone attentively and tried to have a chat with as many people as possible to find out who they were and what they did. Soon it became clear to her. *The tight-lipped are probably visionaries.* And this taciturn group was in the majority. Everyone admired the painting; Freeda saw jealous looks and caught interesting remarks:

"I wanted it for myself. It was too expensive for me."

"Now he has it his way, now he can show off and tell us so we'll all know how terrific he is."

"Can you feel it? That radiation... This is a good buy, the painting is worth much more than two million."

"He's so quiet. He isn't bragging about it. There must be something wrong with him."

Family members started working in the kitchen preparing a buffet for everyone who stayed till evening. Someone played classical music on the white piano. Freeda watched as Mars disappeared into a side room and closed the door. She knew it was a big room used by him as a study. She started to worry when he stayed away for ten minutes. She decided to wait another five minutes, then she would take a look. No one seemed to notice his absence. The guests filled their plates and enjoyed the food. The piano player touched a final chord and suddenly it was strangely quiet. Some of the guests sat down at the table, on the couch, or the armchairs, but most of them stood with a plate or a glass in hand in the middle of the room.

Suddenly there was a loud bang. The glass that covered The Reading Man shattered. Thousands of glass fragments flew up against the ceiling. Plates and cutlery clattered to the floor. One man shrunk back tumbled and fell. Two women held on to each other and started to scream. A rain of glass came down, fragments bounced across the parquet floor. No one got hurt. The painting remained undamaged, still standing on its black glass pedestal.

"How can this happen?" someone cried out.

Freeda shook fragments of glass from her boa and looked at the people around her. Here and there she saw lips moving from across the room. She knew immediately what was said; she was alert, observing, registering, and understanding everything around her.

Everyone uttered two words, as the second word came out of their mouths, Freeda watched their lips press together making the *m* for Nimbus.

"Nicolaes Nimbus," they whispered to each other; instantly Freeda knew they were visionaries. Fear oozed from their pores, their eyes wide.

A door opened. Mars stepped into the room. His eyes were huge, he looked around in a panic, walking up to the piano and banging his fists on the keys. A salvo of false notes filled the room. A member of the family – Freeda didn't know if she was a sister or a cousin – tried to drag him away. He pushed her away and continued his crazed behavior. All of a sudden he seemed to have his fill. He straightened his back, turned around and bowed like a concert pianist who thanked his audience for a standing ovation.

Then he said in a loud and clear voice, "My gift of prophecy has been taken away from me." He bowed again and went back into his study. The door was slammed behind him.

Everyone started talking. What just happened, they asked themselves. Some people wanted to get home as soon as possible, others started to clear the glass away and clean the floor. The woman who had tried to drag Mars away from the piano decided to go to the study with two others in tow.

"Wait!" Freeda yelled in an authoritarian voice, "allow me to talk with him first. I am a psychologist, I know what to do in situations like this." The three stepped aside when she went to the door. "Thank you, in this case, a professional approach seems to be the best." She slipped inside and closed the door behind her.

Mars Kronacher was sitting behind a big, imposing desk with his elbows resting on the sides of a keyboard and his face hidden behind his hands. He was staring between his cupped fingers at a blacked-out monitor as if something was worthy of viewing on it.

Freeda walked through the room, leaned over the desk, and pushed his hands down. Then she took a ballpoint pen that sat next to the keyboard and held it in front of him. "The interplay of lines, remember? Take a sheet of paper and show me how it is done."

His mouth fell open as tears ran down his cheeks. He shook his head slowly. "I cannot do that, I mean... no longer... I'm very sorry, Freeda, I cannot help you with anything anymore."

"What's happened?"

"My gifts are being taken away from me, one-by-one."

"...By whom?" Freeda started to swear, she had to control herself in order not to smack him in the face.

"Everything will be taken away from me if I tell you that, everything... I cannot help you, I cannot help anyone anymore. Fortunately, I have enough money to survive. Please, leave me now, let me be..."

She knew enough to give in. Mars had let his tongue run away with him. He was a true visionary and the punishment was light – he had lost his gifts of prophecy, but he was not deprived of his wits like Thodor Baron or Regina Thule's father. Freeda threw the ballpoint on the desk, turned around, and left the study.

People were waiting by the door, hoping for some good news, any news. "One moment, please," she said, while she passed them. "I'll give you a full report in a while. First I have to look for something in my car. Some medicine... I'll be back in a minute."

She left the house, walked up to her car, opened the door, stepped inside, started the car, and drove away. She swore up a storm to the A9 and only then did she calm down after taking several deep breaths.

The glass that covered the painting was supposed to be unbreakable. Enormous pressure must have built up inside to make the casing burst apart – *how was that possible?* Countless fragments of glass had been flung upward coming down like hail without hurting anyone. *Mars promised to show me the interplay of lines and now he can't even do that, no more fortune-telling or predictions.* Again she began to swear as she stomped on the gas pedal. "Keep your big mouth shut!" she yelled to herself. "Keep that big mouth shut, will you?"

Freeda didn't want to curse continuously and she wanted to slow down but she couldn't control herself or her emotions, driving like a maniac. *Who is the boss in my head at the moment? Which Freeda is sitting at the wheel? I've got no time for psychological reflections; I have to concentrate on the road. It feels like this morning all over again. I am repeating the same sorts of behavior.* Exactly like that morning, she looked angrily at the people she was passing.

When she reached Munich, she had to adjust to the speed of the traffic. She drove to some hotel she had never been to before and decided to spend the night after a delicious dinner.

Dieter Brunn was in a bad mood. Since he had returned from Munich, after swearing an oath with his friends that they would find Nicolaes Nimbus and sacrifice him to science, his behavior had changed as well. On Friday evening he had quarreled with his wife.

Saturday he had stayed in his workroom for a long time, engaging in long telephone conversations with Antonius Heck. Now and then Katja heard him using abusive language. She found that very strange because he had always treated his father's old business associate with respect. He had always looked up to Antonius, had admired his creativity and his playful look at scientific problems.

On Sunday morning Dieter got into his Mercedes and drove to Antonius Heck's bungalow, a half hours' drive from Lake Constance. The little house was situated among fruit orchards, at the edge of a little village. He parked the car in front and went right away to the big garage Antonius used as a workshop, stepping through a side door, without knocking.

Antonius was seated on a workbench with a big mug of coffee in his right hand. He wore dirty overalls that were much too large for his thin body. Dieter wouldn't have been surprised if it was the same pair of overalls the man wore a month ago when he visited him. Antonius was a widower; he didn't care about clean clothes. He shaved irregularly; his grey stubble was more than a week old.

"Hello Dieter," he said, while he looked at him searchingly. "Do you want a cup of coffee? It will wake you up and perhaps you'll be in a better mood than you were yesterday. I had to hold my smartphone as far from my ear as possible because your voice sounded so loud on the other end."

"Do you think I stepped out of my car half asleep?" Dieter stammered without greeting him back.

"I think you're still easily irritated. But, I understood everything you told me about that painting and the alleged existence of Nicolaes Nimbus. Have a seat. I have something here that will interest you."

Dieter dug up an empty chair and sat down. The workshop was full of equipment Antonius had built himself. It was almost impossible to guess what the function of each piece was because he had made use of identical cases; metal frames, backside, and upper side, bottom and side panels were of plywood and the front pieces were often made of synthetic material with holes for switches, meters, little screens and input devices to connect them to other appliances. Workbenches and tables were full of tools and parts. High metal closets stood against any extra wall space.

"First I have to disappoint you," Antonius explained. "During our calls yesterday, I told you that some things are impossible. One of the things you asked me was how one might see what happens in the brain when someone has activated a method to halt the aging process – or to simulate it in a computer program; we don't have a living person who can do anything like that. Will glands start to work differently, will a certain type of matter be liberated that has a rejuvenating influence... How can you find out which parts of the brain become the most active then, how..."

"Stop it!" said Dieter, raising his hand in the air. "Yes, we have discussed that already. You cannot make something like that for us. Just tell me what you have for me now." Antonius drank the rest of his coffee and for Dieter that took too long, "I have no time for this. Do you hear me? I haven't come here to sit and watch you enjoy your coffee."

Antonius placed his mug back on the workbench with so much force that he broke the handle off the mug.

"Don't you talk to me like that, Dieter Brunn!" he said in a sharp tone. "You know very well I seldom get angry, but this time you have gone too far. Together with your father, I set up different companies. Later, after he passed away, I helped you as much as I could, teaching you the ropes. You are a man of many talents, but you also needed a mentor and that mentor was me. I will sell my shares to you before long, and at a very reasonable price. That way you will own everything! I don't like your attitude right now, I do not deserve this. Is that clear?"

Dieter jumped to his feet and waved his fists in the air. "You are no match for me. I could break every bone in your body in a few seconds."

Antonius let himself slide from the workbench; suddenly he had a big iron file in his hand that he could use as a blunt instrument and a pointed weapon. "Do we really have to come down to this level? Why is that?

What has happened to you that has made you so aggressive?"

The two men started circling each other, almost stumbling across appliances and parts scattered all over the floor. Dieter got angrier and every now and then he could not find the right words to give expression to his aggression; he made strange, hissing sounds between his teeth.

"Don't let that anger drain away," Antonius said. "That is exactly what we need right now."

Dieter stopped, relaxed his facial muscles, and lowered his arms. He stretched his fingers and took a deep breath. "What are you talking about?"

"Come on, let's sit down again. I will keep the file in my hand and if you fly at me, I will hit you as hard as I can." Dieter sat down on the chair, Antonius hoisted himself on the workbench again. "Are you prepared to listen to me now?"

"Yes, but it better be interesting."

"It will be. As I already said, it is impossible to find out what exactly happens with the human body and the brain in particular when certain exertions give the initial impetus to the extending of one's lifespan. As far as that is concerned, we might wonder if we are searching for something that actually exists."

"We have already discussed this," Dieter said in a threatening tone. "Tell me something new..."

Antonius pointed at him with the file. "You have explained everything to me about the painting from the Dutchman and about the phenomenon of Nicolaes Nimbus. We are talking about an entity that seems to be noticeably present now and then. Folco Andermann's cousin, Remco Castor, claims he hit him – a physical entity – with a club! After which his house burnt down to the ground and the painting inside it remained undamaged. Some time ago I invented a machine that makes it possible to register all kinds of paranormal phenomena."

Now Dieter sat up straight. "Aha! That sounds much better. Go on..."

"I will explain it to you; I'll be short and to the point. I have heard recordings of alleged ghosts before, vague voices with a lot of noise in the background. First I assumed the people who operated the equipment were producing the sounds themselves with undiscovered powers of the brain, exactly like scientists who propose that people who organize séances don't conjure up spirits but can read the minds of the people present." Dieter was interested. Antonius spoke uninterruptedly. "Then I came across something strange. In a room where things had happened that evoked different emotions – fear, threat, murderousness – the hypersensitive equipment didn't only register voices but sound as well. I heard piano music in a building where a pub was established a century ago and it sounded clear as a bell. I asked myself, was this real, or is the human brain able to make a melody, played on an instrument, clearly audible via a special recording?" Antonius put the file next to him on the workbench. "It has to be one or the other," he went on. "We produce the sounds ourselves, with our brains, or it is something else – a world we know nothing about, perhaps another dimension, or time exists in a way that we are not familiar with so that the future and the past are just as reachable as the present. That thought haunted me. I bought that special recording equipment and studied it, started to experiment with it, and decided to improve all the properties and build my own equipment that would make it possible to find out what exactly was going on."

When he fell silent, Dieter spoke, "And then?" he asked eagerly. "What happened?"

"I started experimenting." Antonius picked up the file to point at a table in the corner of the garage. An apparatus rested on it that was connected to a keyboard. "I took it to my friend's old barn. The results were, eh... well, let's just say they were encouraging. Vague voices and inexplicable sounds were recorded, everything almost without white noise. My apparatus works and now we have the opportunity to put it into action." Dieter looked at him expectantly. "I didn't lose interest after these experiments," continued Antonius, "but other things demanded my attention. I had to concentrate on Project Riverso, a communication satellite design program and I had to take care of the..."

"...safeguarding," Dieter filled in impatiently, "that is my project, Antonius."

"Yes, yes, I know. I just wanted to let you know I had no more time to spare on the device. There are so many possibilities, the computer registers everything that happens within the entire scale of frequencies; everything that might be of any importance is filtered in a split second and gets saved. And there is more. It does not catch sounds only, it also records the presence of everything that remains invisible to the eye; it even registers brain activity – from anyone in the immediate area. It is measured and analyzed in detail. I said the possibilities are endless because the computer keeps on playing with all the information. Well, Dieter, I notice you are getting impatient... and angry as well. And that is wonderful."

"Wonderful, why is that so wonderful?" Dieter threw out.

"I cannot describe it scientifically. All I can do is try to say it in my own words because it is about phenomena that have never been explained. Something has gotten a hold on you that you and the others at Fort Web have defied for too long. Something... maybe we're talking about a man who has lived for so long that his senses have developed further than ours, or is this a phenomenon we simply cannot understand? Something is influencing you; that is the reason why you are in a bad mood. It is so strong, it even affects me; I seldom lose my temper, and yet I have become angry this very day. I got furious with you! I could have bashed you with that file, or stabbed it in your stomach or your neck. Very well then, Dieter, let's use the machine to find out what you have dragged into my workshop unknowingly..."

Dieter rose to his feet. "Yes, let's do it, Antonius! Let's do it!"

"I know we will receive strong signals," said Antonius enthusiastically, while he walked over to the apparatus in the corner of the garage. He pushed several buttons. Needles slid along scales behind small screens of transparent plastic. Antonius took four wireless microphones from a drawer and placed them at different spots nearby. A monitor flared up. He typed on the keyboard using his middle fingers. After the device was set up to his liking, he took the right shell of his headphone from his ear so he could hear what Dieter was going to say. "If a spirit is present or an entity unknown to us, if a powerful brain can transmit and receive or something else that is absolutely impossible for us to grasp, this will give us a definitive answer. Nothing will escape the attention of this device, my brilliant creation!"

"What is going to happen now?" Dieter wanted to know.

"The computer asks questions. No, we cannot hear them. But it is already busy asking and searching. I will listen in now to find out if I have to adjust anything. Wait, wait... I hear something..."

He put the shell of his headphone back on his right ear. He raised his head, his mouth fell open; he stared at the meters of the apparatus.

"What do you hear?" Dieter shouted. He stared at the moving needles and saw big white figures flash on the monitor without knowing what it meant. Finally, he could relax his curiosity no longer; he leaned against Antonius and pressed his ear to the outside of the right shell. All he could hear was a malignant, deep buzzing as if a mad bee was locked inside the shell.

"What is that?" he cried out.

Antonius took the headphone off and reached out to twist several knobs. "I have found something, now I can turn up the volume... Dieter, we have a visitor..."

Loudspeakers hung in all four corners of the garage. The buzzing had stopped. Two different sounds were audible, sounds that Dieter recognized right away. He could hear a calm, deep breathing and – a little softer – the regular beating of a heart. Now there was also a growing pressure perceptible, comparable to what a diver experiences when he sinks deeper and deeper into an ocean. Dieter turned round and round, expecting someone to enter the garage at any time. The pressure on his ears and eyes began to get annoying and he started to gasp for breath.

There was a third sound now, very much like light, hesitating footsteps.

"Antonius, what is happening?" Dieter asked again."What is happening?"

"I don't know, everything indicates there is something present that has volume, but for the time being it is not showing itself. It gives me the creeps. I feel oppressed..."

Antonius grabbed his chest with both hands. The footsteps seemed to come from all sides at the same time; it sounded as if an entire army was marching through the garage, the breathing noises expanded into a wind that swelled into a storm and the invisible heartbeat pounded so loud as if someone was pounding on a kettledrum. A whirlwind materialized in the middle of the garage. Tools that lay closeby– a hammer, a pair of tongs, and different screwdrivers – began flying across the concrete floor. The appliances that stood on the floor, on tables and the workbench were dashed off their perches and whisked against the nearest wall. Not much later everything was part of the maelstrom. The windows shattered, high, light metal garage doors flew open. The side of Dieter's head was hit by an old-fashioned wooden, and iron toolbox. He was lifted and flung outside, coming down hard on the cobbles in the drive. He lost consciousness right away.

* * *

When Dieter opened his eyes, he was still lying on the cobbles in front of the garage. Two male nurses had knelt next to him. From the corner of his eye, he could see the rear of an ambulance. He must not move an inch, according to one of the male nurses. "Could you answer some questions?" They had to take into account he might have broken his neck or his back. His head wound had already been dressed. A third man knelt, a policeman. The ambulance was running, smoke came from the exhaust pipe, it made Dieter cough.

He was hesitant to answer the questions asked to him. The first thing he said was, "Why is the ambulance leaving?"

"Mr. Heck is being transported," said one of the male nurses.

"Antonius... How is he doing?"

"He's dead."

A second police officer appeared. He remained standing, looking down on Dieter. "Such havoc," Dieter heard him say. "What happened? If it was an explosion, you would expect to see fire damage. All we could see were Mr. Heck's feet; his body was underneath a mountain of his own equipment. The metal frames crushed him..."

Suddenly Dieter sat up. A male nurse reacted instinctively and tried to push him back down. He noticed Dieter was very strong; he would not allow himself to be manhandled. Dieter felt anger coursing through his veins; he would have loved to punch the man in the jaw; he did his utmost to control himself.

"My back is not damaged and my neck is okay," he said. "Only my head, my right shoulder, and my right knee hurt. Let me sit here for a while. Then I will try to stand up. I am ready to answer your questions."

Without warning, he lay down again, rolled over the cobbles on his belly, and rested his face in his hands. His body started to shake. The male nurses and the officers watched him as he cried uncontrollably.

"I have known Antonius well, I live in the neighborhood," said one of the police officers. "He worked with this man's father. So of course Antonius' death has affected him deeply..."

But Dieter wasn't crying. He was laughing soundlessly. He didn't understand himself, but he felt very good. And when he finally managed to calm down, he started to think. He could not come up with a reason for his behavior, because no one would believe him if he told them what he really thought was causing his odd reaction to a very sad event. How can I tell these men that something had gone wrong with an apparatus invented by Antonius that had caused a chain reaction that involved all of the equipment in the garage, that an enormous pressure had come into being, that everything got flung around and blown away. Everything was broken, no one could tell with certainty what any single apparatus had been used for.

Dieter rolled on his back, sat up, and stood. He made a sad face and shook his head slowly. "Poor, poor Antonius," the male nurses and police officers heard him say. "His research has become fatal to him... And he almost dragged me down with him, how fortunate ... I'm still alive!"

The twisted doors made the havoc in the garage visible. When he turned around and looked past the bungalow, he saw people standing at a distance behind an orange plastic ribbon tacked on posts by the police. Only now did he fully realize what had happened, how everything was spun around, and how he had been flung outside, away from the swirling mass.

More policemen arrived to investigate the situation. Dieter pretended to wipe his tears away, bowed his head, and prepared himself to answer countless questions.

❋ ❋ ❋

On the evening of that same Sunday, Castor was seated at a table in a restaurant in Freising. The group had rented a luxuriously furnished house for him in the neighborhood. That Saturday a bank employee and an architect had called him to make an appointment; the banker would take charge of his money and the other man would draw up plans for a house to be built on the old family property, a perfect house designed to Castor's specifications.

All he really knew about his new situation was the fact that Rein's painting had yielded a fantastic amount of money and that his wealthy cousin, Folco, had given it all to him. He should have been a very content man, but that was not in his character; he still had not been able to cope with the tragedy of the fire. He missed Rein's company. The young Dutchman understood his pessimism and could laugh at his wry humor. The cause of the fire was still a mystery to him and he didn't understand one thing he had heard in Fort Web. Time and again he thought about the moment he stepped inside the darkroom and saw the oil lamp move. *I should have hit him harder, much harder*, he was convinced of that, *if I had knocked the burglar down, if I had only managed to break his neck or split his skull, we would have been able to see who he was.*

He ate his schnitzel and drank his red wine. He sat here warm and safe with enough money in his pocket to pig out on everything the kitchen had to offer and order all the wine stored in the cellar.

I should have beaten him to death. His mood became malicious and he felt the atmosphere in the restaurant change. The voices of the guests sounded clear as if they were coming from across the water and the tables seemed like nearby islands in a calm sea. A breeze stroked his face and suddenly the air he breathed was so pure, it made him a little dizzy. Everything in the restaurant changed. Tables that seemed to be like islands were cities with medieval walls, separated from each other by dark forests. The voices grew weaker and weaker until they finally fell silent and then he heard the ringing of bells. Death knolls, *I must be hearing death bells!*

Someone had decided to sit opposite him. He was not able to determine who it was and he wondered why his sight had become blurry. "Rein, is that you?"

The ringing of the bells grew louder, an infernal noise. Castor opened his mouth to say something and the air was sucked from his lungs. He sank forward slowly, putting his arms on the white tablecloth; he rested his head on them. His mouth remained open.

"Anna!" someone at another table shouted, roaring with laughter. "I think someone has fallen asleep. He must have had too much wine!"

A waitress looked at the man as he pointed with his finger. She walked up to Castor. She didn't know the old man, this was his first visit. The moment she stood next to his chair, she noticed Castor wasn't breathing. She didn't dare to touch him. "I think he's dead!" she whispered. Then she covered her mouth with her hand and cried. The sound of knives and forks being dropped on plates echoed throughout the restaurant, hunger seemed to have vanished.

Chapter 13

PAINTING UNDER HYPNOTIC INFLUENCE

Hundreds of people walked past the coffin to pay their respects to Antonius Heck. On the day of the cremation, there were not enough seats, many visitors remained standing. Scientists and other important people from the business world eulogized him; they were all asked to keep it short, otherwise, his acquaintances might not have enough time to take the floor.

"Antonius Heck was a genius," Rosa Linge commented, "I was introduced to him by Dieter Brunn. I saw with my own eyes how he effortlessly solved the most complicated technical problems and came up with new inventions that no one had ever had thought of before." She pointed to the high ceiling in the auditorium.

"Many satellites orbit our planet that contain hardware designed by him. He was a many-sided man! He worked on a way to wipe out undesirable memories to help people afflicted by various traumas. He wanted to make drug addicts forget they ever needed cocaine or heroin and to change criminals into good citizens. Antonius was also fascinated by unexplainable phenomena. He once told me about sculptures in caves that clearly showed there must have been highly developed civilizations more than a million years ago and he was flabbergasted when he found out there were huge temple complexes in India that were cut out of the hardest rock – something we are absolutely not able to do even now. He wanted to go there, to India. But it wasn't meant to be. He was a gifted scientist who brought the word *technique* to a higher level and he helped to enhance our research into the human brain. He was a man who – just like many of us present– constantly searched for ways to extend and improve our lives. He was able to look beyond the borders of science as we know it and see other worlds full of possibilities. His flirtatiousness with the supernatural helped him to approach science in a playful imaginative way. Antonius showed us the way and I thank him for that from the bottom of my heart – that is why I have a deep respect for him..."

Dieter Brunn took his place behind the microphone. He was the most important speaker. Antonius had no children so he always considered Dieter like a son. Together with Dieter's father, Brunnheck was transformed into a large conglomerate and now Dieter possessed his shares as well, which made him the sole owner with one-hundred percent of the stock.

He looked at his audience, staring, trying to find the right words... *I can't stop the memories from assaulting me. I was there, the only one left, the severe head wound, being knocked to the ground. I was spared the sight of Antonious' mangled crushed body. I cannot imagine what his last thoughts were as he lay under a pile of machinery of his own making. I can't stop thinking about that whirlwind or machinery and other small parts and that deafening noise, the wind coming from every direction. The pressure was unbearable and that thing, being, whatever it was.*

Dieter wore a black custom-made suit, black shoes, and a black-tie. He looked serious and sad at the same time. "Antonius Heck..." he started, leaning forward, with his mouth close to the microphone, his voice, with a light echo, sounded a little too loud. Immediately he straightened his back and looked at the people in the auditorium. His wife was sitting in the front row, next to Gabi Stein and Folco Andermann.

"Antonius Heck..." he repeated, now his voice sounded better.

He knew his speech by heart. Five hundred words were enough to praise and honor Antonius and say farewell in a dignified way. Dieter pressed his lips together. There was a strange, guttural sound coming from his throat and his cheeks began to turn red. He laughed uncontrollably.

Everyone looked at him in a dazed sort of way, wondering how to react. After a short time, Lucas Montaigne rose to his feet and ran up to Dieter. He grabbed him by the arm, pulled him away from the microphone, and dragged him toward the exit.

"What is wrong with you?" he shouted in Dieter's ear when they entered the crematorium's foyer.

Dieter was unable to answer but kept on laughing. All of a sudden Lucas started laughing along with him.

Back in the auditorium, Freeda Olbers got up and walked up to the microphone. In her black dress, trimmed with countless red feathers and her coiffed hair decorated with long, blue feathers, she looked like the next fool ready to perform an undesirable act. She remained very calm and her voice sounded friendly as she spoke, "Ladies and gentlemen, for everyone who doesn't know me, my name is Freeda Olbers and as a psychologist, I can assure you these kinds of situations are commonplace. If a man or a woman isn't able to control himself or herself, intending only to utter some serious words, depending on the circumstances, he or she may very well burst into laughter instead. I ask you kindly to forgive Dieter Brunn. Sometimes it is better to forget about reactions that were contrary to original intent. Now and then, under extreme situations, one may no longer be responsible for his behavior...I am sure most of you are aware that Dieter was the last man to see Antonius alive; he is just now recovering from a serious head injury." She stepped aside for the next speaker.

❋ ❋ ❋

Significantly fewer people were present at the cremation of Remco Castor. His cousin arranged everything, even drumming up some family members who had hardly known Castor, the lone wolf. Only one friend was present, someone who had met him only a short time ago, Rein Vulpes.

Rein was also the only one who had something to say; he kept his speech short, "He looked at his surroundings with the eyes of a genre painter and what he saw were abstract caricatures of what could have been his reality. He placed empty picture frames on poles in front of his house. They exemplified tiny parts of our world, probably symbolizing the existence of short-sighted people in his neighborhood – but from his spot, from his chair next to his door, he could see past those frames. He saw the vastness of the universe. He hated life, he loved life and finally... he stopped living. Halfway through a good meal in a restaurant, a special man simply gave up. Castor, you entered my life and disappeared like a comet racing through the sky, but I have known you as a poor man and as a wealthy man. I will always remember you..."

"Rest in peace," was all Folco Andermann had to say.

❀ ❀ ❀

Because Freeda had told him things had to be arranged before she would allow him to paint under hypnosis, Rein made good use of his old Toyota daily, checking out local towns and cities. He enjoyed traveling around, exploring. Gabi urged him to accept some money from her so he could enjoy the luxury of five-star hotels and the best restaurants. He had not made use of her offer to spend his nights in Fort Web, preferring not to be there all by himself at night. He visited Munich several times enjoying weisswurst and beer, roaming the streets till the sun came up. For the time being, he had no desire to go back to Rotterdam. His house was firmly locked and all the bills were paid.

He was part of a game in which his painting – and now he himself– played such an important role, it was so exciting. These scientists were searching for eternal life; they had discovered something they simply didn't understand. Something out there was opposed to the strict rules of science and it intrigued them so much it had become an obsession. Rein had witnessed and become involved in a bizarre conspiracy, willingly. That didn't trouble him at all, as long he could say goodbye to everyone any time he chose and drive back home in his old car.

He didn't fear danger at all; he was eager to know how it felt to work under the influence of hypnosis and was curious about the result. The people who had hired him wanted him to throw his heart and soul into his work to lure the person or entity by the name of Nicolaes Nimbus to a certain place.

During his jaunts here and there he ran his circumstances around in his head...The fox is the bait. Ha! No, no, the fox is never the bait, one only haunts the fox, and more than often he is one too many for the hounds. And Reinaert the fox, who can lead King Lion up the garden path, will always escape from all critical situations. *Painting while hypnotized, I can't wait. I wonder how my painting will be affected.*

❀ ❀ ❀

While Rein was riding around leading a carefree life, a special atelier was being prepared for him. There was a garden behind the CompuStein building. At the back of the garden, hidden from view by bushes and trees, three oblong concrete sheds had been constructed by the builders to store their materials. Now the sheds were empty; they were cleared out after CompuStein was finished. Gabi asked the builders to clean up the area but leave the sheds on the property. One was used by a gardener for his tools, one had been repurposed as a records office and the third would be used as Rein's atelier. The preparations were being done by the two silent men who had guarded the painting when it was in Remco Castor's care. The men had worked for Folco for several years.

"Happiness and satisfaction can be found in little pills," Folco often said to himself, "and the composition is always different, depending on what one needs." The patented medicine his pharmaceutical imperium developed brought in a fortune every year. Folco still oversaw several projects in his labs and he knew the business like no one else – he was still one of the most important scientists within his company. Both men had a police record, they were totally unreliable and often very violent. They had been in the same prison and when they got released, they decided to work together. Coincidentally, they frequented the same pub Folco often went to for a drink or two. As soon as they knew who he was, they made plans to kidnap or blackmail him. One evening they dragged him into an alley and threatened him. The next day he invited them to one of his offices and listened to their demands.

In the meantime, he offered them coffee with sugar, milk, and a certain powder, one that he had conjured. From that moment on, their threats of physical violence disappeared. He had both men in his power. They became his helpers, his guinea pigs, his zombies, and faithful bodyguards; they were dependent on the little blue pills he gave them. He changed the composition of his special pills often until he found the right amount of every ingredient; the aggressive blackmailers became silent men who would do anything for Folco Andermann.

Folco did not regret what he had done. "When certain men tell you about their malicious plans while they sit opposite you, they will surely kill you as soon as they have got what they asked for," was his argument, "because a dead man cannot tell the police anything about himself or his identity," he repeated often and to no one in particular.

The silent men were on the payroll, living in an apartment with a doctor on standby who certified that they were under his care and that they behaved exemplary – the doctor was Folco's friend. He was always in need of money because he gambled frequently. He was in Folco's debt big time.

Now the silent men worked with Rein Vulpes, designing and building his atelier. The flooring, sides, back, and roof of the shed were of concrete. The wooden front, including a window and a door, was removed. They replaced them with a concrete front and a heavy metal door. The door's hinges were precision-made and well lubricated, It was easy to open the door to gain access. It closed without a sound and locked automatically. From the inside it was impossible to open the door; the shed became a concrete trap. Inside they installed a sanitary facility, electricity, and cameras.

Freeda Olbers would ask Rein, as soon as she had him under hypnosis, to think of Nicolaes Nimbus constantly, painting him the way he thinks he looks.

"He is the perfect artist for this experiment. He is willing; it will be easy for me to hypnotize him. If telepathy really exists, assuming Nicolaes Nimbus is a real man, he will visit the atelier, especially if he is curious and in the area. He will step inside, I assure you! He will probably do it at night after Rein has left. This is absolutely viable, assuming he is real; I really think he was in Remco Castor's house that day. The metal door will close without a sound and lock behind him automatically. And this time we will not only have light, we will also have night vision cameras in case the bulbs burst after we capture him. On the monitors in Fort Web, we will be able to see anyone who has entered the concrete shed. He may go on a rampage, but he will not be able to escape. And then we will see how long an immortal person can survive without a bite to eat. Believe me, by a certain point he will do anything for a simple slice of bread!"

Everyone agreed this was anything but a scientific experiment.

Carsten von Haller said, "This goes far beyond the snaring of a hare. The magic ritual has become part of our plan, like hunters who once begged the gods for help before they went hunting for vicious prey. Did it help them, I wonder? Everyone has good reasons to believe what he perceives to be true against the background of the common views of his community. How about us? The shed is the snare, Nicolaes Nimbus is the hare, creating the painting is the magic ritual. Why do we even think this will succeed?"

"We are entering his territory," Rosa Linge uttered softly. "Maybe we can't believe in it entirely, because we have no scientific proof, but Nicolaes Nimbus might be very sensitive to it. We are making use of his own methods, using them against him. And if we succeed... we will have to adjust our opinions and study mysterious phenomena, just like our dear departed friend Antonius Heck did. It's so sad that he is no longer among us, he could have explained so much more to us..."

Rein Vulpes found himself in the office of Gabi Stein on the ground floor of the building; it was situated at the back, the French doors gave entrance to the big garden. Rein was leaning back in a comfortable, leather desk chair.

Gabi was not present, he was there with Freeda. It was easy for him to relax; he had turned the chair to be able to look outside through a window. Freeda sat in an armchair with her eyes closed as she prepared for her task.

She knew everything about hypnosis, studying its history from the time Armand Marie Jacques de Chastenet, Marquis de Puységur, started to experiment with animal magnetism. It was discovered by Franz Anton Mesmer at the end of the eighteenth century.

Freeda learned how to bring people under a hypnotic influence, but it remained, even though she was a psychologist and a neurologist, shrouded in mystery. Her results baffled her over and over again. She had to admit the human brain was an extremely complicated organ; people under the hypnotic influence were able to do the most absurd things. As far as that was concerned, hypnosis intrigued her just as much as sleepwalking. Several sleepwalkers had even been acquitted of murder; one with no knowledge of his dead victim can be accountable for it.

"Are you ready, Rein?"

"Yes, I want to paint and I am just as curious about the results as you are."

Freeda rose to her feet and walked up to him. She wore a tight, green, purple, red, orange, yellow, and blue striped pantsuit. When she stood in front of him, she reached out her hand and let her fingers stroke his face. "Close your eyes, Rein, breathe calmly, and listen to my voice…" It was easy for her to bring him under her hypnotic influence. After she had asked him to raise his left hand and then his right hand, making him drink from an imaginary cup, she gave him further instructions.

"Think of Nicolaes Nimbus, think of him all the time. Try to picture what you think he looks like in your mind and then paint him. Think about him and prepare yourself for his arrival. You must paint him as he actually is. Use the power of your mind to invite him to come and take a look at himself… Listen to me carefully, Rein, this is important. Maybe you will not be able to paint a human figure. If you have thoughts about an interplay of lines, a perfect interplay of lines and If that thought gets very strong, you should concentrate on it to the fullest." She repeated her words several times and asked him if he understood her.

"Yes, I will paint him, I will invite him in. If I am not able to paint him, I will concentrate on the interplay of lines."

"Come on, Rein, let's go…" Freeda led him through the garden to the concrete shed. The two men were sitting on a wooden bench in the sun. She opened the metal door and Rein stepped inside. "You know what you have to do," she said, after which she let go of the doorknob. The door closed without a sound.

Freeda went back to the building without a word to the silent men. Once inside Fort Web she could see what Rein Vulpes was doing on the monitors. She went through Gabi's office to the big hall and took the elevator to the upper story. The moment she stepped out, she saw Lucas Montaigne and Alrik von Hecht standing opposite each other, fists clenched.

"Who the hell do you think you are?" she heard Lucas shout. "Without Rosa's help, you would have achieved nothing at all. Hollow teeth filled with micro equipment... Don't make me laugh! I should kick in those teeth of yours..."

Alrik lashed out. He hit Lucas on the chin. It hardly seemed to affect the strong, broad-shouldered man as he used his fists as well. Alrik fell to the floor and tried to scramble to his feet immediately. His right cheek was red and swelling.

Freeda stood between both men and showed them her brightly colored, long nails. "I ought to scratch out your eyes."

Lucas and Alrik just laughed. "Don't do that, Freeda, please," said Lucas. "We both need our eyes to see what the Dutch painter is doing."

"Well, come with me then, I am certain he has already started."

The men shook hands and tapped each other on the shoulder. They embraced Freeda and kissed her on both cheeks. Then the three of them went to the room where the monitors were installed; the other members of the group were already present.

Rein had been in the shed several times before to see if everything he needed was in place. Of course, he had considered what techniques he would use, although he had no idea what he should paint exactly. He might work in three different phases, as he had done when he created The Reading Man; he could make a sketch and use it as an example, there were more possibilities, like applying very fine contours on the canvas with crayon or a soft pencil. As an art forger, Rein knew all possible techniques, most of them he had already tried. Now he wasn't thinking of any special technique at all.

A high canvas on a solid easel stood exactly in front of him. He just looked at it, with his hands on his hips. For twenty minutes he hardly moved. The canvas shone brightly in the artificial light. No shadows fell upon it. When he finally went into action, his movements seemed a bit mechanical, like those of a remote-controlled robot. He searched the countless tubes of paint, picked up a palette and a brush.

Never before had he started this way; very carefully he covered the entire canvas with a layer of white paint. Before everything dried he allowed thinned grey paint to flow from his brush. Grey lines came into being that crossed each other, slowly but surely the canvas looked like a glass window that had burst into fine fragments. Rein didn't give himself a moment of rest. He started at the upper left corner and worked till he reached the bottom right section of the canvas.

Everyone was there in Fort Web to see how Rein Vulpes began his work: Gabi Stein, Rosa Linge, and Alrik von Hecht, Folco Andermann, Freeda Olbers, Dieter Brunn, Carsten von Haller, and Lucas Montaigne. They shoved their desk chairs close together and looked attentively at the big screen.

Rein Vulpes stood with his back turned toward them; they were not able to see the entire canvas. After his final brushstroke he turned around, they saw his face. He did not show any specific emotions, but suddenly a wide grin passed over his face, he stepped to one side so the eight could see what he had painted for the first time.

Rosa Linge reacted immediately, "Why, that's the interplay of lines..." No one else spoke a single word.

Exactly at the same moment, all eight stood up and came closer to the screen. They were not able to turn their faces away, forced to remain standing still. What they saw had attracted their complete attention. Everything outside the screen no longer registered in their brains. First, they experienced astonishment and admiration, then they were flooded by a feeling of fear – fear of the unknown. Their thoughts were bent and detached from what Freeda would have called their doubtful own free will. They were no longer able to form a single idea about what was happening to them now; eight brains were adrift on unknown waters and that generated sheer panic. While they couldn't look away, they searched for each other's hands with trembling fingers.

Invisible claws pushed sharp nails into their brains, invisible teeth tore their frontal lobes apart; no one could defend themselves against the onslaught.

All of a sudden Rein stood in front of the painting again, he was still grinning. All eight let go of each other's hands, in total shock. The screen turned black.

Five men and three women leaned back in their desk chairs coming to their senses again, ever so slowly. They could not fathom what had just happened to them. Gabi rubbed her eyes and panted as if she had run several miles. She stood up in despair and walked over to the computer that was connected to the monitor. She entered different codes and looked at the monitor constantly to see if anything changed. She continued to work on the keyboard while the others began to talk at the same time. Maybe the light went out in the shed? The night vision cameras didn't work either. Perhaps there was no connection? I can't recapture the images we saw– everything has disappeared.

"I'm scared," she heard Rosa Linge say. "If I can't control the fear I am feeling right now, I'm afraid I'll need a strong sedative."

"I wasn't able to think at all," said Dieter. "If I had been able to, I would have thought about something as terrible as death. I'm sure of that."

"Freeda!" said Carsten, his voice quavering, "you can tell us what happened, can't you?"

"No, no!" Freeda cried, "You leave me alone, Carsten von Haller. Try to figure out your own misery; don't expect any wise words from me."

"Does anyone understand any of this?" Gabi cried out. "The images have not been saved and we are no longer able to see what is happening in the shed. Folco, have your men enter the shed. This is so frightening, this is unbearable; this is agony times ten! Why can't I control myself? Why can't I calm down? Folco, did you hear what I just said?"

"I don't know."

"You don't know what?"

"I know nothing, nothing at all; does that sound better to you? When I panic, I can jump out of the window and kill myself. Don't bother me with stupid questions!"

For half an hour everyone tried to suppress their fears and understand what had happened. Everything was quiet. Unexpectedly, the shed's lights and the monitor came online as the eight stared at the screen. Rein Vulpes had used a broad brush to cover the canvas with a new layer of white paint.

Chapter 14

THE CUP

Rein Vulpes took his time working carefully, as always. First, he painted thin, light blue stripes all over the canvas. Then he started to concentrate near the bottom of the canvas. Much to everyone's surprise he painted a fox running away with a pheasant between its jaws. The watchers became confused when the fox was given human features. In an inimitable and brilliant way, Rein had managed to transform himself into a real fox on canvas! The animal had his eyes and his personality; it was a fox for certain, but everyone who had ever met Rein would recognize him immediately. Details, tiny dots of paint, ensured that the predator looked human and it was impossible to tell which – and how many – of these dots would have to be removed to undo that illusion. The neck of the colorful pheasant between the fox's sharp teeth was clearly broken, as Rein intended.

Freeda Olbers wondered what the symbolic meaning of the dead bird could be. Is it about victory, about a big score of some kind?

As soon as Rein was done painting, several hours later, Freeda released Rein from her hypnotic spell. A chauffeur picked Rein up to take him from CompuStein to a hotel in Munich. He dined in one of its best restaurants and slept well afterward. He had no special recollection of what he had done during the day, all he knew was that he had been painting and he knew he must have been standing for a long time; his legs were aching in protest.

His methods were strange as he worked slowly from the bottom to the top of the canvas. As his painting progressed, a worn boot came into being, right above the running fox. Next to it, a second boot materialized. Then a grey pair of pants were painted full of tears, along with a brown leather jerkin. Next, a tall man leaned on a stick that he held in his left hand. In his right hand, he held a golden cup, encrusted with precious stones: probably garnets, rubies, and amethysts. Carsten von Haller immediately said it had to be a cup from the Carolingian period, "It must be somewhere between the eighth and tenth centuries!"

Everyone waited impatiently for the moment Rein would start painting the man's face. They stared at a painting of a man without a face who, leaning forward on a stick, walked through a green meadow, within a forest background and a running fox with a dead peasant between its jaws in the foreground. It had become a work of art of the highest quality. Over and over again Rein applied accents that made the scene become even more alive.

Freeda became even more impatient so when she put him under the hypnotic influence one morning, she gave him an explicit order to paint the man's face.

It took Rein the whole day to do it. The eyes of Nicolaes Nimbus were bright blue. The face was neatly shaved; his hair was thick, blond, and full of curls.

Carsten von Haller remembered a remark Victor the Visionary had relayed to him,"...Billions of people, billions of faces. But no face is alike. They all differ. The face is only a small part of the body. But there are billions of ways to draw a unique face."

The face of Nicolaes Nimbus was impressive, lively, and full of character. No one believed this was just Rein Vulpes' fantasy.

"Nicolaes Nimbus has found his way into Rein's brain and stimulated his imagination. Rein knew exactly what to paint," said Lucas Montaigne. "It is so scary... we all know this is the real Nicolaes Nimbus for certain!"

"Nicolaes Nimbus will see the result for himself," Alrik joined in. "He will turn up, he will open the door of the shed..."

The group decided the most frightening thing about the face of the man in the painting was the fact that it was so ordinary. Maybe the golden cup was an indication of the time when he was born, the clothes seemed to be from different periods; the boots looked almost modern, the trousers could be from the eighteenth century and the jerkin was probably medieval. A man from all times...

As soon as the work was done, Rein Vulpes made it clear that he wanted to go home. There was no reason for him to stay any longer. Gabi gave him a large sum of money and said she would stay in touch with him, "We might need your help again sometime, Rein. On behalf of everyone, I thank you so much for making this painting. If you had lived in your own country during the Golden Age, you surely would have become a Rembrandt or a Frans Hals. You are such a great artist."

Rein bowed, "And after all his adventures, the smart fox returned to his safe hole with booty in tow."

He used his dice to decide whether he should return straight to Rotterdam or make a roundabout trip. Even numbers stood for the shortest route, odd numbers, for a ramble. He threw a six, double threes, and drove back home straightaway in his old Toyota.

Every night someone was present in Fort Web to see if anything was happening. Gabi was there now and because she didn't dare to be all by herself, she invited Folco to keep her company.

On the monitors, the night vision cameras showed the outside of the metal door and the interior of the shed with the big painting standing in the middle.

To kill the time, Gabi and Folco talked about things that were very important to them. Every time one of them started with a single remark, a lengthy conversation ensued, "It is said by learned individuals there are immortal alchemists. Maybe we came across one without knowing it in the past."

"Alchemy cleared the way for chemistry; did you know that?"

"Our planet will become one big city with parks scattered here and there. If we live in a virtual world most of the time, we won't need personal space anymore."

"Can you eliminate the factor of time in a virtual world, so that you can stay there forever – even after you have passed away?"

"We must get rid of all our physical and mental pains to be happy for a long, long time."

"If life itself is purposeless, we will give it purpose ourselves – because that is our nature."

"All power in the hands of a wealthy élite, or perhaps we should share, that is what it will be all about in the future."

"How will your way of thinking be affected, what will your desires be when one has tinkered with your brain to help you remain equal to others, when you are connected to micro equipment packed with helping programs – equipment in your teeth, maybe, if it's up to Alrik von Hecht and Rosa Linge..."

"Future humans with better-developed brains will be able to comprehend everything; will know the answers to all questions, there will be room for an entire universe with brains like that. No one can imagine how it must feel to have a brain like that right now."

"Will you still care about anything if everything always – day in, day out – goes the way you want it to go?"

"Will we allow our own technical innovations to manipulate us?"

"Will adventure vanish from our lives when we rely on artificial intelligence completely?"

"There is a chance we have changed the human brain completely before we know exactly how it works."

"Magic disappeared from our society. But behind our backs, unnoticed, magic continues to exist."

"I am afraid of Nicolaes Nimbus. I'm scared to death..."

"Don't talk about death; we must strive for eternal life..."

"We're already old, you and I. For us there's no time to wait for new developments, we need Nicolaes Nimbus to prolong our future now."

Now and then they held each other's hands while they talked together. It was hard to realize they found themselves in the winter of their lives, that immortality was something hidden, unreachable for them behind the horizon of time. "The children that will be born tomorrow, they'll get their chance..."

Aside from the cameras, there were also microphones installed in front of and inside of the shed. The volume control was turned up to the max, a constant noise was audible. Suddenly the noise was interrupted by a short creak. Gabi and Folco immediately looked up at the monitors.

"What was that?"

Folco put his forefinger to his lips to make it clear she must remain silent. Now they heard a sound as if someone had heaved a deep sigh – or was it a gust of wind that flew past one of the microphones? The sound was repeated several times; Gabi and Folco assumed it had to be an intensified breathing.

"Someone's there in or near the shed..." Gabi whispered. A night vision camera registered a shadow sliding past the metal door of the shed. A dark, moving mass became visible; Gabi thought it might be the silhouette of a man. The door opened without a sound.

Something slipped inside. The door closed slowly, the click of the lock was clearly audible.

The cameras inside the shed showed the same dark mass. "We got him now...!" said Folco. He tried to focus the cameras when he realized there was also a button to activate the lights in the shed. As he pushed the button, the screens turned white; immediately after that they turned black and all sound ceased. There was nothing to see or hear anymore. The cameras and microphones outside the shed didn't work either.

"I think I have to throw up," Gabi said, as she jumped up and quickly left the room.

As soon as Folco was alone, he took a little plastic box from the inside pocket of his jacket, opened it, took out a pill, and put it in his mouth. His heart was beating much too fast.

Gabi looked deathly pale when she came back. "And what are we supposed to do now, Folco?" she cried out, "what should we do now?"

It was midnight; they were alone in the big building. Folco rose to his feet carefully. He had to lean on the back of the desk chair to prevent himself from falling as he stumbled to the corridor.

"Don't leave me alone!" Gabi ran after him. "Where the hell are you going?"

Folco walked slowly, teetering this way and that toward one of the guestrooms at the back of the building. As soon as he and Gabi were inside, he turned off the lights and slammed the door. Not much later they stood at the window together in total darkness and looked downward. It was a clear but moonless night. The three concrete sheds in the back of the garden were only vaguely visible.

"Who is brave enough to open that door again, you or me?" Folco whispered close to Gabi's ear.

"And when should we open it?" Gabi's frightful voice squeaked next to him.

"We'll have to wait," Folco said with no reservation, "until tomorrow night, late, when the others are here as well."

"...What now? Do you want to go home?"

"I am staying right here," Folco responded. "I don't think I'm capable of driving just now and I want to keep an eye on that shed – and I must try to get those cameras working again, I want... no, wait, you know much more about computers than I. How could the system fail? I, no, we..." He started to pant as he leaned both hands on the window sill. "Good heavens, Gabi," he sighed, rasping heavily, "what have we done?!"

"Try to calm down, Folco. If you panic, I'll go crazy, and if you collapse, I will die!" Gabi almost screamed. "We must do something, we must keep ourselves busy. Yes, I will take a look at the computers. Come with me, I want you to stay close to me, do you hear me? Stick to me like glue."

Gabi concentrated on the computers for a long time. It seemed impossible to get the cameras and microphones working again, finally, she gave up.

"Everything is alright; the equipment should be working properly. I have checked everything a dozen times or more and I even tried some new programming. I cannot find failures where there are none to be found..."

They went back to the same guestroom to look out the window after grabbing a cup of coffee from the kitchen. Later Gabi went to one of the guestrooms to lie down; she slept for about an hour. Folco paced through the corridors, looking at his watch constantly *Never before have I longed so much for the break of dawn.*

CompuStein Hightech was already bustling when Gabi came down the elevator. She went to her office straight away and contacted Rosa Linge, Lucas Montaigne, Carsten von Haller, Dieter Brunn, and Freeda Olbers. Everyone reacted in the same manner, everyone promised to come to Fort Web that evening, especially after Gabi told them what had taken place the night before.

"I will inform Alrik," said Rosa "he will come with me."

Folco had driven to his own offices as soon as Gabi woke up, waving to his silent hires as he left the grounds.

That night everyone was present in time for dinner in Fort Web. The hearth was burning in the kitchen. Little lamps in the shape of burning candles strengthened the impression that one found himself or herself in the taproom of an old inn, far away from the modern world.

"We will wait till the cleaning crew has left the building," said Folco. "My two guards will still be present of course. They will come with us to the shed and see to it that nothing happens to us. Believe me, they know no fear; they will open the door and step inside without hesitating."

Rosa looked at Folco. "What will they find there?"

"A hungry man, if he doesn't like eating paint," Folco grinned at his own pun. "There's no food in the shed."

Freeda shivered, "Just imagine... what if it isn't a man..."

"What else would it be?" asked Lucas.

"How am I supposed to know?" Freeda threw out. "An entity, something spiritual, immaterial, something beyond our comprehension... none of us has ever had to deal with something like this before."

"If it's a man, we'll talk with him," said Folco. "What we decide to do with him depends on his behavior. He will have to serve science; willingly or unwillingly. I hope we all agree about that, right?"

Everyone nodded.

"Imagine..." said Rosa, "if he turns out to be a man of flesh and blood and is really that old, we will soon discover his secret. That will be an enormous breakthrough; such knowledge will give us unimaginable power."

Much of the food remained untouched, no one was hungry. It grew darker and darker outside while they waited.

"It is time," Gabi finally said, "let's go."

"One moment, Gabi, let me radio my men to meet us in the hallway on the ground floor. Let's not take any unnecessary chances." Gabi nodded and they headed down the elevator.

The silent men were standing there, waiting for them in the hall on the ground floor. They both wore a security uniform with the CompuStein logo on the jacket.

"Now I feel a lot safer," whispered Freeda. "I know they fear nothing and no one."

Everyone went into the garden through the French doors of Gabi's office. The building was dark, only the hall lighting on the ground floor was aglow. The ten people followed the winding path to the sheds. Gabi gave one of the men a big key.

"Wait a minute," said Folco, breathing heavily. "Don't open the door yet. I need some time to catch my breath; my heart is racing a mile a minute ..."

"That's a good idea," said Rosa, "let's rest for a moment; I want to prepare myself for what is going to happen." Not a single leaf rustled in the calm evening. Everyone stood wrapped in their own thoughts.

"Before we use the key, let's do something different," said Lucas Montaigne all of a sudden, "I will knock on the door. Maybe we'll get a reply."

Because no one reacted, he walked up to the door, hesitated for a moment and took a deep breath.

"Do it, do it!" Freeda pushed him.

Lucas pounded on the metal with his knuckles and the flat of his hand. Nothing happened. Lucas pounded harder and again there was no response. He stood right in front of the door and beat on it furiously with both hands.

"Hello!" he shouted, "Hello! Who's there, anyone inside?" He started kicking against the door. No one dared to interfere because Lucas was such a strong man. Folco didn't want his men to step in. Finally, Lucas stepped back breathing heavily.

"Open that door now," he said to the two men, lightly panting. "If anyone comes outside and even tries to escape, I will knock him down and restrain him."

Folco nodded at the man with the key. The other man switched on a powerful flashlight. The key went in the lock and was turned. The door was slowly opened and the two men slipped inside. Lucas stood in the doorway. His hand slid past the metal frame and pressed a button he found there; the mechanism that would make the door close was deactivated.

There was an explosion in the shed, the uniformed men were flung outside. Lucas and the other two tumbled to the ground. The others shrunk back. A sudden blast of wind made the branches of the trees creak and crack. Inside the shed, the flashlight lay on the floor, a figure was visible – someone was moving around in there. Something rushed forward and jumped outside. Freeda Olbers and Alrik von Hecht screamed as they were knocked aside. One of the silent men shot up and fell upon the dark figure. A fight broke out, Lucas Montaigne got involved and soon everyone got into the action.

"Kill him!" Folco cried out. "Kill him! Dead he's worth exactly as much as he is alive!"

"Oh, yes, let's kill him!" another voice sounded and someone else remarked, "Hasn't he already lived long enough? This will be his last moments!"

The men in uniform grabbed someone and the others lashed out as hard as they could. The figure let himself fall to the ground. The men had to let go of him as they were both yanked to one side; he jumped to the other side and started to run. No one was able to stop him as he disappeared into the darkened garden.

"Get him! Get him!" Folco screamed at his two helpers. One of them had a flashlight hanging down from his belt, he grabbed for it.

Lucas Montaigne was the first to enter the shed and search along the wall for the light switch. Gabi and Folco were baffled as the interior suddenly lit up.

"How on Earth is this possible..." muttered Gabi. The walls, the floor, and the ceiling were smeared with paint. Several tubes seemed to have exploded. Broken brushes lay everywhere. A chair had tumbled over, a table lay upside down on the floor; two of its legs had been broken off. But the canvas was still standing on the solid easel. The image of Nicolaes Nimbus had disappeared. It was no longer covered by a new layer of paint– the canvas was nearly blank. But at the bottom, the running fox still looked very much like Rein Vulpes and the pheasant with a broken neck between its teeth was still there...

"This fiasco is totally insane!" Carsten von Haller screamed.

The uniformed men came back, they both shook their heads; they had not been able to find the fleeing figure anywhere on the property.

"We should have given your men a baseball bat, Folco," Dieter Brunn commented. "Then we would have a body we could drag to one of our labs."

"Or to all of our labs," remarked Rosa, " cut into pieces and shared among us."

"We must get out of here," Alrik decided. "We have no business being here any longer."

They left the shed area. Folco turned off the light and one of his men locked the door. Suddenly Gabi started to scream. She stood there in the garden, flabbergasted, her eyes were as big as pie plates.

"Everyone, look at that. I don't believe it. Who turned all those lights on?" Lights were shining brightly behind all the windows of Fort Web. *Who is in my building if we are all standing here?*

Then Gabi's entire body began to shake and she cried hysterically. Freeda burst into tears as well. Rivulets of fear ran down Folco's cheeks. Everyone looked upward fearing the moment someone would pop up behind one of the lit windows.

They stood in front of the French doors of Gabi's office. Gabi managed to stop crying a few minutes later and mustered up the courage to unlock all the doors. Folco sent his men inside first. The group gathered in the illuminated hall, waiting and hoping.

"We have to go to Fort Web; we must know what is going on there.   It would be nice if we had weapons.

Are there any weapons in the building, Gabi?" Lucas asked her.

"No, of course not..." Gabi replied.

"I remember Remco Castor using the leg of an old chair like a club," said Folco.

"That is a good idea," Lucas chimed in. "Now, let's see..." He walked back to Gabi's office and switched on the light. Next to a large desk, he saw a fern on the side table and a modern table with heavy cast-iron legs. Lucas knelt and noticed the top of the legs was fastened with faux woodblocks that were screwed down against the underside of the tabletop. He put the pot on the floor and unscrewed all four legs. Back in the hall, he gave a metal leg to both silent men, the third he gave to Alrik, and kept the fourth for himself. "You can easily split someone's skull with these," he said. "Come on, everyone, let's go!"

Gabi led them to the big elevator, the one mainly used by the cleaning crew. They all stepped inside. She pushed the button for the top story and the elevator went up to Fort Web.

"We'll stay together and search all the rooms one-by-one," said Lucas. "Pass the instructions on to your guards, Folco."

"Hit him as hard as you can," said Folco to the silent men. "Don't hesitate for a moment. As soon as you see someone, eliminate him."

The elevator stopped, the doors slid open.

"Magic has left the modern world," the philosopher whispered, "but it has snuck inside through a side door..."

"Don't say such things!" said Freeda. "Don't make us more scared than we already are, Carsten."

The two men went in front. The lights were on everywhere. All the doors were open, all the rooms were searched. It was deadly quiet. The monitors in the control room still showed the outside and inside of the shed. Dieter Brunn saw a shadow slide past the metal door. "Look! There! Something's happening right in front of the shed!" But nothing was registered by the night vision cameras.

Fort Web was like a mansion of many rooms and there were plenty of places where someone could hide; living rooms, guestrooms, archive rooms, bathrooms, the kitchen, the library, the control room, the meeting room. Everyone followed the silent men. Every inch of Fort Web was combed. Finally, the eight conspirators stepped into the meeting room while Folco's men remained waiting in the corridor.

The extensive search had yielded nothing. But they discovered something very special on the table. The golden cup, encrusted with garnets, rubies, and amethysts stood in its center. This was undoubtedly the beautiful object Rein had painted; Nicolaes Nimbus had held it in his right hand.

"He has been here..." Rosa whispered.

"How did he manage to get inside?" Gabi wondered out loud. "All the doors were locked. Can a magician walk straight through walls, I wonder?"

"Who will be the first to touch the cup?" asked Alrik. "Who dares to pick it up?"

Much to everyone's surprise it was Carsten who leaned over the table and reached out his hand. He took the cup, straightened his back, touched it, and turned it round and round. "I know I often brag about my own qualities," he said then. "But please, believe me when I tell you I know something about antiques. I come from a family of antique dealers and I worked for one of my uncles for many years, he owned a big shop in Munich. He taught me how to tell if an object is real or not – no matter if it's furniture or..."

"Tell us more about the cup!" Folco interrupted in a gruff voice.

"Immediately when I saw the cup in the painting I said it had to be Carolingian from the eighth or ninth century. Now I know I was right. The object is actually that old and it is pure gold. I have doubts where the precious stones are concerned, maybe the original stones were replaced at one time. But the cup itself is authentic and absolutely priceless. This is a rare piece of art that should be in a museum."

The cup went from hand to hand, everyone wanted to touch it. When Carsten had it again, he held it high above his head and said, "Come with me! All of you!"

He walked to the door and disappeared into the corridor. The others followed him. He still held the cup above his head as if it was the Holy Grail. He put it on the table in the kitchen. Gabi opened a high closet and took out a bottle of champagne.

Before she was able to open it, Folco snatched it away from her. "Are you out of your mind?" he said angrily. "Champagne is very inappropriate at this moment!" He threw the bottle on the floor, where it shattered into countless fragments. "Red wine, that's what we need," continued Folco. "The best, the most expensive you've got."

Gabi nonchalantly moved her foot through the fragments and fizzing champagne and then opened the closet for the second time.

"This is perfect," she said, while she leaned over and took a bottle. "Pomerol is worth a small fortune." She went to the wooden bar and searched for a corkscrew. Then she opened the bottle carefully. Carsten took the cup from the table and put it on the bar. Gabi filled it with red wine. "Let's drink," she said in a solemn voice. "You first, Folco, you are the oldest."

"You will drink after me," Folco said as he picked up the cup.

The others watched him bring it to his lips and take a sip. Then he gave the cup to Gabi and she drank the wine. No one seemed to wonder what this ritual was all about. Everyone felt a great need to drink from the cup and no one questioned it. Rosa, Freeda, Alrik, Carsten, and Dieter drank as well, Lucas took the last sip. The cup was refilled twice, the bottle was emptied. Gabi went back to the closet for a second bottle of Pomerol, she opened it just as carefully as the first one. And again the cup went round three times.

After drinking from the chalice they went back to the meeting room, the silent men still stood at the door. The eight sat down on their thrones. Gabi shoved her hand under the table and pushed her fingertips against the underside of a deep secret drawer. The drawer opened without a sound. It contained a fountain pen she'd never used. Now she put the golden cup inside and closed the drawer again.

"What have we learned today?" she asked, while she looked at the others one at a time. "Did our ways cross and do we remember where we have come from?"

"The Jura was a time between the Cretaceous Period and the Triassic," reacted Dieter. "But we cannot imagine how long two hundred million years might be."

"The main point is not to be found in philosophy," said Carsten. "The power of speech has given us the possibility to make clear what we think. But no cities have ever been built with words. Foundations of vanity have never existed."

"I want to hear the conclusions!" Folco said in a loud voice.

Rosa started to sob softly, tears ran down her cheeks. "Not a single human being in this world feels pity for the crustaceous lichen," she said. "Everyone walks over it just like that, without noticing."

Alrik, who was sitting next to her, leaned over and tapped her on the shoulder. "Do you ever wonder how many different sorts of cubic measures there have been over time before one started counting in liters? That is unimaginable!"

Lucas Montaigne looked at the metal table leg he held in his hand. "Leonardo da Vinci sketched tanks, helicopters, and robots. And we must not forget that one found stone mortars and pestles that turned out to be thirty million years old – made by men, of course..."

Freeda nodded. "Is it wise to thank life, because you are alive yourself? Let's consider that for a moment. We cannot stop time and we have no idea why things are the way they are."

"Freeda is right," said Gabi, "I ask for a moment of silence." The eight thinkers bowed their heads, folded their hands, and remained that way for a very long time...

Chapter 15

THE SWIMMING FOX

It was late when a woman in a coat with a turned-up collar walked through the luxury district of Ingolstadt, Mars Kronacher's hometown. She walked stooped over with her hands deep in her pockets, then ran as she got closer to his house. Impatiently, she shifted her weight from one foot to the other as she rang his doorbell. The outdoor light went on and the door opened; Mars Kronacher, dressed in a long, white bathrobe stared at her in surprise. Stepping aside, he let her in.

"Theresia... You're here at this hour? What are you doing here so late? I was sleeping..."

"Now is the time to help you," the woman said. "We felt it. Don't go away from the door, you will have more visitors very shortly."

"But, but..." stammered Mars.

"We had to make a long journey," said Theresia, while she took off her long coat. "And I know you will appreciate that."

"Yes, of course," Mars hastened to say and suddenly he seemed to be wide awake.

The bell rang five times in succession. Two men and then three men stepped inside and Mars recognized them, calling them by their first names: Hanke, Franka, Sander, Ditmar, and Walden. Two of them had been present at the party he had given when he had purchased The Reading Man. There was a special bond between them; they knew about each other's extraordinary gift of prophecy.

"I know I am not bragging when I say we are Germany's greatest visionaries at present," Theresia said after everyone had found a place to sit in the living room. "It doesn't give me a good feeling to be here together. No one is supposed to know what we are doing here. Fortunately, I haven't felt the presence of evil all day. I think we are safe for now."

"No presence of evil," confirmed Sander, a thin man in his mid-fifties. "We should be able to concentrate here. Yes, Mars, we are here to help you. We heard you'd said too much and now your talent has been taken away from you. We understand. You are ambitious; you are a snob and a boaster, it is in your character, you cannot help yourself. Still, we think your punishment was too harsh."

"Well, according to medieval standards, the decision to remove his mind's powers was actually rather mild where that is concerned," Walden voiced, he was more than twenty years older than Sander and dressed in black. He pointed at The Reading Man hanging on a wall. "It could have been far worse for you."

Franka, young and energetic, slender and lively, jumped up and walked over to the painting to have a good look at it. "Brilliant! If I'd had more money, I certainly would have bought it myself. You outsmarted us, Mars. You paid for the painting with money you earned honestly as a great visionary. Yes, you were probably the greatest among us and we hope you might be like that again."

"First, tell us how you are doing?" Hanke said to Mars.

Mars Kronacher had lost a lot of weight in a short time and the way he sat in this white bathrobe, they could tell much of his flamboyant personality had left him. He left the room without looking at them and was back again in a couple of minutes, this time dressed in a light brown suit but still barefooted. "Is anyone hungry? Are you thirsty?"

"We didn't come here for that," said Ditmar, "maybe later. Hanke was asking you how you're doing."

"I am not doing well as you may have noticed," Mars intoned softly. "I have had to disappoint people, those who I have been able to help through the years by giving them my best advice. It is useless to receive them because I have nothing more to say to them or give them. My health is failing, I don't enjoy my food and I am bored to death. I spend my days sitting in my armchair and now and then I take a walk along the Danube. At times I feel inclined to jump in and let the river take me to who knows where... Oh well, life isn't exactly pleasant for me these days and there is nothing to look forward to anymore."

"That is exactly why we are here," said Hanke. "This is entirely new territory for us; we have never found ourselves in a situation like this before. We thought we could try and help you. We are still connected, Mars, we will try to restore your clairvoyance. There are still people who rely on you, who need your advice before they make any business decisions. I suggest we start right away..."

"Who will draw the interplay of lines?" asked Franka.

"I will do it but first let me light a fire in the hearth," said Theresia. "Are we all convinced it is safe here?"

Mars nodded, "I am alone here as always. No one will disturb us I assure you. What are you going to do?"

Theresia looked at him with a surprised look on her face. "Oh, but of course... you don't know about things like that anymore. As far as that is concerned, your memory is failing. What you knew yesterday will be forgotten tomorrow... Just wait and see, Mars, it will be alright in a little while."

She had a big bag with her; she opened it and took out a sketchbook and a pencil. Therese sat down on her knees and started to draw lines on a blank sheet of pure white paper.

The others looked on, whispering, "We hope to succeed and that you will be able to function again Mars; there are not that many competent visionaries at our level."

"Our interplay of lines may mean nothing at all compared to that of someone like Nicolaes Nimbus, but we will be able to concentrate and step outside the boundaries of time."

"The secret ritual... No one is supposed to see it, no one..."

"I have no idea what you are..." Mars started to say.

Sander repeated what Theresia had said, "Just wait and see, Mars, soon it will be alright.

Theresia worked hard, concentrating for three-quarters of an hour. She looked at the result and the expression on her face changed. There was a tender look in her eyes and suddenly she seemed years younger. She tore the sheet of paper loose and gave it to Hanke, he stared at it and handed it to Walden. Finally, Mars took it, his jaw dropped and the wrinkles in his face disappeared.

"This is so beautiful..." he sighed.

Everyone stood up and came over to stand in front of the painting. Theresia glanced over at the fire and began to incant, "It is true," she said in a firm voice, "it is true; visionaries that dispense false information have to be punished severely. Everything changes when a man or a woman follows bad advice. It can cause a chain reaction that ends in disaster. We all agree on that. Now we ask forgiveness for someone we admire very much. He has talked too much, that's true. He should have known better. Mars Kronacher is a special man, though conceited, extravagant and bombastic – no matter what we say about him, he has always been honest, and he has proven to be a great visionary in the past. Please give him the talent to predict the future. That is what we are asking. Make it happen... now!"

Mars Kronacher stumbled backward and flopped down in a chair. Theresia went to the hearth and set the sheet of paper on fire.

"Make it happen," she repeated. "Give him back his talent."

The flames engulfed the paper but she only let go of it after almost nothing was left. Even the tiniest fragment was burnt to ashes. The six visitors stood in front of the chair and looked down at Mars.

"...And?" Sander asked him, "did it help?"

Mars stared down at his bare feet. Tears ran down his cheeks. "Nothing has changed, nothing at all. I am no longer a visionary. You have come here in vain."

All of a sudden the visitors were in a hurry. One-by-one they took their leave of the crying man and disappeared into the night. Mars Kronacher remained sitting in his chair. He knew he wouldn't be able to sleep that night.

Theresia walked to her car, which she had parked on another street. She felt herself becoming more uncertain with every step. Something inside of her had changed. *What is it – what has happened to me?* When she stood in front of her car, it dawned on her. *What have we done?* She, Hanke, Franka, Sander, Ditmar, and Walden had made a mistake. They had performed a ritual and showed the interplay of lines to someone who was not supposed to see it at all! Mars Kronacher had been punished and was no longer a member of the inner circle of true visionaries. Mars had been robbed of his gifts and would never get them back again.

She stepped into her car and stared through the windshield at the dark street. "Please..." she whimpered, "don't take away our gifts as well... Please!" But she realized begging was useless.

❀ ❀ ❀

Everyone had left Fort Web. They stood in the big hall on the ground floor. "It is nighttime," said Carsten. "That brings dark thoughts with it."

Lucas still had the metal table leg in his hand. He walked up to the corner of the hall where a coffee machine stood. He began pounding on it with the table leg. The machine was being reduced to a useless pile of junk with every blow. "Wait for me!" Alrik cried out as he wielded his table leg. "That's something we have to do together!" The machine fell to the floor as they beat on it as hard as they could.

Then they ran to the counter and began smashing little computers and telephones, parts flew everywhere and bounced off the walls. A big robot sat on a desk chair behind a counter. The robot had been given to Gabi as a present by her employees for CompuStein's tenth anniversary. It was a high-tech wonder, constructed by her most brilliant engineers. The designers did not make it look too human, as intended. The head was round, with huge glass eyes, the body was angular and the feet were flat and broad; a touching robot, a king-sized toy.

First Alrik dented the head; Lucas hit the right shoulder with his table leg. The robot came to life and stood up. "How may I he...help yyyou?" the friendly voice intoned feebly. A series of hard blows were the only reply it received. Folco's silent men looked at him with raised eyebrows. He nodded and immediately the men ran up to the counter. They helped Lucas and Alrik destroy the robot as well.

Rosa was watching the action and said to Dieter, who was standing next to her, "Copper!" Dieter didn't react. Rosa continued, "I am thinking of changing the furnishings in our living room. I am thinking of designing a wall full of copper cogwheels that rotate very slowly, copper chandeliers on the ceiling, and copper candlesticks. Everything made of plastic must be thrown away."

The robot staggered. The four men with the table legs told Gabi to unlock the door. She rushed toward it. A light touch with her finger was enough to make the door swing open. It gave entrance to a big room housing long rows of computers standing next to each other on high tables. Some of these computers were being used to construct the interplay of lines, controlled by other computers that were programmed to duplicate the human brain as close as they possibly could. Before Gabi could count to one hundred her computers were smashed to pieces.

Freeda Olbers began to feel oppressed. Walking with purpose she went to the computer room and tapped one of the silent men on the shoulder. The man lowered his metal table leg and looked aside. "Open the front door for me," Freeda said as she turned around and left the room again. She walked through the hall and waited at the big door. The silent man stood next to her and opened the door for her.

Freeda breathed the fresh air. There were not many cars in the big parking lot. She noticed Thodor Baron's Volvo still hadn't been removed and she wondered if the alarm would sound if she kicked the side of it with all her might. As she passed it, she only stroked the roof with her hand.

Her canary yellow Porsche shone in the light of a street lamp. *I will sit down at my leisure and think of different things. I will allow things to come to me spontaneously.* She stepped into her car and started the engine. Thin, floating shrouds of mist were visible when she turned on the headlights. Now she was alone, memories of recent events came back to her. Nothing surprised her and she shrugged her shoulders nonchalantly.

What have I got to do with any of this anyway? The next thought that came to her made her laugh. "Yes, yes, exactly!" she cried out. "How on Earth can I be responsible for anything if I constantly change myself or my mind, if I renew myself all the time?" How does that go again? "Everything needs its own time," she said aloud, whilst driving through the business park. "Every part of the human body must rebuild itself, over and over again. It will take a brain about a year to do it. Exactly as long as it takes skin to renew itself completely. Yeah, I had some wine, not that much, but still... Ah! The liver rebuilds itself in about six weeks. Blood needs four months to do it... You'll notice nothing but you'll never be the same as before... No, no, Your Honor, the murder you mentioned had been committed three years ago. In the meantime, my brain has renewed itself three times, so the person I am now cannot be held responsible for that crime."

One thought called up the next and she became more enthusiastic as time progressed. *The human body is a moving hotel for countless living organisms that are not visible to the naked eye!* She laughed while she stepped on the gas. Six hundred million bacteria live on our skin alone! If we die, we do not die alone... we drag all those countless forms of life down with us...

...Forms of life. ...Dying. ...Renewing. Nicolaes Nimbus. In her mind's eye the man appeared, the man Rein Vulpes had painted. What would have happened to her if she had bitten him in the hand when he ran out of the shed, instead of hitting him? What if she had bitten him so hard that his thin bones were crushed if his skin burst open if she had been able to drink his blood? Would his precious blood have made her immortal? Maybe she should have bitten off a finger, maybe he had the power to regenerate it, like a starfish that loses; it grows back in a short time.

You can build an entire city with the money the members of Fort Web have spent to find new possibilities to prolong life." ...New techniques, new ways. And this is only the beginning. But then, all of a sudden, a name is mentioned that we will never forget ... Nicolaes Nimbus. There is so much from the past that never reached the present, it was all left behind while the clock was ticking, it remained out of our reach and still, it existed once upon a time. But Nicolaes Nimbus turned up, from the past!

She held the wheel firmly, not realizing how fast she was driving. ...The cup! The golden cup! His fingerprints must have been all over it. We have all touched it. Still, we have to take it to a lab. Why weren't we able to beat him to death? If we had only managed to make him lose consciousness, then we could have carried him inside and... oh, that would have given us many possibilities! The power this man can generate is inexplicable to us. Why is there so much we don't know, while we think we know so much?

While driving she hadn't paid much attention to the road. She looked straight ahead and saw an empty dark highway – then she looked at the speedometer and noticed she was driving over one-hundred and twenty-five miles an hour. Much to her surprise, she had no idea where she was. It would have made sense if she had gone to the hotel in Munich where she had stayed, but now she was driving on a highway that took her in the opposite direction.

Faces, there are billions of faces and they are all different; when Freeda looked in her rearview, she immediately recognized the face Rein had painted. It was as if Nicolaes Nimbus was looking back at her. He couldn't be sitting in the backseat, there was not enough space in the Porsche and at this speed, it was impossible to be holding on to the *backside of the car looking inside through the rear window. Where is he? Maybe I can get rid of him by driving even faster.* Immediately she floored it. *Can a chimera still keep up with me when I drive at top speed?* "What kind of an absurd thought is that?" She looked in the mirror again. The face was still there, bright blue eyes, a clean-shaven chin, and cheeks, thick, blond, curly hair.

"Go away!" Freeda screamed. "Go away, do you hear me?"

The Porsche raced at top speed on the straight road. Her tires began to shake now. The face of the man turned up right in front of her, coming closer and closer, it grew unrealistically big –pressing itself against the windshield. His nose flattened against the glass, the whites of the eyes flew out, blue irises were full of yellow stripes and the pupils grew, becoming deep holes. His mouth opened and white teeth tried to bite into the smooth glass in vain.

"Go away!" Freeda screamed again. She was not able to move her right foot. Panicking, she steered to the left. The car bumped up against the guardrail and flipped over several times. The last thing Freeda Olbers thought was, *"Where am I?"*

The car came to a standstill on its right side, in the middle of the A8, a highway Freeda had seldom driven on, facing in the direction of Augsburg. Other drivers stopped in time but the late-night traffic was jammed up. Police, an ambulance and a tow truck were there in no time. The dead body was taken out of the wreck, the Porsche was pushed to the shoulder so waiting cars could drive on again, the ambulance left and the sports car was towed away.

Freeda Olbers had disappeared during the night and when it grew light, there was – except for a damaged part of the guardrail – nothing more to see of the tragedy.

❀ ❀ ❀

The dice had fallen the right way, evens for the shortest route, uneven for a round-the-way trip. Rein Vulpes had thrown a six and asked the utmost from his old Toyota. It took him ten hours to reach Rotterdam. He only stopped to refuel and buy himself something to eat and drink. During the drive, he constantly thought about painting in the shed while under hypnosis.

He hardly remembered anything during the time he had worked on the painting. He remembered sitting in a comfortable chair in Gabi's office and being hypnotized by Freeda Olbers. But what happened next? Did Freeda go along with him when he went to the shed? Who opened the door for him – one of the silent men perhaps? When he woke up from his hypnotical state, he found himself in Gabi's office again.

All he knew was that he had mixed paint and worked with brushes.

But there had to be more. It always took him more effort to get a grip on it and put the colors into words.

Only after he was back in The Netherlands and heading for home was he able to think clearly, My hand had been led. Something was added to my creativity. I used my talent to the limit but it even went beyond that – I reached the height of absolute mastership. After that finally dawned on him, he also knew... This situation is long-lasting. The brushing tail of the fox guarantees art of the very highest level.

Once back home he went to bed right away and slept till late the next morning. It had not been easy to find a parking space for his car that evening in the center of Rotterdam so he decided to sell the Toyota. An acquaintance was interested and offered more than he had paid for it; the sly fox made a modest profit. The remainder of the day he used to buy food and drink, paints, new brushes, and additional stretched canvas.

Rein started working on a hunting scene. Twelve hounds were running along the side of a ditch with armed riders on black, brown, and white horses riding right behind them. In the foreground, a big, green frog could be seen jumping in a pond. There was a tiny ripple in the water, a fox held his head just far enough above the surface to be able to breathe and look around. Rein did not use photos or other examples to paint dogs, horses, faces, clothes, and weapons; it all came to him automatically. But the idea that his hand was being led was no longer the case, painting felt different now, "What once led me has now become a part of myself," he said while he painted. He was able to work very fast. The painting was finished earlier than he had expected. He studied every detail. There was nothing more to do, it was a work of beauty.

As soon as the paint dried, twenty-four hours later, Rein decided to take the painting to Mara Swynckels' shop; his work had been sold there before. It was a thirty-minute walk, but it took him longer because he was addressed time-after-time by curious people who wanted to take a look at the painting. He held the painting up for a while and then went on without waiting for their reactions.

Mara Swynckels was not at the shop; Rein was received by a middle-aged woman, a lady he had never met before. He placed the painting carefully on the floor, with the front top edge leaning against another painting, after which he explained he worked with Mara regularly.

"What should I tell her when she comes back in?"

"Tell her Rein Vulpes said hello and show her my most recent masterpiece. She will probably call me as soon as she has sold the painting. That is the way things always work between us."

"And what about the price?" the woman wanted to know. "We always need to know the minimum price asked for every work of art we display."

"She knows what to ask for it to satisfy us both," Rein grinned. "Just say hello from me and tell her not to hurry. I know she always takes into account that artists are hungry and have to eat..."

Rein was working on three different paintings simultaneously in his atelier. It was six o'clock and he was ready for a stroll along Witte de Withstraat and a good hot meal in a nice restaurant. The only thing he had to worry about today was what to drink with his meal – beer or wine. If he couldn't decide, he would order both or make good use of his dice. Now and then life is just that simple.

At ease, hands in his pockets, he walked through the street and entered a restaurant, the first one he came upon. It was crowded inside; a waitress found him a small table for two. When she asked what he wanted to drink, he ordered a beer.

He had just sat himself down when he got a call. "Hello?" he said in a soft voice in order not to disturb anyone.

He heard the enthusiastic voice of Mara Swynckels on the other end, "Rein? Is that you? Good... Where are you? Are you at home?"

"I'm on the Witte de Withstraat sitting in a restaurant."

"Do you still have to order?"

"Well... yes..."

"Then wait till I get there. We'll have dinner together. And it is on me, Rein. I was on my way to your atelier. I am walking on Witte de Withstraat now. What's the name of the restaurant?"

He had no idea so he looked at the window, the name, as seen from the inside, stood out in mirror writing: kabteE eD.

"One moment, De Eetbak," he said, "The Trough."

"I know where that is, I've had dinner there before. You're alone there, aren't you? Alright, see you soon; I'll get there as fast as I can. Oh, by the way, Rein, you're the best, the very best." The phone went dead.

He had just finished his second beer when Mara stepped inside. She was pretty, in her early thirties; she had long, dark brown hair tied up in a ponytail, wearing jeans and a checkered blouse. She waved at him, walked up to him, and kissed him on both cheeks – something she had never done before. After she sat down opposite him at the small table, she said, "It is so good to see you. I'm going to tell you about the Russians and the Chinese."

"Is this a joke?"

"No, oh no, absolutely not, but it's an incredible story."

The waitress brought her a drink menu and she ordered a glass of white wine.

"I'll join you," Rein was happy. He told Mara he had been in Germany, where one of his paintings had been sold for a very nice prize, without telling her the exact amount, two million euros.

"That doesn't surprise me at all," Mara chimed in, "I already told you you're the very best."

Only after the wine was served and the waitress had taken their order did Mara start to tell her story. "Russians and Chinese, they visit Rotterdam by the thousands; they are wealthy and they spend lots of money here. First I want to talk about your painting; that is what this is all about, of course."

"Cheers," said Rein.

"Cheers here's to you. Such a pity I was not there when you came in to bring me the hunting scene. I turned it around as soon as I got back and couldn't believe my eyes. You have always been a good painter, a master in almost all genres. But there are more artists like that. But now you stand out above the pack. It is just that... well, I'd better tell you what happened. I was so impressed by the painting. I immediately framed it and put it in the best spot in the shop window. It was already late so I had to close the shop. The next morning, I had just gotten there when a Chinese couple entered. Fortunately, they spoke English and they told me they wanted to buy your painting. I had to come outside with them so they could point it out to me As we stood in front of my shop window they expressed their feelings, which were similar to those I had experienced." She looked at him and her eyes sparkled.

"What do you mean?"

"Don't tell me you don't know, Rein..."

"I really have no idea what you're talking about, I mean it. What did they say?"

"The magic, the brilliant illusion... You painted part of the head of a fox, you can see his shining nose, you see his black eyes. And then, unexpectedly, the water seems to get clearer and you can see the entire body of the fox, with his mowing legs and his beautiful, long tail. At first, I thought I was the only one hallucinating, I could not understand what was happening because I had never experienced something like that before while I was studying a painting. But the Chinese couple had the same experience."

"I..." Rein started in.

"Wait, wait, I'm not finished, it gets even crazier. I heard impatient footsteps on the sidewalk. Two Russians walked up to me, a couple! They had been standing in front of the shop window yesterday after closing time. They did not speak Dutch, but their English was just as good as that of the Chinese couple. They had been moved to tears by the painting, they told me. They knew it had to be impossible, but they'd had a strange experience when they looked at your work of art. The fox became entirely visible to them, in crystal clear water. They pointed at the painting and told me they were able to see it again."

"That's great!"

"The Chinese woman asked about the price of the painting. I answered very businesslike that the price had not been determined yet, but that it would be very expensive. The Russian woman told me she would pay me more than anyone else. They started a discussion so I stepped back. There I was, Rein, standing on the sidewalk, watching four people who tried to make it clear to each other that they wanted to have the same painting. Finally, we went inside, they wanted to have a closer look at your painting. I took it from the shop window, brought it inside, put it on an easel, and switched on a light. The Russian man named a price, twenty-five thousand euros. I didn't get a chance to reply, because the Chinese woman bid thirty-thousand euro. The bidding went back-and-forth and it ended at fifty-thousand euros. The Russians topped the Chinese couple's bid. But still, this is not the end of my story. The Chinese couple owns property and companies in and around Rotterdam and they visit our country often, they even have their own house in Hillegersberg. They gave me fifty-thousand euro for your next painting, sight unseen. So you'll have to paint another like that one for them. And after that, you must make paintings for me...till you've become so old that even picking up a brush will be too much work for you! How does that sound, Rein?"

"I'm hungry," he complained, hoping the waitress would turn up soon.

During dinner Mara suggested she would draw up a contract, "I want to sell your work exclusively and of course most of the money will be yours. You will become a wealthy man in a very short time. What do you think about that?"

"I don't know what to say right now," Rein responded, "but I will make a decision soon." The dice were burning a hole in his pocket.

Chapter 16

LIKE A BIRD OF PREY

Rosa Linge and Alrik von Hecht were born on the same date, but not the same year, and they often threw a birthday party inviting family and friends to their big home on Lake Starnberg. Now, shortly after the sudden death of Freeda, they didn't feel like feasting at all. It was hard for them and the rest of the team to believe she was no longer with them. The solemn cremation had made a deep impression on Rosa. She missed the extravagant hyper-intelligent Freeda deeply and thought about her all the time.

Perhaps I'll call Alrik's friend, Regina Thule, we had such a good time the night we spent with her in her house in Bremen. Wow, we sure did. She might be able to help us forget about our sorrows for a while.

"I'm selling my house in Habenhausen. I will be moving to another district in Bremen. I met a wonderful man and we have decided to live together. I know him, just like Alrik, from school. We met accidentally when he entered our shop to buy medicine for his mother. He asked me out and you know how things go, one thing leads to another. We fell in love and we have decided to live together even though I have known him for only a short time. Rosa, he is the ying to my yang. He is the right shoe to my left. You know you can't wear one without the other. He and I complement each other!"

Rosa was very disappointed, she wanted to keep the conversation short, but Regina had more to say, "Remember when you both visited Elise van Vennen in Twente and she told you all about her grandfather and The Society of Tamfana. Well, she told me all about it. I called her recently, just because I wanted to talk to her about my father again. She spoke very highly of you both, but she also said you have to watch out... She is afraid you will start hunting something you might want to leave in peace."

"Nicolaes Nimbus...?"

"Yes, she said that some things are beyond our comprehension. Time has changed our way of thinking and the way we interpret things. I remember her words very well, 'You can reject old ideas because they do not fit the facts of modern opinions, but you cannot ignore phenomena from the distant past when they turn up – and how are you going to defend yourself against powers that don't seem to have a scientific foundation, that seem to originate from forgotten magic?' Honestly, I didn't understand much of what she was saying. Perhaps you know what she tried to help me understand ...?"

Rosa shivered. She didn't want to talk about it so she changed the subject and, not much later, she wished her well with her new friend, her new house and her new life.

It was Saturday afternoon and she was home alone thinking about their rather dull birthday plans. Alrik had driven to his dental practice because the host of a reality program airing live on television that night was suffering from a serious toothache. He had left in his new sports car she had given him as a present for his birthday – Alrik had given her a white gold diamond ring. Rosa felt restless and frightened after the conversation with Regina. Since they would not be organizing a party, Rosa suggested they go to Munich and have dinner in an expensive restaurant, then visit a nightclub afterward, but ultimately they decided to stay home.

She was trembling all over when she went to the kitchen to open a bottle of wine. *Maybe a drink will calm me down.* But as soon as she emptied her first glass, she felt even more afraid. "What if Alrik drives too fast like Freeda did? I shouldn't have given him that sports car, not now... What had Regina Thule said? You cannot ignore phenomena from the distant past when they turn up..."

Nicolaes Nimbus, she felt his presence when a sound came from another part of the big house when she looked out a window and saw birds fly up when a shutter flapped in the wind – and she felt his presence even stronger when it was quiet. *How do I defend myself against powers that don't seem to have a scientific foundation, that seem to originate from forgotten magic?*

"I cannot defend myself at all!" she suddenly cried out, her own voice scared her as she burst into tears. "Please, don't do anything to Alrik, let him come home soon!"

Her hearing seemed to be as sharp as that of a dog; there were sounds all around her she had never noticed before. There was a certain singing in her ears and an irritating pressure on her eardrums.

Alrik had been extremely happy with his new silver-grey BMW. She had paid one hundred and fifty thousand euro for it. Time-after-time he told her he felt embarrassed because the ring had been so much cheaper, 'I am not as wealthy as you...' she remembered him saying.

Perhaps I should call him. Maybe he's still busy with the television host, or maybe he's already on his way home. Rosa was sitting on a kitchen chair, leaning forward, with her elbows on her knees and her hands pressed against her ears. Suddenly she heard the typical crunching of car tires rolling over a gravel path and she jumped to her feet. Through a side window, she saw the silver-grey BMW.

She cried again when Alrik came inside; she could see through her tears that his face was covered with sweat and he looked worried. He was the first to say something, "I drove away this morning and immediately I felt so strange, I was seized by feelings of fear, mortal fear. I was so worried about you, but also about myself. It is..." he searched for the right words, "It is as if something has taken possession of me, something I cannot shake off. What about you... What is the matter with you, why are you crying?"

"I know exactly what you mean. I am feeling the way. I was afraid you would crash while driving your new sports car. There is something in my head and it just won't go away. What are we supposed to do, Alrik, what are we supposed to do?"

Alrik took her wine glass, filled it to the brim, and emptied it in one gulp. Then he refilled it and gave it to her. While she drank greedily, Alrik said, "I am not hungry. Wine seems better to me right now, or maybe we need something stronger."

Rosa choked and started to cough. She was still crying. She hadn't managed to calm down. All of a sudden she said, "Alrik, he's here!"

"Yes, Rosa, he's here. We both feel it. Now we have to stay close and help each other. We will get through this together"

"But what are we up against?"

"How the hell am I supposed to know? What do we know anyway? We know nothing, Rosa, nothing at all really!"

They left the kitchen and entered the hall; Alrik hurried to lock the front door. They still felt they were not alone as he took her by the hand and dragged her to a staircase that led to the cellar. "Maybe he will leave us in peace once we are in the pool."

There was a broad corridor at the bottom of the stairs with a room for their wine stock on the left and a fitness room at the right. The swimming pool was at the end of the corridor. Lights went on automatically. Alrik didn't take off his shoes or his clothes, he jumped into the water right away – Rosa didn't hesitate for a moment as she jumped in after him. The water was up to Alrik's chest and Rosa's chin. They waded to the middle of the swimming pool and held each other tight.

"Are we safe here?" Rosa asked. "What if you suddenly get dragged to the bottom..." He did not answer but looked around searchingly. "Where are we?" was her next question, her voice sounded like that of a little girl.

His voice sounded very boyish when he answered after a long silence, "We have to hide. Come with me..."

❋ ❋ ❋

Monday morning at half-past ten, their cleaning lady, Wanda, arrived from a neighboring village. She had already worked for Rosa before Alrik moved in with her. She parked her Volkswagen Golf, stepped outside, walked to the door, and took the key out of her pocket. The moment she put the key into the lock, another car arrived, stopping right behind hers. Wanda recognized one of Rosa's managers, Lotte, whom she had met often before. The women greeted each other and then Lotte explained why she was there, "I tried to reach Rosa all Sunday. There are at least twenty urgent things I have to discuss with her. Normally she is in her office by seven-thirty every Monday. May I come along with you when you go inside? I hope she's at home, but maybe she has gone out with Alrik for the weekend to celebrate their birthdays. Usually, she sends me a message before she goes anywhere…"

"Of course, come with me." Wanda opened the front door. Together they walked through the hall to the big living room, stopped and just stood there, staring.

The couch, easy chairs, and coffee table were placed against the wall to create more space. Alrik had lined up two armies of little toy soldiers while crawling on his hands and knees across the marble floor, carefully pushing a high ranking officer forward. Rosa was sitting at the table holding a doll in her arms.

"Hush!" she whispered in a tiny voice when she saw Wanda and Lotte standing there. "She's finally sleeping... She's a little sick, you know..."

Suddenly a war broke out on the floor. Alrik imitated the sound of rifles, machine guns, and cannon pushing over soldier after soldier.

"Now she's awake!" Rosa sobbed.

"My God..." Lotte sighed. "What's going on here? What are we supposed to do?"

Wanda knew, "I will call Doctor Von Lindern, he has to come here right away! They've gotten all that stuff down from the attic... Just take a good look at them, they've become like children again..."

While the cleaning lady tried to reach the doctor, Lotte walked up to Rosa, trying to pull the doll out of her hands."Don't do that! ...Hands off!" Rosa's high pitched voice screamed. "I told you she's sick, got that?"

Alrik swiped a hand through the ranks and the plastic puppets tumbled over. He laughed enthusiastically and started to put the soldiers upright again one at a time.

"The doctor is on his way," Wanda said to Lotte. "Please, let's wait for him outside. I cannot bear to watch this any longer..."

❈ ❈ ❈

From the moment Folco Andermann had drunk from the golden cup, he had hardly said anything sane.

He had withdrawn into his world and had long conversations with imaginary figures in quick succession about various subjects like alchemy, the origin of the universe, the importance of pepper in every kitchen, the general benefit of spiders, and the influence from medieval wandering hawkers and troubadours who spread the news around. He ate less and his health was failing fast, but he let everyone around him know he should live forever.

His wife, Anna-Margaretha, more than twenty years younger, drove to the head offices of his companies every day to replace him, therefore Folco was alone most of the day. His doctor said he should rest as much as possible. Anna-Margaretha wanted to take him to a psychiatrist and when he refused to come with her, she invited one to their home, but Folco hadn't said a single word to him.

When the weather was bad he remained inside preferring to sit at his desk in his study, staring and talking with imaginary friends. When it was warm and sunny, he went into the garden to cut twigs and branches or dig holes in the grassy fields nearby.

Anna-Margaretha decided to have him admitted to a psychiatric clinic; she would take him there herself. Folco needed professional help and she didn't want to live under the same roof with a man who only talked to himself and destroyed her garden.

But it never came to that. One afternoon, when he was home alone, he cut down three young conifers and sat down on a chair on one of the terraces to rest. Folco never saw the silent men until they were standing right in front of him. He didn't recognize them so it never dawned on him to wonder what they wanted from him. The men were nervous as they talked to him for what might have been the first time in a very long time. They told him they had searched for him everywhere and were craving his pills.

"See to it that we get them right away," they demanded. "Our lives have become unbearable without pills. You gave them to us for such a long time. Don't make us angry. You wouldn't like that!"

Folco pointed at someone who only existed in his fantasy and said, "The problem that always comes up when one discusses alchemy is that the one is talking about fortune hunters who wanted to make gold from base metal, while the other one is mentioning the search for eternal life." He leaned to one side and cupped his hand behind his ear listening to a voice only he could hear. "Exactly," he said. "Yes, yes, we agree on that."

The men kept begging for their pills. And when they finally realized they weren't going to get them, they became violent. "Then we'll search your house till we find them ourselves, but first we'll teach you a valuable lesson, you old fool!"

They dragged him from his garden chair by force and when he stood staggering on the terrace, one of them punched him in the jaw. The other man caught him when he fell and shoved him away from him as hard as he could. Folco staggered forward like a drunken sailor and received another hard blow to the jaw. Then the men started to beat him up, one punch after the other. Folco lay full-length on the stoned terrace; the men only stopped beating him when he no longer moved. Next, they went inside to vent their anger on the furniture. Closet doors were yanked from their hinges, expensive paintings were ripped from the walls to see if there was a safe hidden behind them and a chair in their way was thrown through a large expensive decorative window pane.

"Maybe he keeps the pills in a medicine cabinet in the bathroom," one of the men said, "let's have a look upstairs."

Before they ran upstairs, they smashed everything in the kitchen and the hall. Neighbors heard the noise and called the police right away. Soon two cars arrived. Four policemen ran around the house. One of them stayed with the lifeless body of Folco Andermann, the others went inside and heard sounds on the second story. The silent men wanted to fight, but they realized they could never win against determined police officers holding guns in their hands.

❋ ❋ ❋

Lucas Montaigne was an enthusiastic pilot; he had bought his third Cessna, one with a strong six-cylinder engine, recently. The plane had four seats so he could take his wife and children with him on pleasure trips. Now he was alone. He parked his car in his hangar at a small airport not far from Munich, taxiing early that morning headed for Geneva.

His secretary had made an appointment for him in Geneva where he would meet engineers who could help him with a high-tech project for the army. It was a short flight, only about three hundred and seventy-five miles. The Cessna had more than enough fuel for the trip; the tank held enough fuel to fly more than eight hundred and seventy miles. Lucas smiled when he thought about that. Above him, there were blue skies, below him green pastures with the greys and whites of villages and towns and shining lakes scattered about.

But Lucas Montaigne was not alone. The three passenger seats were unoccupied, but he felt the presence of a strong, forceful personality.

Scientific minds had started to search for immortality and Lucas was, together with a large group of people who gathered regularly in Fort Web, one of the leading figures in this big expensive operation. A smaller group – eight people to be exact – had split off and gone further than the rest. Together with them, Lucas had gotten lost in a magic world where everything was strange and frightening. A voice from the past had made itself heard, the eight had agreed to the hunt and swore they would not rest before they had caught Nicolaes Nimbus, dismembered him and scattering his body parts to their labs, where they would find out everything they could about the secret of his immortality.

Are you sitting right behind me, or are you in my head? No scientist in the modern world was able to make this influence from the past disappear. That was the true reality of the situation.

"There is no place for you in our society," Lucas voiced loudly, "yet still you have turned up. There is no way to describe you, our knowledge falls short; we cannot understand who you are exactly and what you do to confuse us so much."

He changed course. Soon he was flying over the Alps and after a quarter of an hour, he started to circle. "Am I doing this right?" he cried out. Those were his last words. He had intentionally forgotten to refuel the Cessna after his last flight. All he had to do now was wait until the engine started to protest, to splutter, and finally stop. The propeller would come to a standstill and then he would make the plane dive, like a bird of prey, headed for the alluring, white Alpine mountain peaks. It happened sooner than he expected. The fall to his absolute end ...

Chapter 17

Worn-out, fragile, and close to a nervous breakdown, Gabi Stein sat down on a throne in the big meeting room of Fort Web. She was caught between two horrors, she was afraid to die and she was afraid to live. Circumstances beyond her control demanded that she be alert and decisive. Now that Rosa Linge had been admitted to an institution, managers had asked her to take charge of Rosa's companies. CompuStein Hightech and Rosa's Noncha had many common interests and it was only logical that Gabi should take the helm until someone was found who could replace Rosa permanently. It had become clear that Rosa and Alrik would never outgrow their current intellect, that of carefree playing children. She missed the extravagant Freeda, who had known so much about the workings of the human brain and had always been able to explain it. She missed her good old friend Folco and she was shocked when she heard the news about the crash on an Alpine peak, Lucas' plane had nearly disintegrated!

Carsten von Haller was seated to her left. He had lost so much weight that his chubby cheeks had disappeared. His philosophical reflections had been suppressed by one single thought... How can a man like me rid himself of the unbearable fear of death?

Dieter Brunn sat to the right of Gabi looking more like a hobo than the almost total owner of the conglomerate of Brunnheck companies. Katja and he now slept in separate rooms and divorce seemed inevitable. He had become an unpredictable partner who tried to chase away his fears with sedatives and liquor. He wore the same shirt for five days and hadn't shaved for nearly a week. His eyes were deadpan and his hands shook violently.

Footsteps sounded in the corridor. All three heard them. "Patience..." Carsten sighed. "It will take some time, I understand that. Please, let's talk to each other in the meantime. Just to kill time. Tell me something, no matter what..."

It was Gabi who reacted first, "You have heard it already, but I will tell you one more time. I had a meeting with twelve people from Fort Web, seven from Germany, three from Switzerland, and two from Italy. We sat down in the meeting room. I wanted to show them the golden cup so I opened the drawer. Believe me, when I tell you, no one else can open that drawer without leaving traces of damage. The only thing I found was my fountain pen. The cup had disappeared! How do you explain something thing that?"

"Please," Carsten moaned, "I don't want you to tell us something depressing or talk about something we cannot answer. It will only make us more nervous. I want to hear something about beautiful holidays, great parties, or interesting information, something upbeat."

"We're not in the mood for things like that, Carsten," said Dieter. "I didn't come to Munich for the umpteenth time to hear about the holidays. Just have patience..."

Again there were footsteps in the corridor. They were coming closer and becoming louder; two seconds later they faded away.

Every time Carsten put his hands on the table and removed them, his sweat stains slowly dissolved. He stared at them as if they were the trick of a conjurer. Dieter stroked the stubbles on his chin, Gabi tried to concentrate on the classical music that sounded softly from the ceiling-high speakers in the meeting room.

Again they heard footsteps in the corridor. "There he is," whispered Dieter. "Oh yes, there he is..."

A man was standing in the doorway. Rein Vulpes entered the meeting room and occupied an empty throne next to Carsten. He had come to Munich on an urgent request from Gabi, Carsten, and Dieter. He had bought another old car especially for the trip – this time it was a little Peugeot convertible and because the weather was perfect, he had driven with his face to the sun for the majority of the trip.

Gabi had called him often and they had long conversations. She had informed him about everything that had happened, "Now there are only three of us and we are waiting for the next disaster. Freeda had a severe car accident; Rosa Linge and Alrik von Hecht behave like little children these days, my good friend Folco Andermann died recently... His attackers have confessed and will never leave prison again... Lucas Montaigne crashed his plane into the Alps. Remco Castor is no longer among us; you know what happened to him... I am well aware of the fact that we behaved very badly, that we tried to kill someone on that dark night by the shed just after you made the painting. The price we have to pay is so high now, so high, Rein, the thought of another fatal accident is slowly but surely destroying us. We're scared to death, all of us." Rein was shocked by everything he heard even though Gabi had told him mostly everything during their last phone conversation.

❦ ❦ ❦

Rosa had also been in contact with Rein by phone not too long ago and she had called Gabi to relay the conversation right after she had spoken to Rein. But when Rosa asked him for help, he didn't understand what she meant. "How do you feel?" Rosa had asked him.

"I'm fine," he had answered. "I'm very fine indeed. I work hard and my paintings are already sold while the paint is still wet. One way or another I have risen above myself."

"You see? You have become involved with everything unwanted and you went back home with an enormous bonus."

"A Bonus?" he had repeated.

"But of course! You have risen above yourself, your talent has grown and you have been rewarded instead of punished. And there is more! While you were under a hypnotic influence, you were able to paint the interplay of lines that forced us all to look at it, after which it did unexplainable things to our brains. Perhaps you could do that one more time. Please, come and visit us. Try to get in contact with our tormentor and ask him for forgiveness on our behalf. Rein, you are our only hope, please, come to Munich!" Those were her last words to him.

❁ ❁ ❁

And now he was here. He tried to sketch the interplay of lines. He set to work with a ballpoint and concentrated to the max; he drew lines on more than twenty different sheets of paper. He even tried it with closed eyes, hoping it would happen automatically while he thought about other things in the meantime. But all his efforts were fruitless.

But something else happened. He retired to a room in Fort Web and while he made the ballpoint move across the paper, he got the feeling he was no longer alone. He could not explain how it felt to have something or someone with him he could not see; he only knew that it was real. He walked back to the three desperate Germans who had gone to the kitchen to have coffee and something to eat.

"The interplay of lines leads to nothing," he said. "But there is something else. I can only describe it as a kind of contact. Give me time to make these feelings stronger. It wouldn't surprise me if I were able to reach a point where I was able to communicate with it, whatever it is. I want to be alone, to walk through corridors and enter rooms, to find out where the will that affects me is the strongest."

"Yes, yes, please do so..." Gabi begged him.

She went back to the meeting room with Carsten and Dieter. All three took their coffee with them. Sitting on their thrones, they listened to Rein's meandering footsteps and now, finally, he was back. "Dear Queen Lioness, philosophical bear and sloppy wolf," Rein started in, "ultimately it is always the fox that turns out to be smarter than all the other animals put together." He raised his hands in the air to state his innocence and continued, "You probably know the expression: don't shoot the messenger. Keep in mind that I am not sitting here as your judge, I only get information through..."

"Oh, but that is just terrific in itself!" Gabi whispered as if she was afraid to force Rein out of his concentration by saying it louder Carsten and Dieter didn't even dare to open their mouths.

Rein nodded. "We have to take our leave soon." Gabi looked at him, eyes full of fright. "But before we go I will do something for you, something that has been suggested to me."

He rose to his feet and walked up to Gabi, leaned forward and embraced her. He shook hands with both men. He remained standing and took his die from his pocket. "Listen carefully," he said, "you must remember this well. Uneven numbers are negative, even numbers are positive. One stands for mental health deterioration, three means a short life that will be dominated by mortal fear; five will bring you an immediate death... here and now. A two will set you free from all negative influences, four brings you luck, six clears the way that leads to immortality, scientifically speaking." He showed them his die in the flat of his hand. "This is the way it was told to me. Through a voice I was not able to hear, the words entered my brain straight away. I only pass something on to you... Of course, there is another possibility as well; I could put the die back in my pocket. No matter what you decide, I will leave you immediately. You have asked for my help and this is all I can do for you."

"Throw the die," Gabi Stein whispered.

Carsten von Haller and Dieter Brunn repeated it, "Throw the die."

Rein didn't hesitate for a moment. He took Gabi's empty coffee cup and put the die in it. He shook the cup so fast that the die raced along on the inside like an out of control Ferris wheel, he quickly turned it upside down and placed it on her saucer. They heard the die fall on the saucer under the cup. Carefully Rein pushed the cup and saucer to the middle of the huge table. He bowed, turned around, and left the meeting room. His footsteps faded away down the corridor.

Gabi, Carsten, and Dieter stood up, afraid to move a muscle. No one dared reach out to grab the upside-down coffee cup, hoping one of the other two would do it. Only Nicolaes Nimbus knew how the die had landed...

❊ ❊ ❊

Rein took the elevator, whizzed down through the transparent shaft, stepped out, and walked through the hall of CompuStein heading to the exit. The weather was great so he'd left the convertible open when he'd stepped inside. He decided to drive in the direction of Freising, over the narrow country roads, to have a look at the spot where Castor's house had stood; then he would stop at Restaurant Etzel for a big glass of cool beer and a good meal.

But he knew he was not alone, although no one was sitting in the passenger seat and he didn't see anyone when he looked in the rear-view. "It is about time that you left the fox alone. We don't need each other's company any longer. I wish you well." He held the wheel with his left hand and waved with his right hand. It was a calm day, but he had to clasp the wheel with both hands due to a sudden gust of wind that tried to push the car to one side.

Looking toward the side of the road, he saw someone up ahead who wore the same clothes as the man he had painted while he was in the concrete shed; he also had the same build. When he passed him and looked in the side mirror, he seemed to have disappeared. Rein felt relieved. *All I need is a new pair of dice.*

THE END

About Koos Verkaik

Koos, a 'Dutchy' with spunk and an inexhaustible drive and fathomless imagination, is one of the most prolific authors of Sci-Fi and children's books in The Netherlands.

His novels, *All-Father* and *Wolf Tears*, earned him the moniker, the Dutch Stephen King.

He wrote his first Sci-Fi novel, *Adolar*, on a weekend when he was 18 years old and the manuscript was published shortly thereafter.

Koos has published over 60 books, both children's books, and novels, many hundreds of comic scripts, and he has worked as a copywriter. He is currently working on several screenplays and new novels.

To read more about Koos and his work visit his website at www.koosverkaik.com or follow him on Facebook:

https,//www.facebook.com/koos.verkaik.5